FATAL DOSE

FATAL DOSE

BRIAN PRICE

This edition produced in Great Britain in 2023

by Hobeck Books Limited, Unit 14, Sugnall Business Centre, Sugnall, Stafford, Staffordshire, ST21 6NF

www.hobeck.net

ISBN 978-1-913-817-00-6 (pbk)

ISBN 978-1-913-793-99-9 (ebook)

Cover design by Jayne Mapp Design

Printed and bound in Great Britain

Are you a thriller seeker?

Hobeck Books is an independent publisher of crime, thrillers and suspense fiction and we have one aim – to bring you the books you want to read.

For more details about our books, our authors and our plans, plus the chance to download free novellas, sign up for our newsletter at **www.hobeck.net**.

You can also find us on Twitter **@hobeckbooks** or on Facebook **www.facebook.com/hobeckbooks10**.

Hobeck Advanced Reader Team

Hobeck Books has a team of dedicated advanced readers who read our books before publication (not all of them, they choose which they would like to read). Here is what they said about *Fatal Dose.*

'Brian is a master storyteller. I would say, and I read a lot, the best.' Carole Gourlay

'I almost read it in one sitting.' Sarah Blackburn

'Kept me gripped throughout.' Sarah Leck

To our magnificent and over-worked and underpaid NHS staff, whose dedication and endurance, during Covid and at other times, is unappreciated by those who hold the purse strings.

Note from the Author

This novel is set around the late spring/summer of 2021. Covid is still about and there are some restrictions in place but no lockdown. People are allowed to gather in pubs and elsewhere, but masks are still required in some circumstances. Where possible, detectives and civilian support staff are encouraged to work from home and participate in online meetings using platforms such as Teams and Zoom. For the purposes of the plot, I may have described more face-to-face contact than would be ideal, but I hope you will bear with me on this.

Similarly, I have telescoped some of the timescales for post mortem and forensic test results and omitted much of the paperwork which detectives have to complete – otherwise it would be a rather boring book!

Just for fun, I have hidden numerous musical references in the book, plus a couple of 'Easter Eggs'. See how many you can find. Email hobeckbooks@gmail.com and they will let you know if you have spotted them all!

Prologue

Some years previously

It started with *You Only Live Twice*, his fascination with poisons. Not the film, the book by Ian Fleming. A whole section was devoted to the poisonous plants in Blofeld's suicide garden. He lapped it up, amazed that innocent-looking plants could wreak such havoc on the human body. Then he turned his attention to real life poisoners such as the Borgias with arsenic, Neill Cream with strychnine and Graham Young with thallium. This was power, he thought. With skill and dedication, you could poison someone and get away with it, especially if you had no previous connection to them. But you couldn't just go into a chemist's and buy arsenic and cyanide like in Agatha Christie's day. The chemicals he was really interested in were tightly restricted and you needed a licence to possess them. But perhaps there were other ways.

The internet was a wonderful source of information, and the local library had links to online medical and scientific journals that provided him with a wealth of details. He was fascinated to find that, although you couldn't buy controlled poisons on the net, you could buy the seeds of poisonous plants.

He studied science at A-level and began a pharmacy degree, but those unproven allegations about the theft of drugs forced him to leave. He wanted to know more about what made people tick and was fascinated by psychology experiments where some of the subjects were given power over others; power that they inevitably abused. So, he took a mixed degree with the Open University, following courses in psychology and the arts.

He still thought endlessly about the power that poisons represented. In all his reading, this power had been used for nefarious purposes: to get rid of a troublesome spouse, to claim insurance for murdered babies or from pure sadism. But what if that power could be used for good? He used to think that the justice system was fair. He wouldn't get fooled again. Many people escaped the net of justice, or received punishments far less than their offences deserved, while innocent people had their lives ruined by police incompetence or a failing system. His step-mother, for one. Perhaps he could fill the gap? So, with a decent degree under his belt, he resolved to pursue a career that would enable him to find out about such cases and administer his own brand of, terminal, justice.

Chapter One

Day 1

GORDON HOWELL LEFT the Greek deli with a look of anticipation on his face and a bag of sticky pastry in his hand. He was looking forward to eating his baklava in the park, as close to the children's playground as he could get. His thoughts were curtailed abruptly when someone collided with him, knocking his honeyed treat from his hands.

'Oh, I'm so sorry,' said the stranger, reaching down to pick up the bag. 'That was really clumsy of me. Are you hurt? Here's your cake.'

Gordon scowled but grudgingly admitted that he wasn't injured. He wasn't one to start a row and didn't want to draw attention to himself, so he just grabbed the bag and stalked off, with further apologies from the stranger floating in the air behind him. He reached the park and sat down on his usual bench, the afternoon sun warming his face. He knew he shouldn't be there but he couldn't help himself. He pulled out the baklava, which seemed none the worse for its impact with the pavement, and bit blissfully into it. Perhaps it was the incident outside the shop that affected his mood, but it didn't taste as sweet as usual. Nevertheless, a baklava was a baklava and he wasn't going to waste it.

Half an hour later Gordon had finished his snack, the playground was empty and he decided to head for home. He stood up and noticed that his muscles were tingling and twitching slightly. He felt odd and noises seemed to be more intrusive than usual. By the time he reached the park gates he was feeling distinctly uncomfortable. It must have shown, because a man in a paramedic's uniform, wearing a face mask, stopped him and asked if he was all right.

'Yes. Just feeling a bit odd, that's all.'

'Can I give you a lift anywhere?' the man asked. 'I've just come off duty and I'm in no particular hurry.'

'That's kind of you. But I think I'll be fine.'

Gordon debated with himself. Was this person to be trusted? He'd had plenty of experience of people turning on him, but no-one here knew his real name, so it should be safe. And, by now, he was feeling rather ill.

'OK then. Thank you. I live in the flats on Felton Street. It's not far.'

'No problem. I know where the flats are. We've been called out there a few times. This van's mine.'

He gestured to a dark blue Transit parked a few metres away.

'Sorry it's not a more comfortable ride, but I do some light removals when I'm not working. I'll just put my rucksack in the back.'

The man opened the back doors, dropped in his bag and turned to Gordon. A lightning blow to Gordon's stomach doubled him over. He could hardly breathe and offered no resistance as the man pushed him into the van, sweeping up his legs from under him and slamming the doors.

Gordon's head banged against the side of the van as it

accelerated away. He felt sick, disoriented and, above all, terrified.

'Why are you doing this? Who are you?'

'Who I am is irrelevant. You don't know me. But I know who you really are. And you can guess why I've taken you.'

The kidnapper put a CD into the van's player and pressed play.

'Here's a song for you to listen to while we drive. It's by an American singer, Tom Lehrer. It's called *Poisoning Pigeons in the Park*. He sings the praises of strychnine, and you, my friend, are my pigeon. Enjoy.'

For the next two hours the van was constantly on the move with the song playing repeatedly. Gordon vomited. His muscle twitching turned into excruciating bouts of convulsions. Periods of calm, during which he sobbed and pleaded for his life, gave way to ferocious cramps when he felt his muscles were being torn from his bones. Every sound, bump, or flash of light through the van's window triggered more pain. Eventually, he could breathe no more and he expired in agony, his face scarlet and his body arched as the contracted muscles in his back pulled his spine out of shape.

The driver switched off the CD player and parked the van in a public car park, avoiding CCTV cameras. It would stay there until the middle of the night when he would dump Gordon's body in the location he had selected. A message sent.

Chapter Two

Day 2

THE CORPSE LAY on its back, just outside the school gates. Only the head and feet touched the ground, and judging by the terrible grin on the dead man's face, he had stared into the depths of hell and laughed.

'This wasn't an easy death,' commented Dr Durbridge, the pathologist. 'I'll take some samples, but I'm ninety percent certain this is strychnine poisoning. Though where anyone would get strychnine these days beats me. The last case I heard of was a suicide who had brought some back from India.'

'Definitely suspicious, then,' said DI Emma Thorpe. 'So, we've got a crime scene. I'll get the SOCOs in.'

Within an hour, the inner and outer cordons were set up and a PC was on guard with a clipboard, to record anyone entering. SOCOs Dave Graham and Kate Bartlett, in forensic suits, were photographing, examining and sampling the body and the scene. When they had first looked at the body they had recoiled at the macabre death mask before getting on with their jobs.

'Nasty,' commented Kate.

'Yes, give me an old-fashioned bludgeoning any time,' her colleague replied.

Thunder clouds were building and the air was thick with sticky electricity, adding extra urgency to the processing of the crime scene.

'We'd better get a wriggle on,' said Dave. 'When that lot hits it'll wash away what little evidence we've got.'

Kate nodded and continued taking photographs.

As the storm started to break, the body was loaded into a plain van for transport to the mortuary and the SOCOs dashed to their vehicles, leaving only a mournful and soggy PC guarding the flapping crime scene tape, clearly wishing it had been his day off.

Chapter Three

Day 4

AFTER THE PM on Gordon Howell's body, Emma called the team together in the incident room.

'OK, folks. Gordon Howell. Dr Durbridge called in a favour at the university and they analysed the samples he sent them immediately. The results confirm his suspicions that Howell was poisoned with strychnine, most likely in a sweet pastry of some sort, although it was difficult to be precise about that. And it's highly unlikely to be accidental or suicide.'

'Where d'you get strychnine, guv? Boots?' asked DC Martin Rowse, absent-mindedly scratching a scar on his stomach through his shirt.

'Basically, you don't. It's effectively banned in the UK, although it was used for killing moles until fairly recently. It's horrible stuff, a really cruel poison. However, the lab discovered a related chemical, called brucine, in the samples, which suggested that the source was one of the plants that contain it, rather than a chemical supplier.

Apparently the two substances are found together in nature.'

'A garden centre, then?'

'Nope. These are tropical plants and would only grow over here in a hothouse. But, according to Dr Durbridge's report, you can buy the seeds of one plant, *Strychnos nux-vomica,* on the internet. He suggested that the killer either grew the plant under special conditions and harvested the strychnine from its leaves, together with brucine, or extracted the chemicals directly from the seeds. It's not particularly difficult, according to the report.'

'So, who would know about this, boss?' asked DC Trevor Blake, dipping a biscuit into his coffee.

'Anyone who'd heard about strychnine and wanted to get hold of it, I suppose. I had a quick chat with one of the lasses in the forensic lab, and someone with A-level chemistry would have no problem with that side of it. All they'd need would be a coffee grinder, if they were using seeds, fifty quid's worth of glassware and a few basic chemicals. Of course, they'd need to be careful to avoid poisoning themselves, but that needn't be a problem.'

Most of the team looked astonished.

'Now,' continued Emma. 'Gordon Howell is known to us. I asked Martin to do some digging. What did you find, Martin?'

'He was the caretaker at the school where he was dumped, convicted last year of possessing indecent images of children. Bad ones. He served four months and is on the Sex Offenders Register. There were suspicions that he had been interfering with some of the children at his school, but there was not enough evidence to charge him. His body was dumped just out of range of the CCTV cameras. Fortunately, the schools are on holiday, otherwise the sight would have terrified the kids.'

'Shit,' said DS Jack Vaughan. 'The killer was obviously making a point by dumping him there. Can we find out who he was supposed to have abused and interview the parents?'

'I'll do that if you like,' volunteered DC Mel Cotton, thinking that her gender might be an advantage for a change.

'Thanks, Mel,' replied Emma. 'Did you get anything else on Howell, Martin?'

'Apart from his nasty habits he seems to have avoided trouble with us. He doesn't drive or own a motor vehicle. He was knocked off his bike a couple of weeks before his trial and got a broken wrist. It was probably deliberate but the car driver wasn't identified. He had an unpleasant time inside, as you'd expect, but wasn't seriously injured. It just seemed to take a long time for his wrist to heal. He was unemployed and wouldn't have been able to get a job involving contact with children or vulnerable people – he'd have failed the DBS check every time. He was banned from living or walking within a mile of a school or children's playground and lived in a flat in Felton Street under a different name.'

'OK.' Emma nodded her thanks. 'Jack, can you get someone to look through CCTV for the day before he was found? See if we can track his movements. With so many people wearing face masks, it's probably a waste of time, but we've got to do it anyway. Get someone to search his flat for threatening letters, IT – anything relevant. Does he have any friends, relatives or former work colleagues? Also, we need door-to-doors, but I doubt we'll get owt from that. If anyone knows who he was, they'll not help us catch his killer. I'm expecting the report from forensics in the morning, so we'll meet up again at lunchtime tomorrow. Thanks, folks.'

Chapter Four

Day 5

The Mexton Messenger

Paedo poisoned: police perplexed

The man found dead outside Greyfriars Primary Academy three days ago was convicted paedophile monster Gordon Howell. He had been living in Mexton under an assumed name. Police are not releasing any further details but the paper understands that Howell was poisoned with strychnine, a particularly nasty chemical used to kill moles. How and why he was killed has not been disclosed and the police appear to have no leads as yet.

The Messenger *does not condone murder, but wouldn't it be safer for everyone if predatory perverts like Howell were kept locked up? It would certainly have been safer for Howell. Enter the readers' poll and text your answers to the following questions to 75957892, with the heading Poisonpoll:*

- *Should Gordon Howell have been kept in prison?*
- *Do you regret that Gordon Howell was poisoned?*

'Have you seen this shit in the paper, guv?' asked Mel, standing behind Emma in the coffee queue. 'It's an unsigned leader but it's got Jenny Pike's nasty hands all over it.'

'Yes, I have,' Emma replied, wearily. 'Why do these buggers try to make our job so bloody difficult? One day they'll need us and perhaps they won't be so critical, but until then we've got to keep putting up with their bullshit. And I'd like to find out who's talking to that rag and leaking sensitive information. If I only had the time to investigate. Come on. Incident room in ten minutes.

'Has anyone found out anything useful?' asked Emma, standing tall in an elegant trouser suit, against a whiteboard that had little on it. 'Forensics haven't got back to me yet as they're short of staff. How about the CCTV, Jack?'

'Addy's been through hours of stuff and managed to find Howell coming out of a deli at about three, holding a paper bag. Someone wearing a baseball cap and a mask bumped into him outside the shop and he dropped the bag, The stranger picked it up and then Howell headed off to the park, which is probably in breach of his licence. Addy checked with the owner and, apparently, Howell's a regular customer. He always buys a baklava.'

'Does he put it over his head?' joked Mel.

'No, Mel, it's a sweet, sticky pastry. Don't be silly,' Jack replied.

'That must be how he was poisoned,' said Emma, frowning at Mel. 'The stranger switched his cake for one with strychnine in it. And the sweetness would disguise the taste of the chemical, which, Dr Durbridge told me, is very bitter. Where did the stranger go?'

'In the opposite direction to Howell,' DC 'Addy' Adeyemo chipped in. 'He ducked down a side street and I couldn't see him again. He probably changed his appearance or got into a vehicle. It's busy round there so we can't track every car and van in the vicinity.'

'Fair point. Thanks, Addy. How about door-to-doors around Howell's flat?'

'Nothing, guv,' said Martin. 'No-one seemed to know him. He kept himself to himself and rarely went out, except on weekday afternoons, shortly before the schools finish. His immediate neighbours said he was quiet and never had visitors.'

'Hmmm. We know he has no relatives in the area and, obviously, has no work colleagues. What about enemies? What sort of person are we looking for? Suggestions, please.'

'Someone who hates nonces?'

'A pharmacist or chemist. Maybe a botanist?'

'Someone who's been abused?'

'A parent or teacher at the school where he worked?'

'I hate to suggest it,' said Mel, 'but someone in the Job? Or a prison officer?'

Emma sighed. 'All these are possible, but the field covers about half of Mexton. It's certainly worth talking to the headteacher at the school. Digital forensics have got Howell's phone and will look for any threatening messages. But we can't go talking to everyone who knows a bit about chemistry or plants. I'll talk to the DCI and see if he thinks a public appeal is worthwhile. Somehow, I doubt it. Right, Mel, can you track down the headteacher and arrange an interview?

Then talk to those parents. Please remember, everyone, and I'm sure I don't need to remind you, that whatever Gordon Howell did, he deserves justice. Thank you, all.'

The killer read the newspaper with a feeling of deep satisfaction. Not only had justice been served but his target's vile history had come to light. He would wait to see the result of the paper's poll, but he felt sure that the public would be on his side.

Exerting this power gave him a thrill like no other. The fact that he was ridding society of vermin made it all the sweeter. He had a list of names for future projects. They'd none of them be missed, but who to choose next? Yes, this one. He would have to be careful that no-one else was harmed, but that shouldn't be too difficult. He smiled contentedly and opened his chemicals cupboard, humming the melody from *Danse Macabre,* as he selected a bottle and a jar.

Chapter Five

Eight months previously

LONDON, Barcelona, Prague and now Mexton. 'Why the hell did I end up back here?' Valentina Malenka, aka Marnie Draycott, asked herself, albeit rhetorically. She had unfinished business to attend to and Mexton would be the last place anyone would look for her. The plastic surgery, which took a large chunk out of her savings, should prevent her from being recognised, and her secluded cottage on the outskirts of the town would make doubly sure. She had a mole in the local police force and, courtesy of the internet and 5G, she would be able to rebuild her finances, order provisions and carry on her business, leaving her home only occasionally.

Valentina's business was blackmail. Her time running a high-class escort agency in London had enabled her to gather a wealth of material on rich, and prominent, clients. Previously she had used this influence to build up a network of corrupt police officers and customs officials, which eased the flow of drugs imported and distributed by the Maldobourne gang. But now she needed to cash in, and blackmail was much less risky than drugs. Or so she hoped.

It only took her a few days to set up two new online identities and a couple of cryptocurrency accounts. Her most valuable asset, apart from her ruthless personality, was a flash drive that contained the details of potential victims, all of whom would hand over substantial sums to prevent their marital lapses or peculiar proclivities becoming public knowledge. She copied this information into both new cloud accounts and also made physical copies. Just in case.

While she was recovering from the plastic surgery, in an anonymous private hospital in Slovenia, she had befriended a hacker who had undergone a similar operation to avoid the vengeance of the Ukrainian mafia, from whom he had purloined several million dollars. He explained a number of techniques for disguising email addresses and remaining anonymous on the internet. She showed her gratitude physically and he promised to advise her if she needed help in the future.

So where should she start? The cabinet minister who, as a back-bench MP, had enjoyed dressing up in women's clothes while using the services of the escort agency she used to run in London? The police officer with a penchant for snorting cocaine off young women's breasts? The gutter press would just love the photos. Or the former newspaper columnist and senior politician who not only had a wife and mistress but vigorously enjoyed the services provided by her agency while dressed as a bus driver?

Once, the list had been long and varied, opening many windows on the peculiarities of human nature, and offering the prospect of a substantial income if used properly. But now it was no longer enough. Some targets had confessed to their indiscretions, or been outed by the press, and were no longer vulnerable. A few had been arrested and two had died. She needed new blood, to replenish her bank balance.

She would start locally, she decided. There were two or three individuals in or around Mexton who could contribute moderate sums to her retirement fund: the new MP, for a start. She still had contacts in the escort agency, which was now run by a couple of former employees, and the MP had let it slip that his brother, the owner of a meat processing firm, was in line for a substantial contract providing anti-viral sprays and wipes to the NHS, thanks to his influence with the Minister. The fact that they were virtually useless didn't seem to matter. The nine-bob-note simile sprang to mind. Then there was the police officer. He was local, too. But she did need to expand her portfolio. She picked up one of her phones and dialled a burner number.

Chapter Six

'Do you swim?'

DC Karen Groves flinched when she heard the voice. She had hoped she would never have to do anything for the woman who had been posting her a modest amount of money each month, but it looked as though she was about to collect.

'Err. Yes. A bit.'

'Meet me at Mexton sports centre at six this evening. I'll be in the pool wearing a navy one-piece and a yellow cap.'

The phone beeped off.

Karen shivered. Decision time. Should she confess and turn her blackmailer in or prepare to betray her colleagues? She couldn't bear the thought of her indiscretion with a senior officer being splashed over the internet. The video would ruin her career. But she had taken an oath to uphold the law and she hated the idea of breaking it. Perhaps she would go along and see what the woman wanted. Then she could decide.

The pool was quiet when Karen arrived. The evening swimming clubs were yet to start and those wanting a quick dip before their evening meal had left. Once changed, she spotted her nemesis immediately and lowered herself into the water to join her. The two women swam slowly up and down the middle of the pool, clear of any other swimmers who might overhear them.

'Time to earn your money, Karen,' said her unwelcome companion.

'What do you want me to do?' Karen's nervousness interrupted the rhythm of her strokes and she had to work to keep up.

'Nothing too difficult, or dangerous. I need to know a couple of things. Firstly, the names of any public figures under investigation for crimes, before they are arrested. Secondly, I need to know of any officers who might be vulnerable, whether it's through potential misconduct, drinking or gambling.'

'Why do you need this stuff?'

'I'm surprised you haven't guessed. I intend to invite them to contribute to my pension fund.'

'That's disgusting. You're just a common blackmailer.'

'Half right. I am a blackmailer but I'm certainly not common. Oh, two other things. I will need an early warning of any investigations that may affect my activities. And I am concerned for the safety of your DC Cotton. Keep me informed about her.'

'Why Mel?'

'Never you mind. It's personal. Now, is everything clear? You'll get a bonus as well as your retainer every time you give me something useful. Enjoy the rest of your swim.'

Valentina pulled away with a powerful crawl, leaving Karen treading water and feeling sick to her stomach. No way would she pass on information about vulnerable fellow officers, but what was the woman's connection with Mel Cotton? Obviously something she couldn't ask her colleague about, but was the woman protecting her in some way? It wouldn't be difficult to keep her ears open for information about prominent citizens in trouble, but surely she wasn't expected to search the PNC? Unless she had a good reason to do so, she could be sacked and prosecuted for misconduct in public office. Karen's tears mingled with the chlorinated water as she swam listlessly to the poolside and hauled herself out. 'I'm screwed,' she thought, terrified that she might be forced into doing something desperate.

Chapter Seven

Day 6

IT WASN'T hard to follow the little creep to his lair. After all, he had no reason to believe he was being followed. He specialised in spying on others, but why should anyone spy on him? The man watched as his target entered the empty flat, and then stepped quietly up behind him. Jamming his foot in the door, he shoved the gangling youth in the back and produced a replica semi-automatic pistol from his coat pocket. It looked just like the real thing, but lacked the orange paint that would have allowed him to carry it legally in public.

'Show me your darkroom. Now.'

He emphasised his command by jabbing the pistol in the young man's ribs.

'In here. I'll show you. Please don't hurt me,' the youth sobbed, his trousers dampening as he lost control of his bladder.

He led the man to the back of the flat, drew aside a heavy black curtain and opened a door. A red light came on, illuminating an array of photographic equipment. An enlarger, bottles of chemicals and several plastic baths were set out along a bench, and drying prints, mostly showing young women with little or no clothing, hung from pegs on a line that stretched across the small room.

'Now turn around and put your thumbs together behind your back.'

The intruder tightened a plastic cable tie over the proffered thumb joints, immobilising the young man's arms. He pushed him to the ground and pulled a glass bottle and a small jar from a small rucksack. He poured hydrochloric acid from the bottle into one of the plastic baths on the bench. Unscrewing the top of the jar, he paused.

'Remember Stacey?' The youth looked guilty and then nodded cautiously. 'The Bannisters send their regards.'

With that he tipped a cascade of orange crystals into the bath full of acid and stepped briskly out of the room, grabbing the youth's bag and jamming the door shut with a wooden wedge retrieved from his rucksack. While he taped a notice to the door carrying the warning 'Hydrogen Cyanide. Do not Enter' he could hear the youth's pleas to be let out. These soon turned to screams, followed by a painful gurgle. Then there was silence.

Chapter Eight

THE CRUNCH CAME WHEN SHEILA, the female eclectus, deposited a large streak of shit on Mel's freshly dry-cleaned jacket as it hung in the bathroom.

'Tom,' she yelled. 'We've got to do something about these bloody parrots.'

'What's up? What's happened?' Tom rushed into the bathroom, an anxious expression on his face. 'Is one of them hurt?'

'Never mind the birds, you idiot. My jacket's ruined. It'll need cleaning again and I doubt the stain will come out. Look at it.'

Tom looked sheepishly at the splattered garment and tried to make excuses.

'I'm sorry, love. But they can't stay in their cages all day. They have to fly a bit so they can build up their flight muscles. Especially Sheila. She's still learning and she had no freedom until we rescued her from that warehouse.'

'That's all very well. But this used to be a clean and tidy flat before they moved in. Now it's like a parrot's toilet. And it's really beginning to piss me off.'

'You know what this means, don't you?' said Tom, his face set. 'It's not working.'

'What?'

A flicker of apprehension crossed Mel's face.

'We've got to move.'

She relaxed slightly.

'But I thought you liked living here,' she said.

'Yes, I do. But you're right. We need to find space for the parrots, where they have some freedom but don't wreck the place. And, also, where the noise won't disturb the neighbours.'

Mel looked around the flat, taking in the chewed paintwork, spilt bird food, the half-shredded curtains and the ubiquitous evidence of the birds' bowel habits, stains that were almost impossible to remove.

'So where did you have in mind?'

'Nothing specific, yet. But I think we should start looking. We're getting married when this virus thing is over so let's make a new start in a new home. What do you reckon?'

'I think that's a wonderful idea,' said Mel, hugging Tom and removing a scarlet feather from his hair. 'We'll work out what we want, and what we can afford. We'll look at the online estate agents at the weekend. In the meantime, is there any way you can persuade Bruce to stop mimicking the sound of orgasms?'

'Sadly, no. A parrot's got to do what a parrot's got to do. Speaking of which...'

His hand moved downwards to her behind. Mel pushed him away, smiling.

'Stop it. You're supposed to be cooking the dinner. I've got an appetite.'

'So have I.'

He ducked as Mel threw a towel at him, and ambled off to the kitchen.

Chapter Nine

Day 7

PATIENCE PAID OFF. After three weeks grabbing his latest subject's rubbish on the night it was put out, and returning it after a thorough search, he struck gold. The screwed-up invoice and receipt from the supplements company, which included the customer number, was exactly what he needed for his next project.

It took him less than half an hour to mock up a letter with the company's logo.

Dear Mr Foreman,

Ergophyto Plus!

As a loyal customer we thought you should be among the first to try our new energy leaves. This careful blend of organic plant material is specially tailored to release the energy from your food in the most effective way, ensuring you can draw upon it as and when you need it most. Try it with a kale and carrot smoothie before breakfast or half an hour before your evening meal. You'll be amazed at the results and will definitely want to order more when Ergophyto Plus! comes onto the market in a month's time. Use the special offer code at the bottom of this letter to get a 20% discount and try this free sample today!

Stay strong, stay healthy,

The Ergophyto Plus! Team

Offer code EP20

He slipped the letter into a slim cardboard box with a plastic bag containing plant material. He stuck on the box an address label, bearing a copy of the company's logo and Foreman's name, address and customer number. A mocked-up postage label completed the deception, and when his target had left for work, he posted it through the letter box. Then all he had to do was wait.

Gary Foreman picked up the cardboard box along with his other post. 'That's odd,' he thought. 'I've only just had an order.' He opened it immediately and read the letter. 'Cool,' he thought. 'Worth a try. Never heard of Ergophyto Plus but these guys know what they're doing.' He mixed most of the contents of the plastic bag with some water, chopped kale and carrot, as instructed, added a scoop of peanut powder for protein, and whizzed it into a smoothie. It tasted a bit odd, perhaps rather bitter, but it wasn't too unpleasant. He knew from experience that supplements were not always a delight to take, but he was convinced they did him good. He had the muscles to prove it, although the steroids obviously helped as well.

He changed into a vest and shorts and started his workout on the home gym equipment installed in his front room. It wasn't as good as going to the proper gym. He would do that later. But it was useful exercise to be going on with and would work up his appetite for dinner. He never drew the curtains while he worked out. He wanted passers-by to see the power of his muscles and the effort he was putting in. Not that any of his neighbours commented, but he was sure they admired him.

He spent some time on the cross trainer and then moved to lifting weights. By then he was feeling slightly nauseous. 'Perhaps it's the new stuff,' he thought. Still, no pain, no gain. He pressed on and was puzzled to find that everything he looked at had a yellowish tinge to it. The light bulbs and the LEDs on his music system seemed to have haloes around them.

He decided to finish off his routine on the exercise bicycle and then have a shower and some food. Clamping his hands on the grips he was surprised to find that his heart rate, monitored by the machine, was all over the place. He could feel irregular beats in his chest. Sometimes extra fast, sometimes slow. He was determined to finish his workout so he carried on pedalling until, a few minutes later, he vomited, collapsed over the handlebars and died, as his heart finally stopped.

Chapter Ten

Day 8

'CAN you take a look at a dead bodybuilder, Jack?' asked Emma. 'The postie spotted him this morning slumped over an exercise bike. She called the paramedics, who thought it a bit odd. Take Mel with you.'

'OK, Emma. Give me the address and we'll drop round.'

When the two detectives arrived at Foreman's house, they found a paramedic waiting for them.

'What's bothering you, Jim?' asked Mel, reading his name from the badge on his uniform.

'Come and see.'

He led them through the forced-open door into the front room.

'He's obviously fit, yet he's just collapsed. He vomited over the bike, but it looks as though he kept pedalling for a moment after he threw up. You can see from the way the pedals have sprayed the sick over the frame.'

'Quite the detective, aren't you?' said Jack, slightly sarcastically.

'I don't mean to trespass on your patch,' said Jim, huffily. 'But I'm just telling you what I saw. He was probably confused. For some reason his heart stopped while he was exercising. It could be he's taken too many steroids or it could be something else. I think he'll need a post mortem.'

'Oh shit. Not another bloody poisoning,' moaned Jack.

'I didn't say that,' said Jim. 'But it's worth bearing in mind. Anyway, I'll leave you to it. My mate had to dash off to an emergency but he'll be picking me up in a few minutes.'

'Thanks for calling us, Jim,' said Mel. 'We'll have a look around. You did the right thing. Better leave your details, and your mate's name, in case we need DNA samples for elimination.'

She smiled at him, hoping to compensate for Jack's grumpiness. Once he had left, Jack and Mel put on nitrile gloves and approached the body, carefully avoiding stepping in the pool of sick. Finding no obvious signs of violence, they turned their attention to the contents of Foreman's kitchen.

'Supplements! Load of rubbish,' grumbled Jack as he looked through the assorted tubs, jars and packets spread out over the deceased's kitchen worktop.

'You can get all you need from a proper diet. Haven't you noticed that the people going into health food shops never look very healthy?'

'Yes, but not everyone gets a proper diet, do they?' replied Mel. 'And guys like this try to boost their muscles by any means possible. They're suckers for clever advertising from charlatans and woo merchants. I bet he took steroids as well. So, you're not a fan of alternative medicine then?' she teased.

'Nope. I prefer to get my health advice from a qualified doctor, not some fanny-steaming film star with the scientific qualifications of a gerbil.'

Mel laughed.

'What's this then?' she queried, holding up a plastic bag containing bits of plant material.'

Jack sniffed it, cautiously.

'It's not weed. Perhaps it's another barmy supplement. Look, there's a letter from a supplier. Ergophyto Plus, they call it. I think we'd better bag it up. I reckon the paramedic's right. This is fishy. I'll get Emma's authorisation to move the body and we'll seal the house in case it's a crime scene. The SOCOs can have the pleasure of sampling the puke before he's moved.'

'What's got into you today, Jack?' Mel asked. 'You've been a grumpy sod ever since the boss sent us here.'

'Nothing really. Sarah and I were at the pub quiz last night and there was a bit of a row. One of the other teams cheated. Their leader had a Bluetooth earpiece and someone else in the pub, not officially playing, was using a mobile phone to look up the answers and feeding them to him. I called them out and there was an argument. One of them took a swing at me and I decked him. Self-defence, of course. But I'm worried he'll make a complaint.'

'I hadn't got you down as a pub brawler, Jack,' chuckled Mel. 'But I'm sure you'll be all right, if he started it.'

'I hope so. No-one at the pub knows I'm a copper and I don't want it to come out. People behave differently when they realise. We love doing these quizzes. It doesn't really matter if we don't win, and I'd hate to have to stop.'

Mel smiled in sympathy while Jack phoned Emma.

Chapter Eleven

Day 9

'OK, people. What have we found out about the bodybuilder?' asked Emma at the morning briefing.

'He's a muscle freak,' replied Martin. 'He belongs to two local gyms and has loads of equipment at home. He's a scaffolder by trade, working for several firms on a casual basis. He often puts up rigs for a builder called Terry Barwell and also for Overton Windows and Mexton Maintenance Services.'

'Any previous?' asked Emma.

'A few speeding tickets. He drives, or rather drove, a Porsche and regarded speed limits as merely suggestions. He was within two points of losing his licence, so he's behaved himself for the past few months. One thing of interest: when he was stopped the last time, he was found to have anabolic steroids in his possession. They're Class C, but he wasn't prosecuted as we couldn't prove he was supplying them to someone else. There was a scandal about steroids in a local gym a year or so ago after a kid died of a heart attack from abusing the things. We interviewed several people and Foreman's name came up, but we couldn't prove where the kid got the drugs.

'There's a lot of that in Mexton's gyms,' continued Martin. 'I used a gym when I was recovering from my injury and I'm sure people were selling steroids. No proof, of course, and they knew I was a copper, so nobody offered me any.'

'A Porsche is a bit pricey for a scaffolder, isn't it?' said Trevor.

'Makes my point, I think, replied Martin. 'There's money in steroids.'

'Was that what killed our bodybuilder?' asked Mel.

'I was coming to that,' replied Emma. 'I've had the results of the PM. It seems that he died from heart failure. The interesting question is what caused the heart failure? Dr Durbridge found the remains of a vegetable drink in Foreman's stomach. Some of the material resembled the chopped leaves in that supplement we found in his kitchen. He sent samples to a botanist at the university, who identified them as being from two species of plant: Stevia, a natural sweetener, and Foxglove.

Jack whistled. 'That'll stop your heart, won't it?'

'It will,' confirmed Emma. 'Dr Durbridge has sent the stomach contents for analysis, requesting a fast-track test for the poisons in Foxglove. It may take a couple of days, but in the meantime, I want someone to contact the supplement firm to check the toxic leaves didn't get into their supplement by mistake, although that's highly unlikely.'

'I'll do it, guv,' said Karen.

'Thanks. We also need someone to go round the gyms Foreman used and ask if he had any enemies, did they know about steroid sales and so on. They'll deny he sold stuff, but we have to ask. We also need to look deeper into his background, social media accounts, etcetera. Check his finances, too, and do a full search of his house.

'Now. Gordon Howell. We've found nowt. No more CCTV of any use and no witnesses. As to motive, I suppose anyone who read about him in the papers would like to have a go at him. Everybody hates paedophiles. But this was carefully planned. Someone knew about his routine and also about the rumours at the school that weren't in the press. You talked to the headteacher, Mel. What did she say?'

'Two families had their suspicions, she told me, and the school safeguarding lead looked into it. Apparently, he was getting a little too friendly with a couple of girls. They said he never touched them, and the school believed them. He insisted he'd done nothing wrong, but he was warned about his behaviour and the school recorded the incident. They're very hot on this. I've had a word with the families concerned and they were horrified when he was convicted for possessing those images. I wouldn't put them in the frame, though. If they went after him, it would be with fists and baseball bats, not some hard-to-get poison.'

'Did you find anything in his flat, Trevor?'

'No evidence of threats or vandalism, so I guess his false identity was protecting him. He did have a laptop, and Amira took a look at it. She said there was some disgusting material on it, so prison clearly didn't deter him from his nasty interests.

'A woman thought she recognised him in the park,' said Martin. 'She saw his photo in the paper and phoned us. He was sitting on a bench near the playground when she walked past with her toddler in a pushchair. She said he looked "creepy". We looked in the rubbish bin next to the bench for the wrapper from his baklava but it had already been emptied.'

'Do we think these two cases are linked?' asked Karen. 'They're both poisonings.'

'I don't think so,' replied Emma. 'The MOs are different,

as are the victims. We'll keep an open mind, but there's nothing to suggest it at the moment. Jack, can you allocate tasks, please? Thanks, everybody. Grab your coffees and get to work.'

An hour later, Karen knocked on Emma's office door.

'That supplement firm, guv. I spoke to their operations manager, who did some checking. Firstly, they've never heard of Ergophyto Plus. Secondly, they never have Foxgloves, in any shape or form, on their premises. And, thirdly, they haven't sent Gary Foreman any free samples of anything. The manager checked their records, and the customer number on the letter was correct. Foreman bought some whey powder and nut butter a few weeks ago, and that was the last order they sent him. I've also spoken to the supervisor at the Post Office delivery depot. She's going to ask the local postie if he remembers delivering the package.'

'Thanks, Karen, that's really useful. Well done. It's pretty obvious he was deliberately poisoned with the fake supplement. It looks as though the killer obtained his customer details from somewhere. Possibly his rubbish. Could you check with the Council when the bins are emptied in his street? Perhaps we can narrow down the time when his bin was raided, but I doubt we'll get any witnesses.'

'OK, guv. I'll get on to it.'

As Emma tucked the ends of her auburn hair into the cycle helmet and swung her leg over the saddle, she pondered over Karen's suggestion. There were no obvious links, apart from the fact that the killer was clearly intelligent, could plan things in detail and knew something about poisons. But suppose there was a serial poisoner starting work in Mexton? They were getting into Agatha Christie territory here, she remonstrated with herself. Things like this don't happen in real life. Then she remembered Harold Shipman.

Chapter Twelve

Day 10

The Mexton Messenger

Poisons puzzle pathetic police

A second person has been found poisoned in Mexton and the police are clueless. Gary Foreman, a popular local scaffolder, was found dead in his home yesterday. The Messenger *understands that he is thought to have been killed with Foxgloves, but the police are not confirming this.*

Is there a modern-day Borgia at work in Mexton? The Messenger *wants to know. We will be watching the situation closely and keeping a very close eye on what the police are doing – or not doing.*

The article in the *Messenger* was short but typical of the paper, and of its crime correspondent in particular.

'Where the hell did she get this?' a vexed Emma asked, semi-rhetorically.

'Well not from any of us, I'm sure,' replied Jack. 'They all know better than to talk to the *Messenger* and that grudge-bearing cow, Jenny Pike. Perhaps it's someone linked to the mortuary? A hospital porter? An undertaker, even, although they're usually pretty discreet. People do love to gossip, though, and poisoning is a really juicy topic.'

'I suppose you're right. I'll remind the team to be careful who they talk to, at the next briefing. I'll also speak to Dr Durbridge, although he won't be pleased at the suggestion that one of his colleagues is indiscreet. Is there any point meeting Jenny Pike and trying to improve relations?'

'I doubt it. She was always a bit sniffy about us, but since she was done for drink-driving, she's been vitriolic. Maybe one day she'll need us and perhaps that'll change her tune.'

'OK. Thanks, Jack. I've a meeting with the DCI and I'll let him know about the article, if he hasn't already seen it.'

As Emma walked slowly towards DCI Farlowe's office she wondered, once again, what was wrong with the paper. Jenny Pike might have a chip on her shoulder, but the editor chose to publish her rants. Of course, the police should be called to account, and challenged if they were not doing their job. But Jenny Pike seemed to be running a campaign, which had impeded their investigations in the past. Emma had never encountered problems like this when she worked in Sheffield.

'So, the paper thinks the cases are linked. More than the police do,' he supposed. 'It won't be long before even the dumbest copper makes the connection, and they'll have plenty to connect by the time I've finished.' He stepped out into his garden and admired the plants growing there, most of them lethal if eaten. 'That will do,' he thought, putting on gloves and gently handling a tall, shrubby plant with dull purple flowers. 'And I know just the person for it.'

Chapter Thirteen

'Come on. She'll have got her tits out by now,' Stevie urged. 'Her brother promised.'

'All right, all right. I'm just syncing the camera with the laptop. Stop being a dick,' his mate replied. 'She'll be there as long as the sun shines.'

The two boys crouched over the drone as it sat on the tarmac like a giant, malevolent spider. Eventually, Eddy was satisfied and reached for the controller. The rotors whirred and the machine took off, lurching at first then stabilising as Eddy's confidence grew. Stevie's eyes were glued to the laptop's screen as the drone headed for the garden two streets away where Susie Evans regularly sunbathed topless, protected by high hedges on three sides and the wall of her house on the fourth. But there was no protection from eyes in the sky.

'Stop, Eddy. Go back,' shouted Stevie as the drone soared over the rooftops. 'There's a body on that roof.'

'Stop pissing about. We've got a video to make.'

'No. I mean it. Go back to that house on its own. In the

trees. Look at the screen. There's something on a square bit of roof. It looks like a body. I swear.'

Reluctantly, Eddy retraced the drone's path and held it hovering over a detached house, set back from the road and screened by trees.

'You're right. There's something on that flat bit. I'll go in closer. Oh shit. You're right. What the fuck do we do now?'

'We gotta tell someone. The police.'

'Yeah, but what do we tell them? We were spying on a naked bird? Get real.'

'But we didn't get that far, did we? We were just flying around.'

'Don't think even that's legal.'

'But s'pose it's someone injured? They'd need help.'

Eddy scowled and eventually agreed.

'OK. Phone the cops. But don't say anything about Susie. We'll get her next time.'

Half an hour later PCs Reg Dawnay and Sally Erskine knocked on Eddy's parents' door. Eddy himself let them in and explained that they had been test flying a drone with a camera and had picked up something disturbing. He showed them the footage on the laptop.

'You were right to call us. That does look like a person, on what seems to be a garage roof,' said Reg. 'Where is this house, exactly?'

'It's in the next road along. That way.' Eddy pointed. 'It's bigger than the rest and behind those trees.'

'OK. Thank you. We'll go round and take a look. It was very responsible of you to call us. But just one thing.' Reg paused. 'You wouldn't be thinking of putting this out on the internet, would you? Because if you were, we might have to confiscate the laptop. Also, you do know that there are laws covering drone flying, especially in residential areas, don't you? And you're not allowed to film or photograph people without their consent?'

'Yes, officer,' said Eddy, meekly. 'I'll delete the footage.'

'Good lad. You can do it now, can't you? And from your trash bin.'

Eddy complied, furious inside at the loss of something that would have gained him much more respect than shots of Susie Evans' breasts.

'Could we really confiscate his laptop?' asked Sally, as they returned to the car.

'I doubt it, unless there was footage showing evidence of a crime,' Reg replied. 'But the bluff worked and the kid deleted the film. I can't stand it when people exploit others' misery by posting scenes of road accidents and fights on social media. We'd better get round to that garage sharpish.'

When the officers arrived at the house on the video, the iron gates guarding a gravelled drive were open. They drove in and had to squeeze past a BMW saloon that appeared to have veered off the curving drive on its way to the entrance and crashed into a tree. They parked in front of an impressive modern house that must have cost at least seven figures. To the left of the building was a flat-roofed garage containing ladders, a cement mixer, a wheelbarrow, bags of sand and cement and odd lengths of wood. A van parked outside bore a logo of a cheery bricklayer and the slogan 'Build with Barwell. Build with confidence', with a web address and mobile phone number underneath.

A ladder was propped up against the garage, and Sally, younger and more nimble than Reg, climbed cautiously up.

'The kids were right, Reg. There's someone up here. He looks dead but I'll check for a pulse. Better call for paramedics and let the duty inspector know.'

Chapter Fourteen

HALF AN HOUR LATER, a paramedic had confirmed that life was extinct and the scene had been sealed off. The outer cordon covered part of the drive, while the inner tape stretched around the garage. Emma signed in at the outer tape and approached the garage, where SOCOs were removing their equipment from shiny aluminium cases that glinted in the sun.

'Any idea how he got there?' she asked Mark Talbot, the Crime Scene Manager.

'Can't really say until the guys have taken a good look. There's a window overlooking the garage roof he could have come out of but it looks shut. There's also a length of rope round his torso. It's early days yet.'

'OK. Let me know when you've finished and I'll take a look at the body before it's moved. I don't want it spending too long up there in this heat. Cheers.'

Emma spent an hour sitting in her car, dealing with emails on her phone. Needing a break, she got out to stretch her legs and strolled down the drive to where the BMW was crashed. There was considerable damage to the front of the car, and as she peered in through the windows, she could see what looked like traces of blood inside, just above the windscreen. The airbags had deployed and deflated, but she wondered whether the driver hadn't been wearing a seatbelt and had hit his or her head on the roof. She would tell the SOCOs to take a look and maybe ask for an RTC investigator to give an opinion.

When she returned to her car, Mark gave her the all clear to approach the body. She suited up, signed in again and followed the stepping plates to the ladder.

'You can climb up. We've processed the rungs and side bits,' he called.

When Emma reached the garage roof, she saw the body of a slim but muscular man who looked to be in his forties. He was lying on his front, his face turned towards Emma, and whitish dust was visible on the back of his clothes. Emma could see blood on the top of his forehead, and his hair was matted. She climbed back down the ladder and spoke to Mark.

'What's that powder on his clothes?' she asked.

'Looks like cement. We've sampled it and the lab will identify it in due course.'

'OK. Thanks. You can get him moved to the mortuary. I've seen all I need here. Thanks.'

Emma drove back to the station wondering how someone involved in a car crash could end up on top of a garage a hundred metres away. Definitely a suspicious death. She would talk to the DCI and set up a team to investigate.

Chapter Fifteen

Three hours earlier

TERRY BARWELL RETURNED HOME at lunchtime to finish off some paperwork. His VAT returns were due shortly and he had to check the dodgy invoices his accountant had provided for him. He knew the lads could be trusted to get on with the current job, a loft conversion, and the building inspector had been well paid to turn a blind eye to any corners they might cut.

He was pleasantly surprised to see a cardboard box on his doorstep, which, when he opened it, contained a fruit pie. Just the job for lunch, he thought. A note was attached bearing the message 'This is to reward you for all the work you did on my home. Yours sincerely, Nemesia Fortune (Mrs)'. He couldn't, for the life of him, remember a Mrs Fortune but assumed she was a satisfied client who had paid in cash. There was no record of her among the invoices, fake or genuine, that cluttered his desk. But the pie was tempting so he ate a large slice, smothered with cream, after his sandwiches. It was a bit sharp, he thought, but blackberries and blueberries can be like that. He would add some sugar to the next bit.

Half an hour later, Terry began to feel strange. He couldn't quench his thirst, no matter how much water he drank, and his heart was racing. He felt hot and wondered if he was going down with a fever. He hadn't consulted a doctor for years but decided to call in at the surgery and ask to be seen at the end of normal hours, without an appointment. He'd done some work on the building, which no-one had complained about, so he hoped they would see him this evening, as a favour.

Grabbing his car keys, he stumbled to his BMW and climbed in. Turning it round, he floored the accelerator, ignoring the seat belt warning bleep. Everything was blurred and he kept blinking to clear his vision. It didn't work. His heart continued to pound as he hurtled down the drive. He was finding it difficult to breathe. He didn't see the tree, as he failed to take the bend in the drive, until too late. The juddering crash as the car hit the trunk, and the simultaneous explosions as the airbags operated, were the last things he heard before he was hurled from his seat, striking his head on the roof of the cabin and lapsing into unconsciousness.

The man hiding among the trees sat patiently for half an hour, just in case the car caught fire and saved him the rest of the job. Not that he wanted it to. He had a mission to fulfil. A statement to make. So, he approached the car cautiously and looked inside. It was fairly obvious that Terry Barwell was dead, and there was now a small logistical problem to solve, given that the car was immobilised. He sauntered back up the drive, running over in his mind the scene in Barwell's garage. That would do it, he thought. Five minutes later he was trundling a wheelbarrow down the path. He managed to open the driver's door of the BMW and dragged the body into the barrow. Pushing it up a slight gradient through gravel was difficult but he managed it, and when he got back to the house, he stopped for a rest.

Barwell wasn't heavy and it was important that his body should end up on the garage roof. But how would he get it there? Finding a length of blue nylon rope in Barwell's van, he tied it around his victim's chest, under his arms, and tested the knot for strength. He leaned a ladder against the garage wall, climbed up and began to haul. Gradually, a few centimetres at a time, Barwell's body slid up the ladder until it could be dragged across the roof.

Almost exhausted, he climbed down, his hands sore despite his gloves, which had torn on the rough wood, and returned the wheelbarrow and ladder to the garage. The door to the house was unlocked, so he slipped in and found the remains of the pie, still in its cardboard box. No point in leaving easy clues, he said to himself, as he dropped it into a plastic bag. He missed the note, which had slipped under the table and was half-hidden by a chair leg. He rinsed the used plate under a tap before putting it in the dishwasher and did the same with the dirty spoon.

'Another job well done,' he thought, as he strolled back to his car, parked a few streets away. 'Easier than I expected. But hard work nonetheless. The next one had better be a little less physical.'

Chapter Sixteen

Day 11

'WE'VE GOT a potential witness to the Howell killing,' said Addy. 'A uniformed patrol pulled this kid in, on suspicion of drug dealing, and he asked if we'd let him go if he helped us.'

'In his dreams,' replied Emma. 'Who is he?'

'Devon Wilson. According to the drug squad he runs a click-and-collect service for customers, providing just about anything they need to get off their faces. People send him a text saying what they want and he tells them where to collect it, and how much cash to leave. They never actually meet. No-one's been able to prove it yet, but the squad is watching him.'

'Did he have anything on him?'

'A small amount of cannabis, for personal use, he said.'

'OK. Tell him we'll let him off with a caution if he's got anything useful. If he's buggering us about, we'll apply to charge him.'

'Will do.'

Addy returned to the interview room and outlined

Emma's terms. Wilson shuffled in his seat, fiddled with a gold chain around his neck and agreed.

'I was ridin' me bike through the park on Wednesday afternoon, mindin' me business, gettin' fresh air.'

Addy looked sceptical. 'Go on,' he said.

'I saw this white guy, lookin' funny. Not walkin' proper. Ambulance man was helpin' him in a dark van. That ain't right, I thinks. That ain't an ambulance.'

'Then how did you know it was an ambulance man?'

'Cos he had them green clothes on, innit. Then I saw the dude's face on TV. 'Im what got murdered. Figured it was the same guy.'

'Are you sure it was Mr Howell?'

'Definitely. Maybe. Yeah, I'm pretty sure.'

'I see,' sighed Addy. 'I don't suppose you got the van's number?'

'You fink I'm on *Countdown* or somethin'? Got the letters, though. LSD. Easy to remember, innit.' Wilson grinned.

'How about the man in the uniform. What did he look like?'

Wilson shrugged. 'Tall. Not fat. Not thin. Wore a Nike cap. Had a mask on. Cheap white trainers.

'Did you notice anything else?'

'Nah.' Wilson shrugged. 'Do I get to go now?'

'If that's all you can remember, yes. We won't charge you. The officer at the desk will caution you, so don't get caught in possession again.'

'Yeah. Can I have me weed back?'

'Don't push it, mate. But thanks.'

Addy steered Wilson back to reception and went to find Emma.

Chapter Seventeen

Day 12

When the preliminary results from the PM on Terry Barwell came in, Emma called the team together in the incident room.

'OK,' she began, trying to ignore a strange buzzing from the room lights.

'Terry Barwell, local builder, found dead on top of his garage roof, his body spotted by a couple of lads flying a drone. From the rope around his chest, fibres on the ladder leaning against the garage and scuff marks on the roofing material, it looks as though he was dragged up there, by a person or persons unknown, when already dead. It seems as though he crashed his car going down the drive. But the impact didn't kill him. The airbags operated, and although he struck his head on the inside of the car roof, the pathologist didn't think that was enough to cause a fatal injury. Physically, he was in good shape and had no underlying heart disease or brain issues. A possibility is that he was feeling ill and was going for help, although there's no record of a call to the NHS helpline or his GP.

'There is another, more sinister, scenario. Barwell could have been poisoned. Dr Durbridge is looking into that, but it will be some time before he has anything to report. SOCOs have already been through his place, but I'd like a couple of DCs to look for evidence of anyone having a grudge against him. Also, look for anything toxic he could have taken by accident – you know what to do. Mel, can you go with Karen, please?'

'Yes, guv. But how did his body get from the crashed car to the garage roof, if he was already dead?'

'SOCOs found traces of cement on his clothing that resembled samples taken from a wheelbarrow at the scene. So, if he was murdered, someone, for some reason, wanted him on the roof and wheeled him back up the path. It goes without saying that someone physically fairly strong was involved. If it was an accident, which seems unlikely, someone must have put his body on the roof. Which is weird.'

'Perhaps it was meant to send a message,' suggested Martin.

'OK. But what was the message and to whom was it sent? Worth bearing in mind, though. Right then, jobs to do. Thank you.'

'What's with the long face, Karen?' asked Mel, as they drove out of the station car park.

'Nothing.'

'Nothing? You've had a face like a wet Monday ever since the briefing. D'you have a problem working with me?'

'Why should I have a problem working with Wonder Woman?' snapped Karen.

'What the fuck do you mean by that?'

Karen looked uncomfortable but eventually replied.

'You're quite the little star, aren't you? Daughter of two respected coppers, defuser of bombs and catcher of killers, with a hot, clever boyfriend. You're one of the youngest coppers to get a QGM and you're protected. Makes the rest of us look inadequate.'

Mel pulled the car in to the side of the road, furious and concerned that Karen's outburst might affect her driving.

'Well, I don't know what your problem is, Karen. I do not swan about the station like a diva, I never mention my parents or the medal. As to the rest, I was just doing my job. I happened to be in the right places at the right times. And I was fucking scared. Yes, Tom is brilliant but there's nothing to stop you getting a partner. There's nothing wrong with you apart from this chip on your shoulder. You've got a nice face, a good figure and you dress well. I've never had any preferential treatment from anyone. In fact, Jack's been pretty hard on me in the past. And what do you mean I'm protected?'

'Nothing. Forget it.'

Mel was confused.

'If I'm arrogant towards you, call me out. But I don't think I am. And if I can help, with advice or just a chat, let me know and we'll go for a drink or a coffee or something. But don't have a go at me for no good reason. OK?'

'Yeah, all right. Sorry,' Karen said, sheepishly. 'I'm just in a mood. Personal stuff.'

'OK. Now let's get back to doing our jobs.'

They drove to the crime scene in an awkward silence, Mel still wondering what Karen had meant by protected.

Chapter Eighteen

Day 13

Emma called the team together to discuss the latest results.

'Firstly, what do we know about the victim? Addy, you were looking into him.'

'Yes, guv. Terry Barwell was forty-three and ran his own building business. He started out working for various firms, then went solo after a few years. He now sub-contracts most of the work to other people. He still does the occasional small job himself, and HMRC suspects that the cash never finds its way into his accounts.'

'Anything suspicious about him, from our point of view?'

'He's been prosecuted a couple of times by the Health and Safety Executive for sloppy safety standards but escaped with fines as no-one was seriously hurt. He's had a few speeding tickets and prosecutions for defects on his vehicles. The main thing of interest is a charge of fraud last year. He was accused of taking five grand from a seventy-six-year-old pensioner for fixing three roof tiles that had fallen off in a storm. The case collapsed when the gentleman in question withdrew his complaint. There's a note to say he died three months later, but the circumstances weren't suspicious.'

'Anything to suggest he was coerced into withdrawing?' asked Emma.

'Nothing on file, guv, but his initial statement is lucid and detailed. He was clearly determined to get some kind of justice.'

'Hmmm. How about the house? What did you and Karen find, Mel?'

'Nothing much of interest. No bottles marked poison, but Karen spotted a note that had fallen on the kitchen floor. It was thanking Barwell for the work he had done somewhere and signed Nemesia Fortune. There's no-one of that name on record, I'm afraid.'

'It's clearly made up,' said Jack. 'Unless the first name is referring to a garden plant, which I doubt, it's from Nemesis, the Greek goddess of retribution. Fortune speaks for itself. It's from the killer.'

'Just goes to show how useful your pub quizzes are, Jack,' grinned Mel.

Jack smiled slightly.

'What have you done with the note, Mel?'

'I sent it to forensics, guv. It looked to me as though it was printed off a computer. There was no handwritten signature. Also, there was a purplish stain on one corner. Looked like fruit juice. There was nothing in the place that colour, though, and there were no dirty dishes. If he was poisoned, either it happened somewhere else or the killer cleaned up afterwards.'

Emma thought for a moment, then picked up her phone and dialled.

'Dr Durbridge? Sorry to bother you. I hope you're not up

to your armpits in viscera. I'm putting you on speaker. It's about Terry Barwell. Did you find fruit or fruit juice in his stomach by any chance?'

'Funnily enough,' the pathologist replied, 'I was going to call you later. Shortly before he died, Mr Barwell ate a large portion of fruit pie. I recognised some of the fruit – blackberries and blueberries – but some I wasn't so sure of. I sent a sample to Kew and they came back to me first thing this morning. The pie contained berries from *Atropa belladonna* – Deadly Nightshade – which, as you know, is highly poisonous. It must have been loaded with sugar, as they're extremely bitter. I took blood, urine, stomach contents and liver samples during the post-mortem, which I've sent off to the lab to see if they can find atropine in them, but that could be difficult as the stuff doesn't hang around long after death. So, it looks suspiciously like he was poisoned by a lethal component of the pie. But please don't quote me on this until I get the results back.'

'Thank you, Doctor. That's very helpful.'

Emma hung up and spoke.

'You all heard that, I take it. This wasn't an accidental poisoning. Barwell picking a few berries by the roadside thinking they're edible. Someone wanted him dead and we need to find out who and why. We need to go through his accounts and see if he's been ripping off anyone else with outrageous prices. Trevor – can you do that? It's your kind of thing.'

'Yes, boss.'

'Karen, can you track down any relatives of the deceased pensioner and talk to them? There could be a motive there, but go gently to begin with. Have a word with any former neighbours, too.'

'Righto, guv.'

'Mel, try and find out where Deadly Nightshade grows around here. Is it common? Have they had any cases of poisoning in A&E that could give us a location?'

'OK, boss. I'll talk to the local wildlife trust and also the botany department at the university.

'Addy and Martin, go door-to-door in the neighbourhood, please. Did anyone see anything strange? Talk to the kids with the drone. Did they see any vehicles or people loitering in the area? You know the sort of thing to ask. We haven't got an operation name yet.'

'How about fiddler on the roof?' called Mel.

One or two people grinned but most looked blank.

'It's a sixties musical,' explained Jack.

'Very funny, Mel,' said Emma, 'but I think we'll wait for the computer to generate one.'

'Now, was there any evidence of threats in Gary Foreman's place?'

'No, guv,' replied Martin. 'I'd've said so earlier if there was. There was a dozen boxes of steroids, though, so he was clearly selling them. They couldn't all have been for personal use.'

'OK. Can you do the same at Barwell's place?'

'Yes, boss.'

'Right, any questions, liaise with Jack. I've got a meeting with the DCI. Thanks, guys.'

'This is the third poisoning case in Mexton in two weeks, all of which look like murder,' she thought, as she headed for DCI Farlowe's office. 'But in each case the poisons were different, and there's no obvious link between the victims, apart from the fact that Barwell occasionally employed Foreman. The poisonings were all carefully planned, too. Could this be the same person, randomly killing people off? Surely not. But if Jenny Pike and her cronies on the *Mexton Messenger* think there really is a serial killer operating, they'll go barmy.'

Chapter Nineteen

Ryan Watts was well stoked. He'd had a few vodkas to calm his nerves and a hit of coke to spark him up. A little bit of meth had given him an edge and he was ready. Clutching a grubby newspaper cutting, he waited in the evening shadows, opposite the back entrance to the police station, for his prey. He'd been there for several hours but no-one noticed him. People didn't notice rough sleepers, and his disguise had done the job. But, as the evening wore on, he was becoming increasingly agitated. If anyone spoke to him, he would probably flare up and that would ruin his plans. He had to remain calm, despite the chemical cocktail in his veins, so he could strike his blow for white Englishmen.

'Night, Jack,' called Mel, as she held the security gate open for him. 'See you in the morning.'

'Yeah. See you. Stay safe.'

Mel had walked home from work most evenings that

week, the exercise welcome after a day spent mostly at her desk. She loved the golden glow of evening sunshine, even in a built-up area like central Mexton, and enjoyed watching the starlings murmurating before departing for their roosts. She never wore earphones or listened to music as she walked. She liked to be part of her environment. That was why she heard the rustling clothing and stealthy approach of the man behind her. She turned just in time to see a ragged shape, a face contorted with fury and the glint of sunlight on a long blade sweeping towards her neck.

Mel's instincts took over. She could not escape the blade by running. It was too long. So she twisted and hurled herself towards her attacker, her wiry frame catching him off-balance. Instead of decapitating her, the blade lodged in her shoulder, sending a wave of agony through her upper body. Her attacker stumbled on the edge of the pavement, tumbling backwards and taking Mel with him. She tried to roll clear but he turned over and pinned her to the ground with his weight.

'You're that fuckin' bint what defused the righteous bomb. It should have gone off and killed those fuckers. And you.'

He straddled her and grabbed her throat. With one arm useless she could do little to fight back. Her head throbbed as he increased the pressure, and her heart began to pound. Dimly, as she began to lose consciousness, she heard a crunching noise. The pressure on her neck slackened and her attacker collapsed on top of her, the impact of Jack's boot on his temple knocking him temporarily unconscious.

Jack hauled the assailant off Mel and swore when he saw the blood pouring from the wound in her shoulder. He ripped off his shirt, formed it into a pad and held it there as he phoned for an ambulance and backup. The attacker stirred and Jack could just reach far enough to kick him again. 'Reasonable force be fucked,' he thought. He tried to kill one of our own.' The man lay still and Jack returned his attention to Mel, who was muttering confusedly and shivering despite the warm tarmac beneath her.

'Stay with me for fuck's sake,' he cried. 'That's a fucking order. For once in your life, do as you're bloody told.'

By now his shirt was saturated with Mel's blood and she seemed to be slipping away. A dreadful anguish shot through him. They might have had their differences, but the prospect of Mel dying was too awful to contemplate. He put his fingers against her slim neck. There was a pulse, but only a faint one. Just as he wondered how you did CPR on someone who was rapidly losing the blood you needed to pump, he felt a hand on his shoulder.

'We'll take over from here.'

In his frenzy to keep Mel alive, Jack hadn't heard the ambulance approaching or seen the two PCs dash out of the station and restrain the attacker. Slumped on the pavement, wiping moisture from his eyes, he watched as the paramedic slipped a line into Mel's arm and forced fluid into a vein from a transparent bag. His colleague put an oxygen mask over Mel's face and kept the pressure on her shoulder, replacing Jack's sodden shirt with cleaner material.

Within a minute of their arrival, Mel was in the ambulance heading for A&E, with blues and twos going. A PC cordoned off the area with blue and white tape while his colleague helped Jack to his feet. As he stumbled back towards the police station, to shower and leave his clothes for forensics, Jack spotted the weapon on the ground and told a PC to guard it until SOCOs arrived. It was some kind of sword, nearly a metre long. He nearly threw up at the thought of what could have happened to Mel. He hoped he wouldn't encounter the attacker in the station, because for the first time in his twenty-year police career, Jack Vaughan felt an overpowering urge to kill someone.

Chapter Twenty

Day 15

'Touch of déjà vu there, Jack. You saving me from another strangler,' said Mel, when he visited her in hospital two days later, referring to a previous incident in the Memorial Gardens.

'Yeah. I'm getting quite good at it. Seriously, though, you scared the shit out of me. How are you?'

'OK. Comfortably numb, I suppose. These machines are a bit of a nuisance. The doc said that if the sword had been sharper, or a couple of centimetres closer, he'd have hit the carotid, which would have saved the NHS a lot of money. He was joking about the last bit. I hope. I can't sleep, though. I keep replaying the attack in my mind. It still gives me the shivers. My dad was horrified, too.

Jack frowned.

'When are they letting you out?'

'A few days yet. And I'll be off work for a while, then confined to light duties. It's gonna take time for the muscles and other bits to repair completely, but I'll be seen by an occupational therapist and a physio before I go home. I'd thought of applying for firearms training, but I don't think that'll be possible now, with a dodgy shoulder.'

'Well, you look after yourself. We can arrange counselling for you if you think it will help. How many lives have you lost now?'

'Lost count, mate,' she grinned.

'The guy that attacked you has been remanded, by the way. Turns out he's some fanatical anti-Muslim racist. His internet posts are vile.'

'I thought as much, from what he said as he was strangling me.'

The two detectives chatted for another half hour, and just as Jack was about to leave, Mel showed him a get well card.

'What do you make of this?' she asked, 'It says "Sorry to hear what happened. I guess I owe you one. The debt will be repaid." It's unsigned.'

'No idea.' Jack shrugged. 'Someone you helped out, I suppose.'

'But surely they would leave a name? And what debt?'

'Well, if you suddenly receive a brown envelope full of tenners, you'd better declare it,' he joked.

'Yeah, right. Anyway, thanks for coming to see me. Give my best to the troops and tell them I can't wait to get back.'

'Will do. Get better. Carefully.'

Ryan wandered into the prison gym after lunch. Two of the long-stay prisoners had impressed on him the need to keep fit inside. They told him he had to be able to look after himself, especially if he got banged up with someone who disagreed with his views on Muslims. So, he had agreed to meet them in the prison gym to learn how to use the weights and equipment. They were the only two men in the room when he entered.

'Come here, mate,' said one of them, a sixteen-stone six-footer with tattoos proclaiming his allegiance to England and Millwall FC. 'We'll start with weights.'

'OK. Ta,' replied Ryan, eying the huge discs of iron with some trepidation.

'Right. Start with these. Not too heavy. Bend your knees, keep your back straight and lift slowly. All right?'

Ryan complied. It was a bit of a strain, but he managed to get the weights bar level with his chest. He was feeling pleased with himself until his legs were kicked from under him and he collapsed on the floor, the weights falling on top of him. The big man shifted the weights so that the bar lay across Ryan's chest, pinning him to the floor, while his accomplice lifted up Ryan's sweatshirt.

'Nothing personal,' he said as he shoved the sharpened toothbrush into Ryan's belly, snapping the head off to prevent its easy retrieval.

'Just doing what we're told.'

Ryan screamed in agony as he started to bleed internally. The two lifers left the gym, jamming the door shut and leaving Ryan to die alone.

Chapter Twenty-One

Cold eyes watched Stephen Brown as he slunk out of the court building, a hat, scarf and sunglasses ensuring his anonymity. He knew he would have to return for sentencing tomorrow, but he was convinced his barrister had done a decent job, getting the charge reduced from manslaughter to causing death by dangerous driving and making an impassioned plea for leniency. With any luck, he would get off with a suspended sentence, a fine and a ban. After all, his character was good, he held down a respectable job as an accountant and he had never been in trouble with the police before.

He didn't notice the watcher who followed him to the bus queue, sat a few seats behind him on the bus and got off at the same stop. Nor did he realise he was being followed to his smart mock-Tudor detached house, in one of Mexton's better suburbs. First and foremost in his mind was his need for a drink. Something substantial. Not a measly glass of wine but a large Scotch. A very large one.

He unlocked his front door, kicked off his shoes and, without taking off his coat, homed in on the drinks cabinet in the lounge. Damn, he thought, as he looked at the three centimetres left in the whisky decanter. Almost out. Still, that would have to do for the time being. He would walk down to the supermarket later, when his nerves had calmed down a bit and he felt confident enough to go out in public. His face hadn't been in the papers or on social media, so the only people likely to recognise him were those involved in the case and the few spectators in the public gallery of the court. He should be all right.

An hour later, feeling pleasantly muzzy, Stephen was about to set off for the shop when his doorbell rang. He put on the door chain and opened the door a fraction, just in case an angry relative had tracked him down. There was no-one there, but he did hear a vehicle driving away. Opening the door further, he was delighted to see an elegant box, bearing the name of his favourite single malt, sitting on the doorstep. Picking it up, he read a note stuck to the top. 'From a sympathiser', it said, with the web address *carlawsarecrap.com* scribbled beneath the capital letters of the message. 'That'll save me a trip,' he thought, and carried the box eagerly inside.

For the rest of the evening, Stephen worked his way through most of the whisky. He thought it didn't taste quite as good as usual, but the strong peaty flavour that he liked was still present. He staggered off to bed, pleased with the thought that the anonymous donor was on his side. He hadn't meant to run the child over, of course. It was just a mistake anyone could have made. The kid should have been paying attention. At least someone could see his point of view. He made a mental note to take a look at the website when he was sober.

Chapter Twenty-Two

Day 16

WHEN STEPHEN WOKE up at ten o'clock the next morning, the first thing he did was vomit. His stomach hurt and his vision was blurred. He staggered to the bathroom and vomited again, all the time finding it harder to see. 'Shit,' he thought. 'Must have overdone it with the Scotch last night. Still, I was under stress. I'd better be more careful in future.' His head was pounding and his muscles started to twitch. He lurched into the kitchen and forced down a glass of water, but before he could replace the glass in the sink he collapsed in a seizure, the vessel flying from his hand and smashing on the floor. Two minutes later he sank into a coma, and he was dead within the hour.

At midday, PC Reg Dawnay knocked on Stephen's door to execute a warrant for his arrest. 'Did the little shit think he could do a runner and escape sentencing?' he mused to himself. Getting no answer from repeated knocking, he opened a wooden gate at the side of the house, walked round the back and peered through the kitchen window. When he saw Stephen's body, prone on the kitchen floor, he radioed for an ambulance. He had no way of forcing a door so he used his baton to break a window and squeezed his bulky frame through, after knocking out the remaining shards of glass. He wriggled his way over the draining board and eased himself to the floor, his left foot landing in a pool of Stephen's vomit. Ignoring this, he searched for a carotid pulse, found none and radioed the station to call in the death.

Paramedics were waiting by the time Jack arrived at Stephen's house.

'Looks like he's drunk himself to death,' said the taller of the two. 'He stinks of booze. Do you need us any more?'

Jack took a quick look round and shook his head.

'No. That's OK. Now you've confirmed death you can get back. It doesn't look suspicious. I'll arrange for the body to be taken to the mortuary. We'll need a basic post mortem, I suppose.'

Jack wandered around the ground floor looking for anything suspicious but found nothing. He pocketed an address book, which, he hoped, would contain contact details for Stephen's next of kin. Before leaving, he radioed for a uniform to guard the premises until an emergency glazier could come and repair the window PC Dawnay had smashed.

Karen slumped on her sofa after work, a rapidly emptying bottle of pinot grigio in front of her. She didn't know how long she could go on providing information to her blackmailer. It went against everything she had believed in when she took the oath as a constable. OK, she hadn't done anything to harm her colleagues, and the people she had provided dirt on were pretty unpleasant anyway. That wasn't the point. She had been forced to betray her principles, and every time she received an envelope of cash, or called the burner phone number she had been given, the guilt made her feel sick.

Should she confess, resign from the police and find another job? She was in too deep for that and would inevitably be charged with misconduct in public office. Even if she didn't go to prison, she would never get a decent job afterwards. There had to be a way out. She was desperate to break her blackmailer's grip and continue with the job she loved. Perhaps it was the alcohol, but she began to think of other ways out of the situation. Some preposterous and some more credible. Would she have the courage to follow a path that could solve her problem, but would put her at risk of even more serious consequences if she failed?

Chapter Twenty-Three

Day 17

EMMA THORPE PUT ASIDE a pile of crime reports when her phone rang.

'Hello, Doctor,' she said, recognising the voice at the end of the line. 'What can I do for you?'

'That alcoholic, DI Thorpe. He was obviously a drinker, his liver indicated as much, but he had a lot of additional organ damage. It may be a long shot, but I suspect he may have been poisoned with methanol. So, I've ordered lab tests on the usual samples. You may want to request a full Home Office PM in due course, but for the moment, I would suggest you consider Mr Brown's death as suspicious.'

'Oh shit. I mean, thank you for letting me know, Dr Durbridge. How long before you get the results?'

'It shouldn't be too long. It's not a complicated analysis, I believe. I'll call you as soon as I hear from the lab.'

'OK. Thank you. Much obliged.'

Emma chucked her biro at the waste bin in annoyance. Another bloody poisoning. Mexton was becoming Borgia

Central. 'If it's the same person,' she mused, 'there must be a link between the victims. But what the bloody hell is it? We're missing something. We must be.' She would wait for Dr Durbridge to confirm his suspicions and then confer with DCI Farlowe. He would probably want to involve the Super and work out a strategy for handling the press. She dreaded meetings, most of which she considered a waste of time, but realised she had to prepare thoroughly. Collecting a coffee from the machine on the way, she walked over to Jack's desk.

'Can you sort out some bodies to look at the Stephen Brown death, please?'

'Not another one?'

'Fraid so. At least, it looks like it. He may have been poisoned by methanol. Can you get SOCOs to look around his place for signs of anything suspicious? Chemical bottles, tampered drinks, that sort of thing. We'll need the place sealed as a crime scene for the moment. And ask someone to find out more about Stephen Brown. I gather he was due to return to court for sentencing and failed to appear. That's why Reg Dawnay went round.'

'OK, Emma,' said Jack, wearily. 'I'll find a few folks. But, with Mel off, we're a bit short.'

'Yes, I know. But I have a feeling this is going to get a lot bigger.

Five out of five so far. He was feeling really proud of himself. He'd got the doses right and the means of getting them to the target correct, and the police didn't have a clue, although they still hadn't found one of them. There might come a time when he would have to ease off for a while, if the police seemed to be getting closer, but that was some way off, he was sure. He was enjoying the power so much he found it hard to disguise his excitement while at his day job. To think that the gangly kid, who nobody picked for their team at school, had grown into a sophisticated adult with the power of life and death over others!

Now for number six. He had collected the materials, watched her movements and planned his moves meticulously. He knew when she would emerge, to the nearest ten minutes or so, and then he would strike. He couldn't wait!

Chapter Twenty-Four

Sharon Cattrall stepped lightly out of Mrs Morrison's hall and closed the front door behind her, clutching the twenty pound note she had taken from the old woman's handbag. 'She won't miss it,' she thought. 'The old bat's got nothing to spend it on. And I got away with it last time when the police dropped the charges. The great thing about caring for people with dementia is they don't know what you're doing, and even if they did, they would never remember.'

Her mind on how she would spend the money, she failed to notice the thin fishing line stretched across the gateway, which pitched her head first onto the pavement. Dazed, and with aching knees and elbows, she looked gratefully at the man in the paramedic's uniform who helped her sit up, with her back leaning against the garden wall.

'You've taken a tumble,' he said. 'Are you injured?'

'I don't think so, she replied. 'Things hurt, but it doesn't feel as though anything's broken.'

'Here, drink this. It'll make you feel a bit better.'

He proffered a bottle of fruity-tasting liquid, which she gulped gratefully.

'Lucky I was passing,' he said. 'I've just finished my shift and I always carry a few odds and ends with me. Just in case.'

'Thank you. You're very kind,' she smiled. 'I'll be all right. I think I'll go back inside and sit down for a few minutes. I'm the carer for Mrs Morrison, the old lady in there. She's having her afternoon nap.'

'Good idea. You be careful now. I'll just give you a hand.'

While Sharon was picking up her handbag and arranging her skirt, the man used a small penknife to cut away the fishing line, attempting to shield his actions from the sight of any passers-by. He didn't notice the woman with the desperate expression, sitting on a wall a few dozen metres away, over the road. He helped Sharon to the front door and watched as she unlocked it and went inside. She was still unsteady on her feet and winced as she moved her legs.

'Make sure you sit down for a while,' he called.

'Will do. And thanks again.'

'Sod that for a shopping trip,' thought Sharon. 'I need a drink.' She tiptoed past her sleeping charge and found a bottle of gin in the sideboard. Sitting at the kitchen table, she poured herself a large measure, put in her earbuds and switched on her music.

Half an hour later, Sharon began to feel sick and her stomach ached. She developed a headache, which she put down to her fall. She got up to fetch some paracetamol from her bag but felt dizzy and stumbled, falling and catching her head on the edge of the kitchen table. Still conscious, she found it increasingly hard to breathe and soon slipped into a coma from which she never awoke.

'An hour should be long enough' he thought, parked in the car opposite Mrs Morrison's house. 'The old lady will be needing help soon.' He picked up a burner phone and dialled the police.

'Hello. Mexton Social Care here. Could you send someone round to do a welfare check on Mrs Morrison, 34 Rose Street, please? I've been trying to phone her for some time and I'm getting no reply. She's alone and vulnerable. I can't attend myself – I've got an emergency on the other side of town. Thanks ever so.'

He gave the name of a social worker obtained from the Council's website and switched off the phone. Before he drove away, he used a credit card to slip back the latch on Mrs Morrison's door, leaving it slightly ajar so the police wouldn't need to break the door down.

'Mrs Morrison. It's the police. Can I come in?' PC Sally Erskine tapped on the door and called the woman's name gently. Getting no reply, she pushed the door open and called again. No reply, still, so she looked in at the doorway on her right. An elderly woman was asleep in a recliner chair, the remains of a meal on a tray on her lap and an untouched cup of tea, developing a layer of scum, on a table beside her. She stepped towards the figure and was relieved to see she was breathing. The woman's eyes slowly opened and she looked at Sally with an air of bafflement.

'Sharon? Why are you dressed as a policewoman?'

'It's not Sharon, Mrs Morrison, it's PC Erskine. We had a call from your social worker. He was worried about you.'

'What social worker? I've not seen those buggers since

they took my Ernest away and put him in a home. Tried to do the same with me but I told them where to go. Bloody cheek. But why are you dressed as a policewoman, Sharon?'

Sally decided not to argue and tried a different tack.

'Who's Sharon, Mrs Morrison?'

'You come in and feed me. Look after me. Don't you remember?'

'I see. When did you last see me?'

'Nineteen-forty-four. That's when I was born,' she said, triumphantly.

'Have you got Sharon's phone number?' asked an increasingly frustrated Sally.

'It's on that pad there,' she replied, with a flash of clarity.

Sally took out her own phone and dialled the number. To her surprise, she heard a phone ringing in the back of the house. She followed the sound and found a young woman lying on the kitchen floor, unconscious or, possibly, dead. Checking her pulse confirmed the latter suspicion. She radioed the station and spoke to her sergeant.

'Sarge, I've got a fatality at 34 Rose Street. Young female with what appears to be a head wound. From the ID on her lanyard, her name's Sharon Cattrall. I believe she was the carer of the elderly householder, so can you contact the Social Services emergency number? I'll wait here until the cavalry arrives.'

Retreating from the kitchen, Sally returned to the lounge and found that Mrs Morrison had fallen asleep again. She looked around the room, noting the old-fashioned decoration, the furniture dated and worn, and the general air of neglect. In her mind she wound the clock back forty years and pictured a neat and tidy room with, perhaps, a contented couple sitting chatting by the fire, a place for everything and everything in its place, and not a speck of dust in sight. She felt unaccountably sad. Her reverie was interrupted by the arrival of paramedics in an ambulance car, closely followed by DS Jack Vaughan in an unmarked police saloon.

'Well, she's got a head injury,' observed the paramedic as she squatted beside Sharon's body. 'But it doesn't look like it's very serious. Yes, she's dead, but I'd be surprised if that killed her. I think you need a pathologist to take a look.'

'Well, we would anyway,' said Jack. 'But thanks. I'll arrange for her to be moved to the mortuary. Sally?' he called. 'Can you wait here until Social Services turn up? I need to get back to the nick. Make the old lady a cup of tea or something when she wakes up. Ask her if she heard Sharon falling over.'

'Will do, Sarge. But I doubt I'll get any sense out of her.'

Jack left the house with a sense of foreboding. If the head injury didn't kill Sharon, what did? Not another fucking poisoning, he thought. He was used to villains stabbing each other, and domestic disputes escalating to lethal violence, but poisoners gave him the creeps.

Chapter Twenty-Five

Day 18

It was twelve days before the photographer's body was discovered, by which time the cyanide fumes had dissipated, replaced by the foul odours of putrefaction. Nevertheless, the fire and rescue service heeded the warning sign. A fire officer, in full protective gear, cautiously opened the door to the dark room while his colleagues, and the police, waited outside the flat. He used a small pump to suck air through a detection tube and, two minutes later, gave the all clear.

'It's all yours, DI Thorpe,' he said, once he had removed his respirator. 'And you're certainly welcome to it.'

Emma, in a forensic suit and hairnet, took one look at the remains, spotted the cable ties and gagged as the smell assaulted her sinuses.

'There's nowt to be gained from my looking at it,' she said, grimly. 'I'll get the force forensic physician to certify death and then call the SOCOs in. Looks like they'll need a shovel and a bucket. That notice, the fact that the door was wedged shut, and the cable ties round the victim's thumbs mean this was a long-planned murder, not a spur-of-the-moment attack. The flat is now a crime scene. I'll need you guys to leave, please. Many thanks for your efforts and sorry it's so grim.'

'We've probably seen worse,' said the Senior Fire Officer, who showed no reluctance to comply. He and his colleague collected their equipment and left the flat hurriedly, obviously in need of some fresh air.

'He's been dead for more than a week, possibly as long as two,' said Dr Durbridge, as he began the post mortem that afternoon. 'I can't give a more precise estimate as I don't know how temperature and humidity varied in that cubbyhole you found him in. It was well sealed, so insects couldn't get access, which cuts out a useful source of evidence. It's not going to be easy establishing cause of death, either,' he continued. 'But I'll do my best.'

'I'm sure you will, Doctor,' said Emma, watching uneasily from the glassed-in viewing gallery. Even with the high-powered extractor fans running at full speed, the horrendous odour from the decomposing cadaver was permeating much of the mortuary. She was glad she hadn't had a greasy canteen lunch.

After several hours cutting, slicing and scooping, Dr Durbridge stepped back and commented.

'There's no obvious cause of death. No bullets left in the body, knife marks on bones or evidence of blunt force trauma to the head. The hyoid bone is intact, but that's not necessarily proof he wasn't strangled. It doesn't always break. You mentioned something about cyanide?'

'Yes, Doctor,' Emma replied. 'There was a warning notice on the door but the fire service found no traces in the air.'

'Well, hydrogen cyanide would have dissipated, in time,

unless the room was completely air tight. The trouble is, cyanide disappears rapidly from the body after death, so the lab won't find it in any samples I might send them. Hang on, though.'

Dr Durbridge turned back to the body and looked thoughtful.

'A few years ago, someone discovered a chemical marker in the livers of cyanide poisoning victims. Much of his liver's decomposed, but there's enough left for me to take a sample. I'll ask the university if there's anyone in their labs who can look for it. But don't hold your breath. It might not show up.'

'Thank you, Dr Durbridge. Anything you can give us would be grand. What about Sharon Cattrall?'

'I'll get on to her in due course,' replied the pathologist, somewhat testily. 'I gave this one priority to try to prevent any further losses of evidence. You are keeping me busy, you know.

'Yes. Sorry, Doctor. I didn't mean to pressurise you. We do appreciate what you do.

Dr Durbridge turned back to his dissecting with a grunt and a slight smile.

Emma drove back to the station pondering. If cyanide was the cause of death, it would add to the mounting toll of poisoning cases in Mexton. The tally was now six. She decided to park this one until Dr Durbridge sent his report, and turned her thoughts back to the strychnine victim. There was no forensic evidence to identify the poisoner, one, possibly unreliable, witness and nothing from Gordon Howell's phone or computer of any use. It was the same with the other confirmed poisonings. The methods were different, but whoever was behind them was bloody clever. Her team had spent hundreds of hours canvassing for witnesses, checking CCTV footage, interviewing relatives of the victims and looking at phone records and social media. And they'd got nothing. Lack of progress was affecting morale and she sensed impatience in the higher-ups. The press, too, was hounding them. In all the cases she had investigated, she had never felt so frustrated, but she owed it to her team to remain upbeat. Perhaps a session in the pub would cheer them up. She would suggest one soon.

Chapter Twenty-Six

'How are you doing, love?' Tom's cheery smile and affectionate embrace always lifted Mel's spirits.

'Ouch. Mind my shoulder. It still hurts.'

'Sorry. Look what I've got.' He dumped a pile of papers on Mel's hospital bed. 'I've been looking at estate agents' websites. There's a few possibles that we could just about afford between us. Take a look.'

'You're serious about this, aren't you? What have you found?'

For the next half hour, the couple sorted the printouts into three piles: obviously unsuitable; maybes; and definitely interesting.

'So, it looks like we've got a couple of places we need to look at and a couple more that might do,' said Mel, sipping hospital orange squash. 'Both with Edwards and Biggs. They say I'll be out of here by the weekend, so can you set up some appointments? And for fuck's sake make sure there's a room for those bloody parrots.'

'Of course,' replied Tom, looking slightly hurt. 'But it has to be comfortable for us as well. It'll be our first proper home together and it's got to be right.'

Mel nodded. She was looking forward to getting a place with Tom, but she had a slight twinge. She had enjoyed her own space and had happy memories of her flat, although a vengeful gunman and a chemical weapon attack had rather taken the gloss off it. But living with Tom seemed to have turned out well. So far. She only hoped it would last when they owned a house together.

'How's work?'

Tom shrugged.

'You know. Cybercrime is endless and we sometimes feel like the Dutch boy with his finger in the dyke, watching the flood waters pour over the top. By the way, Robbie sends his regards. He's doing great. Computer crime is just up his street. Your lot are in a state over these poisonings, though.'

'Yes. Jack told me. There's been another three, apparently. A drunk driver who killed a kid. He was poisoned before he was due to return to court for sentencing. He had a good brief so it looked like he would be treated leniently. The latest is a young woman who worked as a carer for the elderly. She was poisoned with something, they think, but the PM results aren't in yet. And they've just found the remains of a young photographer, poisoned a couple of weeks ago. They think it's the same killer.'

'So how does he find his victims?'

'I don't know. I think Jack's coming in to see me again soon, so I'll ask him if there are any new leads. I bet someone higher up is thinking of bringing in a profiler, who, no doubt, will say it's a white male between twenty and forty who has a semi-skilled job and had an unhappy childhood.'

'Right, I must love you and leave you. I'll be in tomorrow with a list of viewing appointments.'

He kissed Mel and closed the door of her side room

behind him, leaving her pondering. What jobs could possibly enable the killer to identify his targets? She knew her colleagues would be considering the options, but there was no reason why she couldn't give it some thought as well. At least it would alleviate the boredom and take her mind off her narrow escape.

Chapter Twenty-Seven

Day 19

'OK, PEOPLE,' called Emma. 'Grab your coffees. Incident room in five minutes. The PM report on the photographer is back.'

When the team was seated, she began the briefing by projecting a photo of the decomposing corpse on the screen. Several officers blanched, while others took hasty gulps of coffee, an excuse to avert their eyes.

'That, we now know, is what's left of Marvin Lambton. He was eighteen, lived with his mum and was studying photography at Mexton college. She reported him missing a week ago. A friend had let him set up a darkroom in his flat while he was abroad. He liked the old-fashioned film techniques as well as modern digital cameras. More of that later. I'm sure you're all keen to know how he died. It was cyanide. Dr Durbridge had the results from the university and it looks like he breathed in hydrogen cyanide gas, which killed him.'

'How did he do that?' asked Martin. 'Did someone have a cylinder of the stuff?'

'No,' Emma replied. 'It was made in the darkroom. Forensics found a tray of hydrochloric acid on a bench with cyanide in it. Next to it were some spilled orange crystals – a complicated chemical name that I won't trouble you with. Anyway, the point is that when you mix the orange stuff with acid it releases hydrogen cyanide gas, much like in the US gas chamber. With his wrists tied and the door wedged shut, the poor bugger didn't stand a chance. The killer didn't want to harm anyone else, though. He put a sign on the door – he wanted to be sure no-one else breathed in the gas.'

Looks of amazement and revulsion crossed the faces of the detectives while they waited for Emma to continue.

'So, Jack, can you organise people to look into Marvin Lambton's background, talk to his workmates, friends, family and so on? He seemed harmless, so why anyone would want to kill him is anybody's guess. We need to look at any photos he had, just in case he was up to anything dodgy. I think I saw some nude prints hanging up in the darkroom. Meanwhile, I have a meeting with the DCI to discuss this epidemic of poisonings.'

'You've got to tell them, Stace.' Jodie Bannister hugged her younger sister, who sobbed in her arms. 'If they find out and you haven't come forward, they might think you had something to do with it.'

'But I can't. I'm so ashamed. It was awful. If I could've killed him I would've, but I'm not that brave. But what if Mum and Dad find out?'

'They won't. But even if they did, they wouldn't blame you. We've kept what happened from them so far, so there's no need for them to know.'

'Won't they have to come to the police station with me?'

'No. I could come with you. I'm over eighteen and all they need is an appropriate adult. I've looked it up.'

'Would you?' Stacey's tear-stained face turned towards her sister and she wiped her eyes on a tissue. 'I'll go if you're sure I have to.'

'I am, Stace. I am.'

'Be brave,' whispered Jodie as the two sisters walked up the ramp into the police station. 'I'll be with you all the time. And I can do some of the talking, if you like.'

Stacey smiled weakly and gripped Jodie's hand.

'I'd like to talk to someone about Marvin Lambton, please,' she told the civilian receptionist behind the desk. 'But it must be a woman.'

'OK. I'll see if DC Groves is available. In the meantime, can I have your name?'

The receptionist took down Stacey's details and phoned the CID office.

'Take a seat over there,' she said. Clearly concerned at Stacey's distress, she continued, 'Karen will be with you in a moment. She's very nice.'

Stacey tried to smile and sat down, wondering if she was doing the right thing. But someone had to know what Marvin Lambton had done to her.

Chapter Twenty-Eight

'Would you like to come through?'

Karen guided Stacey and Jodie through the door beside reception and led them to the interview room set up for vulnerable witnesses. They sat uneasily in comfortable chairs, accepting water from freshly opened bottles.

'You wanted to talk about Mr Lambton, I believe. How can I help?'

Karen's calm and friendly manner appeared to reassure Stacey, who began to speak, twisting a tissue in her hands as she did so.

'Is he really dead? I saw something on Facebook. Is it true?'

'I'm afraid so, yes,' replied Karen. 'Did you know him?'

'He was evil.' Stacey's voice caught in her throat.

'Evil? What do you mean?'

Stacey sobbed and Jodie put her arm round her sister's shoulders.'

'He took these photos of me. I was getting dressed. I hadn't drawn my bedroom curtains and he had one of those long-range cameras. He showed me the pictures. You could see my...my...top half. He threatened to put them on the internet and post them up in college.'

'That's dreadful,' commiserated Karen. 'If you'd come to us, we would have arrested and charged him.'

'But I couldn't. You see, our mum's a vicar. It would have been too embarrassing. And I couldn't bear the idea of testifying in court.'

'I understand. So, did anything else happen?'

'He...he said he'd destroy the photos if...if I let him have sex with me. Otherwise everyone would see what I looked like half naked.'

'And did you?'

Stacey howled and nodded her head. 'Yes. I did. And I'm so ashamed. What would my parents think?'

'OK, Stacey. The most important thing is for you to believe it wasn't your fault. What this man did was unspeakable and he would have gone to prison for it. It was rape. There is no need for your parents to know. It certainly won't happen again. And I'm sure they would be understanding if they knew. Can I ask you one more thing? If you'd prefer to talk to a nurse instead that's fine.'

Stacey looked worried but nodded cautiously.

'Did he use any protection?'

Stacey started crying again. 'No. I told Jodie what had happened and she took me to the chemists to get the morning after pill. I was so humiliated. I expect the chemist thought I was a prostitute.'

'I'm sure that's not the case. Honestly. I think you've been incredibly brave to come to us, Stacey. You should be proud of yourself. You've nothing to be ashamed of. We might want you to give a formal statement at some stage but I think it's unlikely, as we can't charge Lambton. Give me your mobile number so I can reach you. Here's my card – you can call me any time if it would help you to talk. Also, here are the details of an organisation that helps victims of crime. There's a nice lady called Ellen Wilkins who works with them. She's lovely and you'll find her very helpful.'

'Thank you. You've been very kind.' Stacey attempted a smile and shook Karen's proffered hand.'

'By the way,' Karen said, as they were leaving. 'What are you studying at college?'

'A-levels. Philosophy, psychology and religious studies. I want to follow Mum into the Church.'

'Well, I wish you every success.' Karen smiled. 'Take care.'

Karen walked back to the incident room, turning over the interview in her head and furious at the actions of the despicable Marvin Lambton. 'Do we have a potential suspect for the Lambton murder?' she wondered. She would have to talk to Emma.

Tom had phoned the estate agents, Edwards and Biggs, and made appointments to view the two most likely properties as soon as Mel left hospital. Still somewhat wobbly on her feet, she was, nevertheless, keen to look for a new home.

The first house they looked at was useless. A motor vehicle workshop, not mentioned in the details, backed onto the garden and the walls between the two halves of the semi were so thin that Mel and Tom could hear conversations in the house next door. This meant that the neighbours would also have been able to hear the parrots screeching, which would hardly have fostered good relations between the two households.

Number 42 Craven Street looked unprepossessing from the outside but had, as the estate agent put it, 'potential'. It was an end terrace, with a small park adjacent. The garden was surprisingly long for such a property, which immediately attracted Tom, and a third bedroom had space for a large aviary. Next door was a second-hand/junk shop with no-one living above it. So, no noisy neighbours or people to annoy.

'The house has been empty for some years,' explained Robbie Biggs. 'That's why it's a bit shabby. The owner cleared off to Australia, following a decent lottery win, and left no forwarding address. His children lost contact with him and there was some animosity between them, I believe. They wanted him to share his winnings but he kept them all for himself, saying only that they could live in the house until he decided otherwise. They didn't fancy living here, and had no authority to let the house out, or sell it, so it's remained empty.

'The children tried to trace their father through the Australian High Commission in London, with no success. Sorry, I don't normally gossip about clients like this. Anyway, he'd been gone seven years last June, so the Court declared him officially dead and they can now sell the house.'

Looking around, Mel and Tom realised that a good clean, a bit of redecoration, and a new bathroom and kitchen would make the place comfortable. It didn't look as though any other major works would be needed, although a survey would confirm that. They stood in the back bedroom, looking out over the untamed garden, and conferred.

'What do you think, Mel?' whispered Tom

'Are you any good with a paintbrush?' she replied. 'I like it. And we could build an aviary in the garden for the parrots to use in the summer. I think it might work.'

Tom nodded, and they returned to the kitchen where the estate agent was waiting.

'We like it,' said Tom, and made an offer several percent below the asking price. Biggs thought for a moment and then smiled.

'It's yours. My client gave me some flexibility over the price, as they want a quick sale. I'll draw up the documents and get them to you asap. Let me know the name of your solicitor.'

Biggs shook their hands enthusiastically, showed them out and promised to be in touch shortly. He left the two police officers thrilled at the prospect of owning their own home, but also slightly bemused by the alacrity with which he had accepted their offer.

Chapter Twenty-Nine

Day 20

'ORDER, ORDER.' Emma mimicked the House of Commons Speaker to get the attention of the noisy group of detectives. Mexton Rovers' victory against Manchester United the previous night was the talk of the office, although Jack, an MUFC supporter, was less pleased.

'Come on. Forget about the football. We've got a killer to catch. First thing, though, Mel's recovering better than expected and should be back at work soon. Now, the poisoner. We'll start with Marvin Lambton. Karen has something for us.'

'Yes, guv. A sixteen-year-old young woman, Stacey Bannister, came to see me yesterday. Apparently, Lambton took some photos of her, half naked, without her consent. He threatened to post them on the net and around the college, which they both attended, if she didn't have sex with him.'

Mutterings of 'Bastard', 'Wee shite' and similar interrupted Karen's account.

'Anyway. She didn't come to us about the pictures and

complied with his demands. She's a vicar's daughter and couldn't contemplate the scandal if it came to court. When Lambton's death was mentioned in the papers, her sister persuaded her to come in.'

'So do you rate her as a suspect?' Jack asked.

'No. Not a chance. Her sister, Jodie, is stronger, and came in as her appropriate adult, but I don't think Jodie's capable of murder, either.'

'Yes, but anyone's capable of killing,' said Martin, pensively.

'True. But I seriously doubt these two could. And, surely, they wouldn't report what happened if they had? But until now we've had no motive.'

'Did the SOCOs find any nude photos in Lambton's dark-room?' asked Addy.

'Loads,' replied Emma. 'Prints and negatives that were clearly unrelated to the photography course he's taking. Digital forensics are going through his laptop as we speak. What does Stacey Bannister look like?'

'Petite, brown hair in a ponytail, brown eyes,' replied Karen.

'OK. I'll ask them to look out for shots of her. You can let Stacey know when we've finished with them. We'll ensure they're deleted or destroyed.'

'Thanks, guv. Though I'm not sure she'd be happy at the thought of loads of male coppers looking at her. Still, at least they won't be all over cyberspace.'

'Well Amira is dealing with it and she's pretty discreet. Anyway, let's try and set up a timeline. When was Lambton last seen?'

'Fourteen days, ago,' replied Addy. 'He finished a college practical session and CCTV picked him up leaving the building at around five, heading off towards the town centre. I talked to his tutor and she said he seemed perfectly normal.

Apparently, he was rather intense but talented. He could well have had a promising career as a photographer.'

'He lived with his mum, who didn't report him missing until a week later. Do we know why she didn't?' Martin asked.

'It seems he would sometimes disappear for a few days. Said he was doing project work. It's probable he was staying at his mate's flat and using the darkroom. We found a sleeping bag and takeaway food and drink containers there.'

'Is there any CCTV near the flat?'

Addy shook his head.

'Nothing of any use. The flat's down a side street. Door-to-door enquiries threw up no witnesses, and we can't be sure exactly which day he died.'

'Thanks, Addy,' said Emma. 'Was there a camera at the scene?'

'Just one, guv. Stacey said he had a "long-range" camera, which is, presumably, digital. We only found an old-style film camera, but he'd have needed a digital one for his course. His phone wasn't there either and has been switched off or the battery is dead. His laptop was at his mum's.'

'So, the killer took the lad's posh camera. Did he have it with him when he left the college?'

'He was carrying a bag,' replied Addy, 'but there wasn't a bag or a camera in the flat. I'll check with the college, but I doubt he would have left his camera there.'

'Good. Yes please, Addy.'

'I'm guessing,' said Karen, 'that the killer took the camera to get rid of the photos. It doesn't look like straightforward theft to me.'

'You mean he knew what was on it?' Martin looked slightly incredulous. 'Stacey kept it a secret and we don't think she could have been involved. And, from what you said, she doesn't have a jealous boyfriend.'

'Bear with me, Martin. Suppose Stacey wasn't the only

victim. There could be other women he victimised. Their pictures could have been in his darkroom or on his camera, too. They may have told friends or relatives. And someone decided to make him pay.'

'That's worth exploring, Karen,' said Emma, thoughtfully. 'Let's see if Amira's come up with anything. If you're right, the killer will have destroyed the camera, or at least the memory card. But there may be pictures stored elsewhere.'

The others nodded.

'Does he have a cloud account?' asked Trevor, brushing biscuit crumbs from his shirt.

'That's something Amira's looking at as well. Can you give her a hand to look at social media sites? Check who's tagged and so on.'

'Sure, boss. Glad to.'

'Martin, can you get round to his mum's and search the place again? Ask her about girlfriends and how he spends his time at home. Seize the laptop for Amira.'

'OK. The rest of you, keep on with the other cases. We really need to make some progress with these poisonings before the press starts kicking off again. I know we're struggling with people off sick, but I'm sure you'll all do your best.'

Chapter Thirty

Day 21

MEL STEPPED into the incident room to cheers and shouts of 'welcome back'. Her shoulder still hurt at times, and the muscles hadn't repaired themselves properly, but she had convinced the force's occupational health department that she should return to work. She had been going crazy, in hospital and at home, envying Tom his involvement in interesting cases, and had insisted that she could cope with light duties.

'No chasing villains or going into dodgy situations,' Jack had warned her, when she phoned him to relay the news.

'Course not, Jack. Promise.'

'Well, I know what you're like.'

He spoke firmly but there was warmth in his voice.

After a quick hello to Emma, Mel walked back to her desk. Beneath sundry sheets of paper and folders she found a large box of chocolates, wrapped in brown paper, with her name on it. She opened the package eagerly and was just about to pop a praline in her mouth when Jack screamed at her.

'Stop! What the fuck do you think you're doing? We've got a serial poisoner out there and someone's already tried to kill you. And you're eating chocolates that just happened to turn up on your desk. Are you mad?'

Mel froze and her colleagues looked at her aghast. The only noise intruding on the shocked silence in the room was the gurgling of the coffee machine. Then Mel started to laugh.

'It's all right. It really is. They're from Ellen Wilkins. She sends us chocolates from time to time to thank us for rescuing her from Charles Osbourne. She must have heard I'd been hurt. There's a note here – "From EW". They're fine. Anybody want one?'

She didn't have to ask twice as detectives and civilian staff fell upon the chocolates like vultures on a freshly dead gazelle.

Chapter Thirty-One

'The paramedic was right,' said Dr Durbridge, when he phoned Emma with the preliminary results of Sharon Cattrall's post mortem. 'The head wound was trivial. She was poisoned with nicotine. The lab found large quantities of its breakdown product in the samples I sent them. I noticed a fruity odour when I examined her stomach contents, so I would suggest she was given it in some kind of sweetened fruit juice to disguise the taste. She wasn't a smoker and had no tolerance, so it would have killed her easily.'

'Where do you get nicotine, anyway, apart from in tobacco?' asked Emma.

'It was formerly used as an insecticide but was discontinued because of its toxicity. Vape solutions contain it, though, and they are often fruit flavoured, so that could be the source. If the stuff was mixed with fruit juice and sugar, the victim wouldn't have known what she was drinking. One other thing. Some bruises appeared on her knees and elbows after death, and there was a horizontal lesion just above her left ankle. These suggest she tripped over something, maybe a wire, and fell, shortly before she died.'

'Thank you, Doctor,' sighed Emma. 'Another one to add to the list and a different poison each time. Where the bloody hell will it end?'

'Don't worry. We're on full alert for poisoning cases here. We normally get about thirty deaths from poisoning each year in Mexton, the vast majority from drug overdoses. You've more than doubled our monthly quota, as it were, so any death that isn't obviously something else gets looked at through a toxicological lens.'

'Well, I'm not too sure what one of them is, but I appreciate it.'

'Sharon Cattrall, age twenty-two,' began Emma. 'Carer for Mrs Esme Morrison for the past three months. She worked for an agency, Mexton Care Services, who also used her for cover when their other clients needed extra support or carers were off sick. Unmarried, lived in a bedsit, surviving on the minimum wage. There was nothing of interest in her room, no threatening letters or anything. Poisoned with nicotine administered in a fruit drink by persons unknown. What else do we know about her?'

'She was suspected of stealing from one of her clients about six months ago,' replied Trevor. 'The charges were dropped because the old lady couldn't be sure how much she had in her purse to begin with. She had Alzheimer's. I spoke to the manager at the agency. They could have fired her but they're so short of staff, especially since Brexit, that they couldn't afford to.'

'Hmmm. Remind me not to get old,' said Jack.

'I thought you already were,' teased Mel.

Jack was about to reply when Emma spoke.

'Save that for the pub, you two. Now, Dr Durbridge said

that nicotine can kill quickly, so it must have been given to her sometime in the half hour before she died. He wouldn't commit himself to time of death, saying only that she hadn't been dead long before she was found. He also said that she seemed to have tripped over something, possibly a wire or length of string, shortly before she died. She had several contusions on her knees and elbows. So, we need bodies to go door-to-door and find out if anyone saw her falling, or somebody pushing her, any time that afternoon. CCTV would be useful, too.'

'There's none in the street outside,' said Jack. 'There should be something in the shopping centre down the road. I'll get it checked.'

'One other thing,' continued Emma. 'Someone allegedly from Social Services phoned us and asked for a welfare check on Mrs Morrison, but no-one in their office made the call. We've played the recording to the manager at Social Services and she didn't recognise the voice.'

'What? We've got a killer with a conscience, not wanting any harm to come to Mrs Morrison?' Martin looked perplexed. 'A relative of hers, perhaps?'

'Presumably yes, to your first point, Martin. Remember that notice about cyanide on Lambton's darkroom door. But Mrs Morrison has no living relatives apart from a daughter in Canada who sends some money over to help pay for the carers. Her husband, Ernie, died seven years ago. But it is worth finding out if the woman Sharon was accused of stealing from has a vengeful relative. OK, people, let's get to it.'

Chapter Thirty-Two

It had to stop. The stakes were too high, and if the secret came out it wouldn't just mean personal ruin but would reflect disastrously on the organisation. Blackmailers never stop, so a permanent solution was needed, one without any blowback. And Valentina's evidence would have to be destroyed, in case it fell into someone else's hands.

Valentina's victim poured another glass of wine and started formulating plans. Reporting it officially was not an option. It would result in long prison sentences for both of them. Flight or emigration? No, a move was impossible and achieving a similar lifestyle in a new country would be difficult. That left only one option. Termination. But finding a hitman would not be that easy. There had been several cases in real life where a would-be employer discovered, to his or her considerable cost, that the person they were attempting to hire was an undercover police officer. So, it would have to be a DIY job. Poisons were out and so were firearms – much too noisy, although a replica revolver from an airgun shop could be a useful prop. Strangulation would need the target to be manoeuvred into a particular position, close up, and bludgeoning was potentially unreliable and could be lengthy, which basically left stabbing. Messy, but effective if done properly, although clearing up any forensic traces could be tricky.

Valentina had always insisted that all communication should be done by text via burner phones, or through an accommodation address. She would have to be lured to a face-to-face meeting, which meant that it would have to be worth her while. Perhaps a package that was too valuable to be entrusted to the postal service? After all, meeting an upstanding and trusted member of society shouldn't be risky, although Valentina was bound to be on her guard. Well, it was worth a try. If she didn't bite, a new strategy would be needed. Her victim finished the bottle of wine and stumbled, leaden footed, towards the bedroom thinking that, perhaps, there was a chink of light on the horizon.

Chapter Thirty-Three

Day 22

'We must assume that these poisonings are all linked,' began Emma, her weariness bringing her Yorkshire accent to the fore. 'Look at the victimology, as the profilers might say. We've got Gordon Howell, possessor of indecent images of children. Next up, Gary Foreman. We think his steroids gave a young lad heart failure. Then there's Terry Barwell, fiddled a pensioner over a roofing job. Stephen Brown, killed a child while driving drunk but likely to have received a lenient sentence. Then we've Sharon Cattrall, probable petty thief who got away with it. Finally, Marvin Lambton, who threatened to circulate indecent images of a girl and forced her to have sex with him. It's achingly bloody obvious. Why the sodding hell didn't we see it before?'

'A vigilante,' said Jack. 'We should have spotted it.' He turned to Mel. 'Didn't you say, when I visited you, that one thing the victims had in common was that they'd all escaped justice in some way, either getting away with something completely or with a minor penalty? I thought you were letting your imagination run away with you, but you were right.'

Mel nodded and smiled at him.

'Well, who are we looking for?' continued Emma. 'Someone who knew about the cases, could be away from their place of work during the day without attracting suspicion and who had knowledge of poisons. Also, they would need to be reasonably physically strong to get Barwell up that ladder. Any suggestions?'

'Lawyer,' said Trevor.

'Doctor,' suggested Addy.

'Police officer,' said Jack, tentatively, at which point the room fell silent.

'We mustn't discount that,' replied Emma. 'Anything else?'

'SOCO or other civilian staff? A forensic scientist?' Martin offered.

'Court officials,' said Trevor,

'What about that paramedic?' Addy, again.

'We checked,' replied Jack, 'There were no paramedics unaccounted for when Howell was abducted. The uniform was fake.'

'A pharmacist,' suggested Trevor.

'A crime writer? Some of them know about poisons,' Martin mused.

'Yes, but I can't see Agatha Christie lifting a builder onto his garage roof. Anyway, she's dead and we don't have any crime writers living in Mexton, at least as far as I know,' replied Emma. 'The trouble is, everyone suggested meets some of the criteria but not all of them. Most of those professions or jobs require attendance at a workplace for much of the day. Court officials may hear about the cases, but would they know much about poisons? Poisoning cases are rare, as a rule. Perhaps we need to look for people who knew about the cases and studied chemistry or pharmacy before going into a different career. Like the DCI. He did science at university before joining the Met's graduate entry scheme. I'm not suggesting,' she added hastily, 'that the DCI is our killer, but you see what I mean.'

'All right,' said Jack. 'I'll split people into two teams. One to look at relatives and friends of the victims. See if there's anyone there who knows about toxic chemicals. They'll do background checks and also ask if anyone unusual has been in touch with them. The other group can look at social media and the local press to find out how widely the incidents were covered. There may be something not generally known, that could point to someone with specialist knowledge.'

'Thanks, Jack. That's a start. We'll meet up in a couple of days to review what's been found.'

As Emma collected coffee on the way back to her office she wondered. Could it be the DCI? She didn't know him very well, as he'd not been in post that long and was somewhat reserved. A science background and the physique of a rugby player certainly ticked a couple of boxes. And he was often away from his desk at meetings. No, that was rubbish. She had no reason to doubt his integrity and mustn't let her annoyance at not getting the job cloud her judgement. But still...

Jenny Pike was pissed off. Not only did she have her own job to do, she had to babysit Ricky Marriott, the new boy, as well. He had come with a good reference from his previous job and had been on the paper for nearly eight months, shadowing her as she talked to her contacts, interviewed witnesses and wrote her copy. He had that slightly arrogant air of many young male journalists, apparently determined to be the next Woodward or Bernstein. But the *Mexton Messenger* wasn't the

Washington Post, and the chances of international fame while working on a declining provincial newspaper were microscopic. But he was keen, and that worried Jenny, to the point of her feeling slightly threatened by him.

Jenny had been the lead reporter on the paper, specialising in crime, for five years. She was desperate to make a break from Mexton and had tried for jobs with the nationals on several occasions. She had broken a few stories of local significance, and even had an account of a discovered bomb factory picked up by internet news services. Unfortunately for her, she had a reputation for being not so much economical with the truth as positively miserly with it. The paper's lawyers had kept her copy just the right side of libel, but she felt sure that the editor would replace her if he could. And Ricky Marriott might be hoping to be her replacement.

Now that she had her driving licence back, she could get around Mexton much more easily. Until she could drive again, Ricky had acted as chauffeur in her car, but in recent weeks he had insisted on using his own, recently acquired, vehicle. This suited Jenny fine. She could make calls to her sources, including serving police officers, without him overhearing. She had to preserve some secrets.

This should have made her happier, but for some time she had felt unaccountably irritated. Since Ricky had started driving his own car, she had become more and more anxious that he was after her job. She had had trouble sleeping and her work had suffered, too. Her former confidence had all but evaporated, and when she did have a story to write, her fingers didn't seem to work properly on the keyboard. She was also tired all the time and began to forget things. 'Surely this isn't the bloody menopause?' she asked herself, but her GP reassured her that this was still some way off. The doctor also checked her thyroid, iron levels and liver function and could find nothing obviously wrong.

She followed the doctor's recommendation to take a few days off and cosseted herself with true crime podcasts, TV thrillers and wine. She was beginning to feel better, but as soon as she returned to work, her problems reappeared. By now the editor was noticing her declining performance and suggested she took on a less demanding role. This made her furious, as she knew that Ricky was waiting in the wings. After a particularly turbulent meeting she called the editor a useless twat, stormed out of the office and scraped her car against a lamp post, leaving massive dents in both nearside doors. She sat and sobbed until a police patrol pulled up alongside her.

'Ms Pike, isn't it?' asked the driver, reaching for a breath testing kit. 'Is everything all right?'

'Of course it's not bloody all right. I've wrecked the sodding car.'

'Are you hurt at all?'

'No. Just pissed off.'

'Then would you mind taking a breath test?'

To the officer's obvious surprise, the test proved negative.

'That's all clear, Ms Pike. Glad to see you've not started drinking and driving again. Mind how you go.'

Jenny fumed but said nothing. She phoned her insurance company, managed to get her car to a garage and took a taxi home.

Chapter Thirty-Four

Day 23

DCI Colin Farlowe brushed an imaginary speck of dust from the cuff of his tailored suit jacket and addressed the team.

'Good morning, ladies and gentlemen. As you may have heard, I will now be leading the investigation into the poisonings in Mexton, with DI Thorpe as my deputy. We have reason to believe that the same killer is responsible for all six deaths and it looks like some kind of vigilante is at work. The new name for the combined investigation is Operation Inheritance. And I'll have no jokes about arsenic, please.'

The team looked puzzled.

'I'll explain later,' whispered Jack to Mel.

'So,' continued the DCI,' 'where are we with these cases? Gordon Howell, to start with.'

'The headteacher of the school where Howell worked put out a few feelers and none of the staff or families had any reason to suspect him of interfering with children, apart from the two families I spoke to,' replied Mel. 'Forensics found traces of rust and oil on Howell's clothing. That suggested to them that he'd been in the back of a van at some point, which ties in with what Devon Wilson said. There were also a few green fibres that may have come from a jacket or trousers, but they couldn't be specific. There was no DNA of any value.'

'OK. Thank you, Mel. What about Marvin Lambton?'

'IT have finished going through his laptop and cloud account,' said Jack. 'There were dozens of photos of women, naked or half-dressed, clearly taken without their consent. A nasty little pervert. Unfortunately, we don't have any names for them, just some initials, so we can't find out whether he'd been blackmailing anyone else for sex. We could put out a public appeal, asking anyone who may have been preyed upon by Lambton to come forward, but we may not get much of a response.'

'Yeah. Do you recognise these tits?' muttered a civilian support worker, attracting a withering glare from the DCI.

'That's a good idea,' responded Emma. 'If we phrase it right, we may find some more victims. I'll get on to media liaison. I'll ask Karen to talk to Stacey again. She may have mentioned what happened to someone else, though it would need to have been someone she trusted.'

'Thanks, Emma. Anything else?'

'Not really. The chemicals used to kill him are easy enough to get hold of. The notice on the darkroom door was printed on a basic inkjet printer and there was no DNA or fingerprints on it. We still haven't found Lambton's digital camera and no witnesses have come forward, despite an appeal in the press and on social media. Basically, we're stuck.'

'Right. Thank you. And the bodybuilder?'

Martin spoke up. 'Firstly, it's not hard to get hold of

Foxgloves. Garden centres sell them, they grow wild on verges in dozens of locations around Mexton and you can buy the seeds all over the place. No leads there. A few 'no comeback' questions asked around gyms revealed that Foreman was selling steroids, and we found boxes of them in his house.

'I spoke to the parents of the kid who died. They were still devastated by their son's death but said they hadn't heard of Foreman. They seemed too fragile and depressed to get involved in any vengeful activity, and they're certainly not fit enough to commit some of the other offences.'

'The package was delivered by the killer,' added Karen. 'The postie had no recollection of handling it and the postage label was fake.'

'And the builder?' Farlowe was obviously becoming impatient with the lack of progress.

'We've been through his list of customers, or at least those he kept records for,' said Karen. 'Several of the people I spoke to were unhappy about the standard of his work but were fobbed off when they complained. Another said he felt intimidated when he expressed concerns. It's obvious Barwell's been overcharging and doing off-the-books work. He had quite a lot of cash on his premises. HMRC were looking at him. There were some fibres on the ladder from generic workwear and a small drop of blood on a splinter. It wasn't Barwell's but the DNA wasn't on the database either.'

Mel spoke up. 'I checked with A&E. They've had no cases of Deadly Nightshade poisoning for several years. I'm still waiting to hear from the botanists.'

'Thank you. What about the drunk driver?'

'The lab found methanol in a nearly empty bottle of whisky,' said Addy. 'There was also a note on the box it came in, expressing sympathy and giving a phoney website address – carlawsarecrap.com. We think the poisoned Scotch was left on his doorstep, but no-one saw it being put there. No DNA or fingerprints, either. And methanol is easy to get hold of. You don't need a licence or anything.'

'And Sharon Cattrall? Somebody give me some good news, please.'

'Sorry boss. No can do,' replied Emma. 'The pathologist found bruising to her knees and a mark across the bottom of her left leg that suggested she tripped over a wire or something. We found nowt at the scene. A neighbour saw a paramedic attending to her, and helping her back inside, but no-one saw anything else of use. There's an outstanding action to find who made the call to the ambulance service that brought the paramedic. It's surprising he got there so quickly.'

'Well, prioritise that, please, Emma.'

'We are, guv. It's the second paramedic we've come across. There was someone in a paramedic's uniform seen helping Howell into a van, although he was probably a fake.'

Farlowe scratched a thin scar that ran from beside his right eyebrow to his chin.

'So, in summary, we've got about ten percent of bugger all. Which won't do. I'm not criticising anyone here. I know you've all been working extremely hard under DI Thorpe's guidance. But we can't have some nutcase running round Mexton poisoning people. There are two areas we need to focus on. What sort of person is doing this? And how are they selecting the victims? The Super is making noises about employing a profiler, although I have mixed feelings about how useful these people are.'

'I agree,' said Emma. 'We could probably spend the money better elsewhere. How are you planning to handle the press? Jenny Pike has already asked if there's a serial poisoner about, and now we've officially linked the cases we need to say something.'

'I'll talk to media liaison. We'll put out a statement and

hold a press conference, emphasising that the general public is not at risk. So, what sort of person are we looking for? Ideas, please. Don't be shy.' The DCI smiled encouragingly.

Emma pulled across the whiteboard on which the team had already listed their ideas. Farlowe perused it for a few minutes and then spoke.

'These are all good suggestions, but I don't think they narrow down the pool of suspects very much. We can't interview every pharmacist with access to a van in Mexton or check on all the police and civilian staff. But please keep thinking. Now, I need to report back to the Super and discuss the press conference. In the meantime, can you collate everything that's known about the victims, and those they've harmed, that's in the public domain? If the killer appears to have had access to confidential information, that may help to identify him. I'll leave you in DI Thorpe's capable hands. Thank you, everyone.'

'What did that remark about arsenic mean?' Emma asked Jack, as they waited in the queue for the coffee machine. 'You know all this obscure stuff for your pub quizzes.'

Jack smiled. 'Arsenic used to be referred to as inheritance powder. It's a translation from the French "poudre de succession". The stuff was used for getting rid of relatives who were going to leave you money and had outstayed their welcome.'

'Charming. So DCI Farlowe knows his poisons, then.'

'So it seems. Not that it's significant, I'm sure. I don't see him sneaking around putting chemicals in expensive whisky. He'd probably consider it sacrilege.'

Emma grinned and carried her coffee back to the incident room. She wasn't sure how she felt about DCI Farlowe taking over. On the one hand, she felt she was more than capable of running the enquiry. They were already following the strategy he suggested. On the other, she realised that a DCI would normally be in charge of such a high-profile case. She got on all right with her boss, so she would wait to see how things panned out.

Chapter Thirty-Five

'OK, THEN,' began Emma, as the team reassembled with coffees. 'If we've got a vigilante, then we need to identify his potential targets and warn them. Mel, can you go through court records, going back a year or so, and look for lenient sentences or acquittals where a guilty verdict was expected? Trev, work alongside her and see what there is on social media. Addy, go through the local papers. I'm assuming the killer is working on victims just in Mexton, but, Martin, have a rummage around HOLMES2 and look for poisonings elsewhere. Look for open verdicts, and verdicts of unlawful killing. If you've got time, look at suicides, but there's probably loads of them. Back here at three, please.'

'Right. What have we got?' asked Emma when the team reconvened.

'HOLMES2 didn't give us much, I'm afraid, guv,' replied Martin, 'but I talked to a Crime Analyst at the NCA. She came up with a possible poisoning. A care home manager in

Weston-super-Mare who died from an overdose of sleeping tablets and alcohol. The coroner recorded an open verdict because there was no reason why she would have killed herself, according to people who knew her. I spoke to one of the investigating officers and it turns out she was a nasty piece of work. She left one care home after it failed a Care Quality Commission inspection, because of alleged neglect and ill-treatment of its residents, but nothing was proved against her personally. She was doing well in her new job, managing another home in the same town. The company that owns it apparently valued her, quote, no-nonsense approach.'

'Thanks, Martin. I'll ask Avon and Somerset to take another look. What killed her, by the way?'

'Zopiclone sleeping tablets washed down with gin. There was also some diazepam in her system, but the coroner didn't think that was significant.'

'Right. How about potential victims?'

'Surprisingly, there weren't that many,' said Addy. 'There was one case I came across in the *Messenger*, though. A cyclist was knocked off his bike in Merchant Street by a lorry. He was badly injured but the driver was cleared of careless driving. There was quite a row about it in the paper.'

'Sounds promising. We'd better contact the driver. Anything else, anyone?'

'Here's a nasty one,' replied Karen. 'Two lads from the Eastside pushed over a teenager with Down's Syndrome, kicked him and taunted him. He wasn't badly hurt so they only got fines and community service. Oh, and they had to pay twenty pounds each in compensation to their victim. A bloody joke. The magistrates didn't accept the prosecution's argument that it was a hate crime, which is why they got off so lightly.'

'They deserve fucking poisoning,' a voice from the back said.

'I didn't hear that,' replied Emma. 'Mel?'

'How about this?' she replied. 'A six-year old was bitten by a pitbull in his neighbour's garden. The dog owner argued that the boy had climbed through a hole in the fence and was taunting the dog, so all he got was a fine and a suspended sentence for owning a prohibited breed of dog without a certificate of exemption.'

'Better warn the dog,' joked Mel.

'Too late. It was put down. But someone needs to have a word with the owner. Anyone else?'

'Another possible, guv,' said Trevor. 'A woman was killed when the steering failed on the second-hand car she had just bought. She lost control on a bend at the bottom of a hill and smashed into a wall. The dealer who sold her the car swore it was roadworthy and pointed to a recent MOT certificate, although it came from a testing station we have suspicions about. The woman had been drinking, but not that much, and the coroner recorded a verdict of accidental death. A prosecution by Trading Standards for selling an unroadworthy vehicle failed, but the dealer was condemned on social media and there was vandalism at his premises.'

'OK. Thanks, Trev. Right, can you divide up the visits among you and warn potential victims to be very careful what they eat and drink? Tell them not to take anything from strangers, watch their drinks in the pub and, preferably, survive on pre-packed food until we've caught the killer.'

'Is it worth a public appeal, guv?' asked Karen.

'No way. It would cause a massive panic. We just need to talk to the people we've identified. As soon as possible, please.'

Chapter Thirty-Six

'Mr Wayne Dyer?' asked Mel, as the scruffy PVC door was yanked open in response to her knock.

'Who wants to know?' the burly, shaven-headed individual in a grimy vest and camouflage shorts sneered.

'Police, sir. I'd just like a quick word with you, if that's OK.'

'No, it fucking isn't. Last time you lot came round I lost my dog. So piss off.'

'I really think it's in your best interests to listen to me, sir,' Mel replied, calmly. 'We believe you may be in danger.'

'Are you takin' the piss? Nobody fucks with me on this estate. I ain't got Tyson anymore but I've got his son.'

Dyer's forehead creased as he realised what he'd said.

'May I come in?' persisted Mel.

'Not without a fucking warrant. Say what you've got to say out here.'

'If you insist, sir. Have you heard about this individual who's been poisoning people in Mexton?'

'Yeah? So what?'

'Well, we believe that he is targeting people whom he

considers have got off lightly after committing an offence. We are concerned that you might fit into that category.'

'What? Cos that little shit came onto my property and provoked my dog? He deserved everything he got.'

'It's not for me to comment, sir, but there was an outcry at the time and some people felt you should have gone to prison.'

'Well, if he comes round here he'll have me and the dog to deal with.'

'Nevertheless, we are advising people to be careful about what they eat and drink. Just in case it has something unpleasant in it.'

'You're wastin' your time. No-one's gonna get to me. You'll be tellin' me to have a vaccination next. Now piss off.'

'Enjoy the rest of your day,' said Mel, as the slamming door drowned out the sound of a growling dog.

'Sometimes I don't know why we bother,' she thought to herself, sorely tempted to kick a green box full of unrecyclable rubbish across Dyer's weed-strewn drive. A handleless carving knife, sticking out of the box, caught her eye and she shuddered, returning to her car as quickly as she could.

Martin knocked on the office door of Mexton Magic Autos and cast his eyes around the yard while he waited for a reply. The dealer's stock consisted of unappealing, scruffy vehicles, lined up against a decaying fence, with optimistic price stickers plastered on half-wiped windscreens. Anyone buying from this place must be desperate, he thought.

The door creaked open and a ferrety-looking, middle-aged man looked at him with suspicion.

'You're a copper, aren't you? I can tell. What do you want?'

'Yes, sir. DC Martin Rowse. You're Terry Cole, aren't you? Can I have a word inside?'

Cole ushered him in, but didn't invite him to sit in the cluttered office that smelled strongly of tobacco smoke and stale chips.

'What's it about? I'm all legit. You can see my ledgers if you want. Look at the cars. I'll even give you a blue light discount.'

Martin, a car fan who wouldn't be seen dead in one of Cole's vehicles, declined the offer.

'It's about this person who's been poisoning people around Mexton,' he began. 'We think he's going after people who, in his eyes, have committed crimes and have got away with it or not been punished enough.'

'What's that got to do with me? I've not broken the law. Well, OK, there was that business with the VAT, but my accountant sorted that out.'

'We think that Mrs McGinty's car puts you in that category. Although the charges against you were dropped, some people still hold you responsible for her death.'

'Now look.' Cole's face flushed with anger. 'That car was OK when I sold it. She was pissed. It was her fault.'

'Be that as it may, sir, you are still potentially vulnerable.'

Cole's colour faded.

'So what do I do? Stop eating?'

'Just be careful what you eat and drink. Stick to food you've bought and cooked, or heated up, yourself. Make sure no-one puts anything in your drinks when you're out. That's all I'm saying. And if you're suspicious about anything, please call us at once.'

Cole looked increasingly worried and let Martin out with a grudging, 'Thank you'.

Chapter Thirty-Seven

Day 24

'So HOW DID you get on with the potential victims?' asked Emma.

'Dyer was hostile and reckons he's invincible, guv,' replied Mel. 'I think he's bred a pup from the pitbull, so we need to get one of the dog guys round there to check.'

'OK. Thanks. I'll sort it. How about the lorry driver?'

'He's on a job to Liverpool,' said Trevor. 'He won't be back until tomorrow, but I had a chat with his wife and she'll pass on the warning.'

'I spoke to Terry Cole,' said Martin. 'He wasn't pleased to see me but seemed genuinely worried when I explained the situation. He'll be careful. It's probably the worst collection of used cars I've seen, though. Guaranteed to the end of the road or for ten minutes, whichever's the shorter.'

The others laughed.

'Did you manage to track down those two lads, Karen?'

'Not yet, guv. I had a hospital appointment. I'll try again this morning.'

'OK,' said Emma, reaching for her phone, which had just started ringing.

'DI Thorpe? Yes ... That's right ... Oh shit ... Where? ... Thank you.'

She turned back to the rest of the team, looking grim.

'I'm afraid it's too late, Karen. They've been found dead.'

'Oh fuck. I'm sorry, guv.' Karen paled. 'It's so hard getting an appointment. I couldn't turn it down. I cleared it with Jack.'

'I realise that. We don't know how long they've been dead, so it may have made no difference. I'm going to the scene now and I'll let you know what the doctor says.'

Karen left the room, visibly distressed, while the others picked up their notes and phones to return to their desks.

'I've fucked up again,' thought Karen, as she sat crying silently in the women's toilets. 'I'm a traitor to the force, I've done terrible things and now I'm responsible for the death of two teenagers. I can't go on like this much longer. There must be something I can get right. I must be the world's most useless cop.'

She wiped her face, straightened her jacket and returned to the office, hoping her colleagues wouldn't notice her red-rimmed eyes.

'I'll come with you to the scene, guv,' she said to Emma. 'I feel I ought to.'

Emma looked thoughtful.

'You don't have to, but come along if you want.'

She picked up her bag and Karen followed her out of the room.

Liam Morris and Trenton Hoyle sat sprawled against a wall, under a walkway connecting two blocks of flats on the Eastside estate. The area stank of urine, overlaid with fresh vomit. A black soot stain, a legacy from a van torched during a gang battle, discoloured much of the wall. A two-litre bottle of strong cider, nearly empty, lay at the feet of the two lifeless youths. A single ribbon of police tape, guarded by a uniformed PC, cordoned off the immediate area, but as soon as Emma saw the tableau, she instructed the PC to set up a double cordon and called for SOCOs. Then she phoned DCI Farlowe.

'Looks like we've got another poisoning case, boss. A couple of lads on the Eastside. Seems like we didn't get to them in time. We'll need some bodies to go door-to-door in pairs. Can you let Jack know, please?'

Karen looked mortified.

'Shall I make a start? I can talk to the parents.'

'No, lass. You know bloody well no-one knocks on doors on the Eastside alone. I've learned that much since I've been here. When the SOCOs arrive I'll come with you to deliver the death messages. Paramedics are on their way to confirm death, so there's nowt we can do for the moment. You'd best wait in the car.'

Karen wandered off dejectedly while Emma phoned the Crime Scene Manager, on his way with the SOCOs, to discuss the forensic strategy.

'The main thing of interest is the cider bottle,' she explained. 'We'll need prints and DNA, and as soon as it's been dusted and swabbed we need the contents analysing. I wouldn't spend too much time on the surroundings. The stuff would almost certainly have been poisoned somewhere else, and there's so much crap here you'll never find anything of significance. Their clothing will need looking at, though.'

She listened to the CSM's responses, nodded a few times

and concluded the call with, 'Thanks, Mark. That's brilliant. See you in a minute.'

Two hours later, with photography and sampling finished, the bodies of the two young men were transported to the mortuary in a private ambulance. Emma and Karen drove back to the station, silent and sick at heart after delivering the death messages to the victims' next of kin.

The uniformed PC removed the crime scene tape, and nothing remained to show where two teenagers had breathed their last, apart from a couple of scruffy bunches of flowers, with cards bearing their names, that someone had dropped there as the police left.

Two for the price of one, or was it kill one, get one free? Neat, anyway. And keeping them unconscious while the poison got to work was clever. He hadn't wanted them to throw it up and avoid its deadly effects. Doing it on the Eastside was tricky, though. He knew the estate by reputation and dreaded meeting some of its more vicious inhabitants. Still, his disguise as a rough sleeper had worked, and letting the two little shits steal the cider from him, not suspecting it was lethal, had been a stroke of genius. They hadn't even hit him, and he managed to leave the estate unscathed.

He looked back over his triumphs so far. Fuck, he was good at this. Perhaps he should write a textbook? Or dress it all up as a thriller? No, that was silly, but he would, one day, like some recognition for his talents. The police, clearly, had no idea who he was and he wanted it to stay that way. He would take a break for a while. Investigate some new toxins.

Perhaps he could arrange for several cleansings to take place on the same day? Tricky, but it would certainly keep them busy. It would be great fun planning it, and what better demonstration of his power could there be than striking down three or four undesirables at the same time?

Chapter Thirty-Eight

Day 25

'THIS WAS AN INTERESTING ONE,' said Dr Durbridge. 'It was clear from the post mortem that they had been poisoned with something, but I couldn't tell what. The lab found Zopiclone, a sleeping medication, in the cider. It would have knocked them out, but there wasn't enough in their tissues to kill them. They also found traces of plant matter that weren't large enough to identify under the microscope.'

'You have worked it out, haven't you?' asked Emma. 'I can see you're pleased with yourself.'

Dr Durbridge smiled and continued. 'Did you know that every British flowering plant and conifer has a DNA barcode on file?'

'What? Like the Home Office DNA database?'

'Broadly the same, yes. Anyway, I persuaded a friend of mine in the university genetics department to produce such a barcode, using the official techniques, and I had it checked against the database.'

'And you got a match.'

'I did. I believe the two young males were poisoned with toxins present in Yew. The principal poisonous material is called taxine and I've asked the lab to analyse the cider for it. The results will take a while to come back, but I'm pretty sure they'll find a lethal concentration there.'

'So could they have been given the Zopiclone in the cider to knock them out and prevent them from seeking help while the other stuff did its job?'

'That's really your department. I'm just reporting what was found. But it's not inconsistent with the facts.'

'Thank you very much, Doctor. Strychnine, Yew, Foxgloves, Deadly Nightshade – it sounds like our poisoner's been helping himself from one of those poison gardens that have sprung up.'

'Not necessarily. Apart from strychnine, the others are all easy to come by and not difficult to recognise. Every churchyard has its Yew, for instance. And the other poisons have nothing to do with plants.'

'Well, I'll look forward to your report. Thanks again.'

Emma drove back to the station wondering where the poisoner could get hold of prescription medicines such as Zopiclone as well as poisonous plants. And there was something about the sleeping drug that rang a bell.

'Hello, Stacey, it's DC Karen Groves. Have you got a moment to talk to me?'

'I suppose so.' The girl sounded uncertain when she realised who was phoning her.

'How are you coping?'

'I feel a bit better after talking to you. Thanks. But I still have trouble sleeping at night and I'm scared someone will see the photos.'

'Well, we don't think that's likely, if that helps.'

Stacey sniffed. 'What did you want to talk to me about?'

'Did you tell anyone else about what happened to you?'

'Only the nice ambulanceman. We were sitting on a park bench. I was holding the bag with the pill in it, crying. He was behind us in the chemists and he could see I was upset, even then. He was so kind. Even with a mask on you could see he had one of those faces that made you want to talk to him, you know?'

Karen murmured agreement.

'Anyway, I explained what had happened and he said that it would be a good idea to see a doctor in case I'd picked up something. I'm not sure I can, though. He's our family GP.'

'I think he's right, but you could see a doctor at the hospital's sexual health clinic. Perhaps Jodie could make an appointment for you?'

'I'll ask her. Probably.'

'OK. Before I go, is there anything else you remember about the ambulanceman? We would like to talk to him.'

'Sorry. No. I was so upset I wasn't really taking things in.'

'That's fine. You've been really helpful. Thank you so much. Take care of yourself and don't worry about the pictures.'

'I'll try.'

Chapter Thirty-Nine

EVERY INSTINCT she possessed told Valentina to refuse. Face-to-face meetings were not how it was done. But the text requesting the meeting hadn't come from some low life; a gang member or someone from the Eastside. It was from a respectable member of society who had something she particularly wanted. There shouldn't be a risk, and the location wasn't in a dodgy area. Could it be a police trap? Unlikely. She wouldn't say anything compromising that could be picked up by a wire, and, anyway, her mole hadn't mentioned anything about her activities being investigated. She balanced the potential risks against the expected benefit and agreed. But she put her pepper spray in her coat pocket, just in case.

Valentina stood outside the jobcentre on Castle Street at ten minutes to eleven at night. The other premises on the street had long been closed and the only passers-by were likely to be solitary drunks, couples, either besotted with each other or arguing, and groups of young people moving from pubs to nightclubs. No-one would be likely to notice the nondescript woman in the shadows. Valentina had a talent for looking inconspicuous when the need arose.

She had arrived early, to check out the location and ensure that her meeting would be unobserved. Nothing she had seen worried her, although she remained on full alert. At precisely eleven o'clock, a figure stepped out of a side road that led to a shoppers' car park, holding out a well-filled envelope. She reached for it, only to find that, beneath it, was the blued steel of a revolver barrel. The figure motioned her to follow, backing into the side road.

'How could I have been so fucking stupid?' she thought, reaching into her pocket for the spray. Before she could use it, the revolver barrel disappeared and a strip of steel, glinting in the light from the main road, replaced it. She barely registered the knife before it was rammed into her chest, piercing her coat, jacket and blouse as if they were tissue paper. A dull thump under her left breast gave way to a searing pain. Her head swam and she could hardly breathe. Everything blurred as she lost consciousness and slumped to the ground, her hands grasping the hem of her assailant's coat in a desperate grip. She didn't feel her attacker clumsily lifting her body into the commercial waste bin parked in the side road. For Valentina Malenka, aka Marnie Draycott, aka Martina Baranska, was dead.

Chapter Forty

THE KILLER RIFLED through Valentina's pockets and removed her car keys and wallet. Taking the cash and cards would make it look like a robbery, but the car keys were much more important. Half an hour's searching the nearby streets, repeatedly pressing the key fob, yielded a result, and the killer was soon on the road, following the satnav history back to Valentina's cottage, having picked up a few items on the way. With the job done, the killer drove back towards Mexton and left Valentina's car in a side street close to a bus route. A taxi home was too risky, but a late bus, full of drunken revellers, provided transport back into town, and a combination of dark glasses, a scarf and a baseball cap preserved the killer's anonymity. A perfect murder? Well, nothing's perfect, but this came pretty damn close.

It took forty minutes for the three fire appliances to reach Valentina's blazing cottage. A motorist passing on the main road had spotted a strange glow at the end of the lane. An ardent UFO-spotter, he resolved to investigate in case aliens were dropping in on Mexton. To his disappointment there were no extra-terrestrials in evidence, so he phoned the fire service.

Five litres of petrol, ignited by a candle burning down to a fuel-soaked collar of fabric, had turned the ground floor into an inferno. The thatched roof had fed the hungry flames, which destroyed almost everything but the stone walls. All the fire service could do was damp down the blaze and prevent it from spreading to neighbouring woodland.

'No way was this an accident,' said Station Officer Alderton to Control, 'It's clearly arson. There's no point looking for survivors: no-one could have survived this lot. We'll get an investigator down in the morning, but this needs to be cordoned off. I'll notify the police.'

By the time the fire crew left, the blaze was out and only wisps of smoke, on the water pooling on the ground, remained.

Two hours later, a bored PC Desmond Barrow sat in a patrol car facing the steaming ruins, now garlanded with police tape, playing Candy Crush on his phone. He hated the countryside and would much rather have been patrolling the streets of Mexton, looking out for suspicious characters and maybe stopping off at a late night chippy. His preoccupation with the game meant that he didn't see a dark-clad figure sneaking into the back of the cottage, playing the dimmest of torch beams over the blackened sludge that covered the floor. Nor did he see the satisfied smile on the intruder's face or hear the muffled sounds of the mountain bike slowly negotiating the moonlit woodland track that led back to the road.

'Nothing to report, Sarge,' he said, when DS Jack Vaughan arrived with the fire investigator at eight in the morning.

Chapter Forty-One

Day 26

Peter Dalgliesh was an experienced fire investigator, with dozens of cases under his belt. He had seen just about every cause of domestic and industrial fires, from faulty washing machines and overflowing chip pans to chemicals combusting spontaneously and skilfully planned arson. It didn't take him long to realise that an accelerant had been used at the cottage, and to his relief, there appeared to be no human remains on site. A few blackened, half-burned beams, remnants of the roof, lay on the stone floor, and several lumps of melted and twisted metal were barely recognisable as the remains of a row of computers and ancillary equipment. He was about to leave the scene when something struck him.

'Jack,' he called. 'Didn't you have this place guarded overnight?'

'Course, Peter. It's a probable crime scene. The PC you just met was here from the time your guys left.'

'Well, someone's been here without him noticing. Look.'

Dalgliesh pointed to a series of footwear marks in the

drying sludge and a trail of black material leading out of the cottage's back doorway.

'These are too small to be made by the boots fire officers wear, and when they left, the muck would have been too wet to take footprints. Someone got in here a few hours later.'

'Shit. The dozy sod must have fallen asleep. He'll get a bollocking for that. OK. I'll ask for some SOCOs to take a look and make casts. I'm wondering why someone would visit a burned-out cottage in the middle of the night. Presumably, either to remove something or to check that everything had been destroyed. More likely the latter.

'That's your job, Jack. But that makes sense.'

'Right. Thanks, Peter. Helpful as ever. We'll look forward to your report.'

As the fire investigator changed out of his overalls, a furious Jack phoned DI Thorpe, requesting forensic help and a couple of uniforms to safeguard the scene. He would deal with the inattentive PC later.

Chapter Forty-Two

'OK,' began Emma Thorpe, starting a briefing after lunch. 'I'm running the poisoning cases for the moment, as the DCI had to take a couple of days' personal leave yesterday. He'll probably take over when he gets back, but for the moment, I'm SIO. Before we start, there was a suspicious fire last night a few miles from town, on Arnold's Lane, just off the Highchester road. A cottage was burned out and it looks like arson. Martin's done a bit of digging and found it was rented by a private company registered in the Cayman Islands, so we'll get nowt about it from there. Can you find out who pays the electricity, water and council tax, Trevor? And check the Land Registry to find out who owns the place.'

'Yes, guv.'

'According to the fire investigator, the blaze was deliberate, with several seats to the fire. He said that the primary seat was ignited by a candle in some way, as he found traces of wax. Trails of accelerant led to secondary seats. He also said that the door had been left partly open, to ensure plenty of air, he assumed. Our SOCOs were unable to determine whether it had been forced open or keys had been used. They did manage to make casts of some footwear marks, which we think were left by someone who entered the cottage during the night, after the fire had died down. There were also tyre tracks from what was probably a mountain bike leading from near the cottage to the main road. Possibly, the arsonist parked his or her car some way away and cycled up to the cottage after the fire was out. A bike would be much quieter, and the lazy sod guarding the scene didn't hear it.'

'But why go back?' asked Addy.

'Perhaps to make sure that something was destroyed,' suggested Trevor.

'So, we're treating this as arson, not attempted murder,' said Martin.

'For the moment, Martin,' replied Emma. 'We've no idea when the cottage was last occupied. The fire was so severe that we can glean nothing about who lived there or what they did. Perhaps Trev will give us something. Can you look at ANPR records of vehicles in that area from sunset to dawn?'

'Sure, boss,' said Martin. 'But I doubt that there'll be much nearby and there won't be any CCTV. The cottage was pretty remote.'

'Sounds wonderfully quiet,' said Karen. 'My flat's on the main road from Mexton to the south coast. I'd love a peaceful cottage.'

'You wouldn't be so happy when it's snowed up in winter,' replied Martin. 'You could slip on the ice and break a leg and they'd never get an ambulance up there.'

'That reminds me. I spoke to Stacey Bannister yesterday, and she told me she was comforted by an ambulanceman outside the pharmacy when she bought the morning after pill. He was wearing a mask but had "a nice face", she said. I asked her for a description, but she couldn't remember anything more.'

'OK, Karen,' said Emma. 'That's helpful. Talk to her again

and ask her for the time and date so we can check with the ambulance trust. See if there's any CCTV in the pharmacy. Has anybody got anything else on the poisonings?'

Only Jack answered. 'Still following up possible leads, checking social media, cameras and so on. But to be honest, we're getting nowhere. He's a clever bastard, but he's bound to make a mistake at some point.'

'I hope you're right, Jack, before anyone else gets killed.'

Chapter Forty-Three

Day 27

EMMA CALLED EVERYONE TO ORDER.

'OK, everybody. Message from the Chief Constable. We've got to look for stolen cats.'

The team looked puzzled, somebody miaowed and Trevor spoke up. 'Isn't that more the RSPCA's job? Not major crime, surely?'

'He didn't mean our furry friends. Catalytic converters. The things supposed to stop petrol and diesel engines buggering up the air. There's been an outbreak of thefts and we've been asked by the Serious and Organised Crime Unit to help find out where they go. Also, and unrelated, the Chief's wife had one stolen from her Toyota Prius. It's now a write-off.'

Somebody sniggered.

'That's fucking ridiculous,' raged Jack. 'We're up to our arses in poisons and now we have to go looking for nicked car parts. Would he like us to look for Lord Lucan as well? Or sodding Shergar?'

'Sorry, Jack,' replied Emma. 'The unit thinks this is part of a much bigger operation and they do need our help.'

'What's the point in stealing these things?' asked Mel. 'Is there a shortage or something?'

'Rare metals,' said Jack, sullenly. 'There's really expensive stuff in the cats. Platinum, palladium and rhodium. That last one's about fifteen times the price of gold and there's a world shortage.'

'Your pub quizzes again?' asked Emma, looking amazed.

Jack said nothing but Martin replied.

'He's a total whiz, guv. His brain's a dustbin full of odd facts that he recycles when needed. I've seen him play. Ferocious!'

Emma let the laughter die down before continuing.

'Jack's right. The converters are sawn off, in about ten minutes, by the thieves and sold illegally as scrap. They're worth about four hundred quid each, just for the metals that can be reclaimed. And it's a bastard for the motorist because replacements are hard to come by. The insurance companies usually write off the affected vehicles. And you can't drive a car without one.'

'So what does the top brass want us to do?' asked Mel. 'Go into the scrap trade? I can see it now. "Jack's Junked Jalopies. Best prices paid. No questions asked." Or maybe "Sid Schrödinger's End-of-Life Cat Company." We could make a fortune.'

'I think you're being a bit daft, Mel. We'll start by visiting a few scrapyards in the hope that the stolen cats are disposed of locally. The Environment Agency will have a list of operating scrappies. Someone needs to have a chat with one of their inspectors. See if they have any suspicions about what's being handled. Dealers are no longer allowed to pay cash for metals, and have to keep a record of vehicle registrations, but we know that some operators ignore the law. Can you organise this, please, Jack?'

'Yes, guv. I'll talk to the EA and draw up a list. But how the hell are we going to manage this? Is the Chief going to give us any more resources? Has he got a magic detectives tree?'

'I'm afraid not, Jack. We'll just have to do what we can. We can't have everyone on it. Give it a couple of days with a few people, and if we find nothing, we'll have to shelve it for a while. Perhaps a press release warning people to be vigilant would be useful. I'll talk to media relations when I've got a moment. But if anything comes up on the poisonings, give it priority and sod the cats.'

'OK. We'll keep buggering on, I suppose.'

'Thanks, Jack. Mel, can I have a word?' She motioned Mel into her office. 'Firstly, I'm really pleased to see you back and looking fit, lass. I meant to catch up with you earlier. Are you getting any problems from the injury?'

'No, not really, boss. It's a bit sensitive, but as long as I don't put any strain on it, or bash my shoulder, I'm OK. The physio's given me exercises to build up the muscles again, but it's hard work. Time will heal, they say, although the doctor said there might always be a slight impairment.'

'How about mentally?'

Mel shrugged and then winced. 'OK, I guess. I'm not keen on blades, I suppose.'

'Are you sleeping?'

'Yeah. Well, sometimes better than others.' Mel averted her eyes.

'Hmmm. I don't want you going into potentially dangerous situations just yet. You don't have to prove yourself all the time, you know. So. How do you feel about attending a post mortem? I seem to remember people saying you've got a strong stomach. It should have been me but I've been called to a meeting suddenly. Everyone else is tied up with the poisoner cases and now the cats. Say no if you can't face it.'

'OK, guv,' replied Mel, thinking she had better skip lunch. 'Who and when?'

'Two o'clock this afternoon. It's a stab victim, a Valentina Malenka, according to the driving licence we found on her. She was discovered in an alley off Castle Street early this morning. We've started a murder investigation, Operation Greenfinch. Take Addy along as the exhibits officer.'

'OK. We'll be there.'

It wasn't how Mel had imagined her return to duty, but at least it was real police work. Emma's comment about proving herself had annoyed her. Had her boss been talking to her dad? The thought infuriated her. She grabbed a quick coffee, collected her things and left for the mortuary with Addy.

Chapter Forty-Four

Dr Durbridge had just begun his examination by the time Mel reached the viewing gallery, and Addy had donned protective clothing. The Anatomical Pathology Technologist drew back the sheet, uncovering the victim's pale, naked body, her clothes already having been removed. Even from the viewing gallery, Mel could see the jagged knife wound, stark against the pale skin, above the woman's heart. The pathologist began dictating into a suspended microphone.

'A well-nourished female of approximately fifty years, 165 centimetres in height, weighing 63.1 kilos. There is what appears to be a knife wound to the left of the thorax and a scar resembling a healed bullet wound to the left hip. There is evidence of plastic surgery to her face. Turn her over, please.'

The APT complied and Dr Durbridge continued dictating.

'There is a healed wound to the left buttock that corresponds to the scar on the front of her hip, consistent with a bullet passing through the muscle. The x-ray showed no damage to the bone.'

At this point Mel zoned out. Some words she had heard,

under terrifying circumstances, came back to her. 'Good job I've developed a fat arse.' Surely it couldn't be? She pressed the button on the intercom.

'Sorry to interrupt, Doctor, but could we have fingerprints and a DNA sample from the deceased, please?'

'Of course, DC Cotton,' replied the pathologist, imperturbable as ever. 'That's routine.'

The APT obliged.

For Mel, the rest of the post mortem passed in a blur. She tried to block out the sight of the pathologist's blades, and her mind kept returning to a forest lodge, with a corpse on the floor, a man with a rifle and a woman with a shotgun. Her hand strayed to her right earlobe, damaged by a stray shotgun pellet, and the earring Tom had given her when it had healed. Mel and Tom's actions had probably saved the woman's life, at great risk to their own, but the armed man had taken a shotgun blast to the face and died. Could the woman, naked and vulnerable on the stainless steel table, be the shooter?

'Jack! I was right! That stab victim. It's Marnie Draycott, aka Martina Baranska. The fingerprints match and I'm sure the DNA will as well. I knew it when I saw the bullet wound. She left the country after the shoot-out in the woods. She's obviously had plastic surgery and dyed her hair. But why on earth would she come back, especially to Mexton, when she's wanted for murder?'

'No idea,' Jack replied. 'Unfinished business? A new scam? Perhaps she thought that changing her appearance would be sufficient protection, as long as she didn't get into trouble and leave DNA or fingerprints anywhere.'

'Well, she certainly found trouble, didn't she?'

Jack nodded. 'I'll let DI Thorpe know. She'll probably

want you in on Operation Greenfinch since you knew the victim.'

'Well, we were hardly besties, but I suppose I did help to save her life when I knocked the shooter over. Oh fuck.'

Mel sat down suddenly.

'What is it, Mel. Are you OK?' Jack looked worried.

'Something's just made sense. That get well card. "I guess I owe you one. The debt will be repaid," that's what it said. And you told me that Ryan was shanked while on remand. She must have been behind the killing and the card. But what kind of twisted logic makes it all right to arrange a killing to repay someone who would arrest you for murder on sight? It doesn't make sense. And how did she know who attacked me? Ryan's name wasn't in the paper or on social media.'

'Well, it looks like it made sense to her. And someone must have told her. Anyway, the next briefing on Greenfinch is tomorrow, when the PM results are in. Probably around midday. You'll be needed there.'

'You bet.'

Mel was excited at being back and involved in a murder investigation. Although the deaths were regrettable, murder cases gave her a buzz like no others. And, despite her absence, she was sure she would be able to contribute. She gathered her things together and waited impatiently for Tom to finish work and drive her home.

Chapter Forty-Five

FATHER McKENZIE, as was his habit, sat in the church thinking, after Mass had finished and the altar boys and deacon had left. It was all so difficult, these days. Everything had changed when Covid took hold. More bereaved parishioners to comfort, but no proper funerals. Grief intensified and unassailable. He couldn't even put the communion wafers on the communicants' tongues any more but had to place them in their hands. Most parishioners had accepted this, but one man had become extremely angry and nearly assaulted him, demanding 'religious freedom' to receive the host in the traditional manner. The same thing had happened at a church in Ireland, apparently. There must be a divine purpose behind it, he thought, but, for the life of him, he couldn't see it. Still, his was not to wonder why.

While he sat in the church, meditating, he noticed how vibrant the colours in the stained glass windows were. He had never realised how rich and achingly beautiful they were. The red of Christ's blood almost pulsated, as if it was freshly shed, and the blue of the Virgin's robes was brighter and deeper than any sky. But why were the colours moving? Were the saints really talking to each other? And why was the font glowing and gliding around the floor of the church like some holy Dalek? The coo of a stray pigeon roosting in the rafters echoed around the church, filling the air with colour. It was the most beautiful sound he had ever heard and he wanted it to go on forever.

As the LSD kicked in, and the chemicals in his brain became completely scrambled, Father McKenzie knew one thing. He had truly found God. And he had to tell everyone. A beatific smile on his face, he ran out of the church. He would preach in the shopping centre across the road and he knew everyone would believe him. He was so sure. Then the van hit him.

Chapter Forty-Six

EMMA WAS FEELING THE PRESSURE. With DCI Farlowe taking the lead on the poisoning cases, some of the heat should have eased off, but he was on leave and she was running both Operation Inheritance and Operation Greenfinch at the moment. She also had to crack the stolen cat thefts. At least Mel was back on the team. She might not be up to mixing it with villains yet, but she had a good brain and had known Valentina Malenka, or whoever she was. Emma was looking forward to cycling home in the evening sunshine and curling up with her husband and a takeaway in front of the TV. But, as she was preparing to leave, her phone rang.

'DI Thorpe,' she answered, wearily.

'Ah, Emma. I'm glad I caught you.' It was the duty uniformed inspector. 'We've got a dead priest, I'm afraid. Outside St Benedict's. It seems as though he committed suicide. Can you take a look?'

'A Catholic committing suicide? Surely not. It's some kind of sin, isn't it? Guaranteed damnation?'

'That's why I'd like your team to investigate. Traffic are

desperate to re-open the road, but I told them to wait until you've okayed it.'

'All right, Jim. I'll get round there now. I'll be ten minutes.'

Emma decided to cycle rather than take a pool car. It would be quicker in the rush hour traffic. When she arrived, the road was full of fuming motorists and the tailback had affected the flow of vehicles half a mile away. A forensic tent had been erected over what she assumed was a body, more for privacy than as an attempt to preserve the scene. An ambulance was parked, half on the pavement, its blue lights flashing while the crew waited for instructions. A man, presumably the van driver, sat on the steps of the ambulance, a blanket round his shoulder, a plastic bottle of water in his hand and an expression of profound shock on his face.

'Can you tell me what happened, sir? I'm Detective Inspector Emma Thorpe.'

'I...I was coming up to the church, doing no more than thirty, I swear. I'd just drawn level with a parked car, when this bloke ran out from behind it, like a bat out of hell. I'd no chance of stopping, honest. He went flying and I swerved to avoid running over him. Hit a lamppost instead.'

'Did you notice anything about him? Did it seem as if he was being chased?'

'I didn't see anyone else. The only thing I remember was his face just before I hit him. He was smiling. Looked as if he'd won the lottery or something. I don't think he even saw me.'

'Thank you, sir. I'm sorry you've had such a dreadful experience. We would like you to come into the station tomorrow and make a proper statement, but for the moment, you can go. Are you hurt? Can you drive?'

'I'm not hurt but the van's wrecked. I've phoned a breakdown firm.'

'OK. I'll arrange a lift home for you. Take care.'

Emma conferred with Sergeant Winwood, the traffic officer in charge of the scene.

'What do you think, Pete?'

'I think he's telling the truth, guv. We've breath-tested him and he's clear. We also checked his mobile and he wasn't using it at the time. You can see skid marks where he braked and swerved. Poor bastard, he'll never forget this.'

'Right, I'll take a quick look in the tent. Unless the SOCOs tell me different, I'll get a van to take the body away and you can start the traffic moving. I take it the paramedics have confirmed death?'

'Yes, they have. Thanks.'

Emma put her head through the flap of the tent. The priest was lying on his side with his legs at an unnatural angle and an obvious injury to the side of his head.

'Any point keeping the tent up?' she asked a SOCO, who shook her head.

'No, boss. There's no evidence to collect from the ground. I've taken photos and Kate here has taken a video. We're done.'

'Right. I'll call for the van and you can get off home when he's been moved. The exhibits officer will bag his clothes at the PM in case we need them. Thank you, both.'

This was seriously odd, thought Emma, as she cycled home half an hour later. What on earth would make a priest run out in front of a van with a big smile on his face? She'd better ask the bishop. He would need to be notified anyway.

Chapter Forty-Seven

When Emma arrived at Bishop Donovan's palace and was shown in by the housekeeper, she half-expected to find an elderly gentleman in clerical dress, possibly wearing a mitre. Instead, the man who greeted her seemed barely fifty. He was red-faced and sweating and was wearing a track suit and trainers.

'Good evening, sir. I'm Detective Inspector Emma Thorpe. I believe you're expecting me?'

'Yes, yes. Do come in. My housekeeper told me you were coming. I must apologise for my appearance. I've just got back from my evening run. It's about this tragic business with Father McKenzie, isn't it?'

'I'm afraid so, sir.'

The bishop led Emma into a study furnished with a large desk, two comfortable armchairs and bookshelves groaning with religious books lining one wall. A series of watercolours depicting local churches, one of which she recognised as St Benedict's, hung above the desk, on which a modern laptop sat.

'Please sit down. Do you know what happened?'

'Well, it seems he deliberately ran into the path of a van, which hit him and caused fatal injuries. He died at the scene very shortly after. The peculiar thing is, the van driver said that Father McKenzie had a huge smile on his face. Can you think of anything that would make him do such a thing?'

The bishop steepled his fingers and pursed his lips, thinking before replying.

'Firstly, I shall pray for the soul of Father McKenzie and also for the poor van driver and his family. I must say, it is most unlikely that Father McKenzie would have deliberately taken his own life. As I'm sure you know, the Church condemns suicide. It is up to God to decide when your allotted span is over. Are you sure it wasn't an accident?'

'Ultimately, that's for the coroner to decide, but no-one saw anyone chasing him and he ran straight into the road. It wasn't as if he had just stumbled off the pavement into the traffic. And why the smile?'

'I'm afraid I cannot explain that,' replied the bishop. 'I've known Father McKenzie for twelve years or so and this behaviour seems completely out of character.'

'What can you tell me about him?'

'He came to St Benedict's ten years ago. I first knew him when he worked in a parish near Portsmouth. He was always assiduous in fulfilling his duties, his faith was strong and there have been no complaints made against him at St Benedict's. The parish accounts were audited recently and were completely in order.'

The bishop appeared to be choosing his words carefully.

'It was rumoured that he liked a glass or two, but I have never seen him intoxicated. We are quite used to spotting alcoholics, and I can assure you that Father McKenzie was not one.'

'Could he have been depressed or suffering from any other kind of mental illness?'

'Highly unlikely, I would have thought. As I said, his faith was strong, and that can provide comfort when things look bad. The person who knew him best was his housekeeper, Mrs Corcoran. She should be able to tell you if there was anything particular on his mind.'

'Thank you, sir, that's very helpful.'

Emma wasn't quite sure how to address a bishop but he didn't seem to mind 'sir'.

'We'll keep you informed of progress in our investigations, but if you can think of anything else that might help us, please give me a call.'

She proffered her card as the bishop led her to the door.

'May God speed you, Detective Inspector. Good evening.'

As the door closed, Emma was grateful that the bishop had been unstuffy. But she had a niggling feeling that he had omitted something in his account of Father McKenzie. Something to think about on the journey home.

Chapter Forty-Eight

Day 28

'So WHAT DO we know about the victim?' began Emma, as she started the Operation Greenfinch briefing. Mel, you've had contact with her, I believe.'

'Yes, guv. Valentina Malenka, better known as Marnie Draycott, aka Martina Baranska. She was part of the Maldobourne gang that we took down towards the end of 2019. A former sex worker in Glasgow, she set up a posh escort agency in London and used it to collect blackmail material on a number of notables, from showbiz, politics and law enforcement. She moved to Mexton and started working with Kelvin Campbell and Charles Osbourne, importing drugs and other illegal items. We believe she was trying to get close to Campbell, who was responsible for trafficking her from Poland when she was a girl, to get her revenge.

'She's wanted for the murder of a corrupt police officer who, apparently, shot Campbell before she managed to kill him. She was wounded but would have been killed if I hadn't knocked the officer's rifle aside as he fired. She felt she owed me a debt and seems to have had the man who attacked me killed in prison.

'Thanks, Mel. Very concise. Clearly, she's been a major criminal in the past, and as she obviously hasn't joined the Salvation Army or some such, we must assume she's been up to something back here in Mexton. Any leads?'

'We don't have an address for her yet,' replied Addy. 'She's not on the electoral roll. There was no ID on her, apart from a driving licence, but the address is false. Someone took her credit cards, cash and phone. We did find a pepper spray, though, which seems to have been imported from Germany.

'So, do we think it's simply a street robbery ending up as murder?' asked Martin.

'It could be,' replied Emma,' but Dr Durbridge said that the single knife blow looked as if it was meant to kill. There were no half-hearted slashes to other parts of the body, as if the killer was trying to intimidate. It seems like murder, perhaps covered up by a robbery. He wouldn't say this in court, of course, but that was his private opinion. Also, there were no defensive wounds, so her killer could have been someone she knew who surprised her with a sudden blow.'

'That makes sense,' said Jack. 'She wouldn't have gone into a side alley with someone she didn't trust or have a hold over. She was far too streetwise. There's no CCTV for a hundred metres in either direction. An ideal spot for a murder. Did the pathologist give any estimate of time of death?'

'No. Sometime during the previous night was all he would say. The street is busy with pub-goers etcetera until about eleven, so any time between then and eight thirty, when a shop assistant on the way to work spotted her foot sticking out of a rubbish bin. Can you get someone to check what CCTV there is, in the street and outside pubs? We may get an idea of when she arrived at the scene. I take it there are no witnesses.'

'No, guv,' replied Trevor. 'Uniform showed her photo to people in the street and bar staff yesterday evening, but no-one recognised her.'

'I guessed as much. We'll put out an appeal for sightings in the press and on social media. We'll need to hold a press conference, but I fear it'll be hijacked by people asking about the poisoner. Did she have a car?'

'There are no vehicles registered to Valentina Malenka,' Martin reported. 'We've asked uniformed patrols and the Council's traffic wardens to keep an eye out for possibly abandoned cars. She probably parked some way away – the roads are all yellow-lined around there – and walked, concealing her face from any CCTV cameras.'

'Well, if we can find a car we may get an address. She's obviously got more than one identity. She's not a ghost. More like a bloody chameleon.'

Emma paused. 'Look, I know it seems as though we are drowning here, with the poisoner, the cat thefts and this killer. Absences because of Covid, on top of the austerity cutbacks, haven't helped. But I do appreciate the hard work you're all putting in, especially in your own time. I'll ask the Super to authorise some additional overtime payments, which may help. He's also asking for some extra officers from the Hampshire force to give us a hand. But please do come and see me if you are finding things too much. This is modern policing for you, I'm afraid. OK, folks, carry on and let me know if you find anything.'

Chapter Forty-Nine

HE FELT sick when he heard the news. That wasn't supposed to happen. He wanted to frighten the old bastard, not kill him. When he slipped into the church earlier in the day, on the pretext of delivering flowers, he had put the drug into the communion wine, hoping it would make the priest freak out. A sort of payback for making him feel so worthless at school.

Didn't Jesus preach mercy and forgiveness? Clearly words absent from Father McKenzie's vocabulary when he made the pupils, to whom he delivered pastoral care, believe that they were bound straight for hell. The same man had refused to marry his friend's parents in his church because they had the same address. You would think he'd try to stop people from living in sin rather than condemning them. In the end they found another priest to perform the ceremony, but a legacy of bitterness remained.

Now he was sure to go to hell. Killing a priest must be high on the list of dreadful sins that God would find hard to forgive. He would go to confession, somewhere away from Mexton. That might help. Should he go to the police and confess? He would have to think about that. He didn't want to go to prison, but maybe that was the only way to rid himself of the guilt that was crippling him. Perhaps the priest would advise him. For now, he wished with all his heart that he had never tried to get his own back on the unpleasant Father McKenzie.

'We're definitely moving, at last!' said Mel, flinging her arms round Tom's neck. She had returned from the station to find him working from home, a letter from their solicitor, confirming that the sale was going ahead, on the table. 'Sorry I've been a bit shitty since that attack. But this will be a new start.'

'Yes, we are. And soon.' He hugged her back. 'Bruce and Sheila can live in the spare room, which should cut down on the crap everywhere, although they'll still need to be let out some of the time, and we'll have the bedroom overlooking the park. We'll get an aviary built for them in the summer. It should be perfect.'

'Weren't you suspicious when the estate agent accepted the offer so quickly?'

'Not really. Covid has stopped people moving, so I expect he was glad of a sale at almost any price. Bit of an odd background, though. Still, it's the solicitor's job to check everything's OK. Cup of tea?'

'I think we can do better than that,' smiled Mel. 'There's a bottle of Prosecco in the fridge. Grab a couple of glasses.'

Chapter Fifty

Day 29

First thing in the morning, the garage phoned Jenny Pike.

'It's all done, Miss Pike,' the receptionist said. 'We'll send the bill to the insurance company as agreed. All you need to pay us is the excess. The technician asked me to mention that they found some strange silvery stuff beneath the mat under the driver's seat. He put it in a jar in the boot.'

'OK. Thanks. I'll pick the car up straight away,' replied Jenny, thinking gloomily about next year's insurance premium. With a fault claim on top of the drink-driving conviction, she would be paying a fortune just to be on the road. Worse, she couldn't claim any of it on expenses or against tax.

When she looked at the contents of the small jar, she recognised the substance immediately. Mercury. One of the few things that had stuck in her mind during school science lessons was the fact that this magical material was a metal but also a liquid. She remembered pushing the shiny globules around the kitchen table when her brother had broken a thermometer. But what was it doing in her car?

As soon as she got into the office, she Googled mercury and found out a number of things. Firstly, there was no logical reason why it should have been there. It couldn't have leaked from any equipment in the vehicle. Secondly, you needed a licence to buy and possess it, unless it was part of a thermometer or barometer. And, thirdly, mercury was highly poisonous if inhaled.

'Fuck!' she thought. 'Is this why I've been feeling like shit for the past few weeks?' Panicking, she signed on to the AskmyGP service, listed her symptoms and suspicions and requested an appointment. Within an hour she had an appointment for the late afternoon.

'I've never come across this before,' said Dr Penny Malton, after taking a detailed account from Jenny of how she had been feeling. 'I've done a bit of research and it is known that dentists and other people working with mercury can suffer psychiatric symptoms, as you describe. You've heard the expression "mad as a hatter"?'

Jenny nodded.

'Hatters used to use mercury compounds to stiffen felt and they suffered as a result.'

'So, am I going mad?'

'No, no. I don't think it got that bad. You told me that you began to feel a bit better when you weren't going into work and using your car.'

'Yes, that's right. Then it got worse again when I went back.'

'OK. I think you've been suffering from low level poisoning that should cease now you are no longer exposed. If you had absorbed a larger dose, we could have injected you with something to extract the mercury, but there are side effects. Would you like me to arrange this?'

Jenny shook her head vehemently. She couldn't stand injections.

'I suggest you monitor your symptoms and get back to me if they don't subside,' continued the doctor. 'Is there something else can I help you with?'

'Just suppose,' suggested Jenny, 'that someone put the mercury in my car to deliberately poison me. How could I prove it?'

Dr Malton thought for a moment. 'Hair analysis could help. Your hair keeps a record of substances you've been exposed to, like a sort of toxic timeline. You could get some analysed, and the results would show roughly when it started. If you suspect a crime, the police might commission an analysis, but it would be quicker if you paid for it yourself. Hang on a minute.'

The doctor rummaged in a desk drawer and withdrew a business card.

'This is a firm the police and the courts use to check people's drug consumption history. They're fully accredited and can do the job.'

'Thank you, Doctor, that's brilliant,' said Jenny, copying down the details. 'I'm most grateful.'

As Jenny left the surgery, she realised that she would have to pay for the analysis out of her own pocket. Her relationship with the local police was coloured with animosity and she doubted that they would take much notice of her. After all, she hadn't been poisoned fatally. But if she had some evidence from her hair, surely they would take her seriously?

Chapter Fifty-One

Gavin Ward had worked for the Environment Agency for over twenty years, protecting the land, water and air in a variety of roles. For the past two years he had worked in waste management, inspecting local companies to ensure they were complying with the conditions of their permits and weren't causing illegal pollution. His current focus was on scrapyards, an industry well known to be on the borders of legality. Some firms were operated by organised crime gangs, handling stolen goods, employing illegal immigrants and laundering money. How firms acquired their metals, and where their workers came from, was not his concern. His job was to make sure that oils and other toxic fluids were handled without causing pollution, and that other types of waste were dealt with appropriately and not just dumped or burned on site.

Delvina Recycling was the last site on his list for the day. He had already warned two companies of enforcement action if they didn't improve their practices and he wasn't looking forward to this next encounter. The operators here had consistently ignored his demands for improvement and often pretended they could speak only Albanian. Gavin had the power to shut the site down and was considering using it.

He followed the guidance received on his hazardous situations course, telling his colleagues where he was and parking his car facing towards the gate in case a quick getaway was required. Stepping past pools of evil-looking liquids and sharp-edged bits of metal, he walked up to the door of a makeshift office.

'Good afternoon,' he began, showing his ID. 'Gavin Ward, Environment Agency. I'm here to check compliance with your permit. I'd like to take a look at some of your documentation, please.'

'Piss off, environment man.'

A shaven-headed man, with a dragon tattoo on his neck, glared at Gavin, his hand closing round a metre-long steel pipe. 'Mind your own fucking business.'

Gavin realised he was in danger and turned to leave, warning the man that he would be back, with a police officer if necessary. Before he could reach the door, the side of his head exploded with pain and he fell to the floor. He realised, dimly, that he was being manhandled out of the office and into the back of a van stinking of diesel. He felt someone rummaging in his pockets, taking his work phone and wallet. A blow to his stomach doubled him over and made him vomit, then the doors of the van slammed. He was in darkness, alone, and very, very scared.

Chapter Fifty-Two

KAREN PULLED the unmarked police car into a parking bay in the scrapyard. So far, they had found no evidence of stolen catalytic converters at the other sites they had visited and she wasn't particularly optimistic about this one. Stepping out of the car, Karen and Trevor looked around at the untidy yard, filled with burned out cars, pyramids of old fridges and freezers and mounds of rusty metal. A muscular, shaven-headed man came out of a ramshackle office and approached them.

'What you want?' he challenged, before they could speak.

'DC Groves and DC Blake, Mexton police,' replied Karen, showing her warrant card. 'Can we have a word, please? We won't keep you long.'

'I'm busy. Go away.'

'I'm sorry, sir, but we do need to talk to you. We're asking all scrap merchants in the area if they've been offered stolen catalytic converters. So far, no-one has refused to co-operate and we have been shown around their premises without any problem.'

Trevor's placatory tone was lost on the man, who crossed his arms across his chest and started to shout.

'You're not fucking coming here. If you're police you get a warrant. Now piss off. It's not safe for you.'

'Are you threatening us, sir? said Karen, loosening her baton in its holster. 'That would be a criminal offence. We can get a warrant if we believe that criminal activity is going on here, or also under the Metal Dealers Act 2016. And you are certainly acting suspiciously.'

The man's eyes narrowed.

'You come back tomorrow with warrant. I show you around. Now fuck off.'

Realising that they would get no further, Karen and Trevor started to walk back to the car. As they passed a decrepit white van, they heard a thumping noise and the van started to rock. A quavering voice came from the vehicle.

'Help me. Help me please.'

Karen spun round to see the shaven-headed man rushing towards her, brandishing a metal pipe, while Trevor ran towards the van. She pulled out her baton, but before she could use it her attacker knocked it out of her hand with a savage sweep. She thought she felt her wrist break. The pipe swung back and caught her in the side, knocking her into a pool of foul-smelling liquid. A vicious pain flared in her kidney and she felt sick. The man raised the pipe above his head, clearly intent on smashing Karen's skull, but before it descended Trevor kicked him behind the knees and he fell backwards. A dose of pepper spray in his face made him drop the pipe and, dodging flying fists, the two officers managed to get the cursing thug onto his front and handcuff him.

'Are you all right?' Trevor asked Karen.

'Bastard's smashed my wrist. My side hurts,' she groaned. 'Who's that in the van?'

'I didn't get a chance to look. I'll phone for backup and an ambulance. Don't argue. You need to get that wrist seen to. I'll stand guard over this scrote, if you're up to checking the van.'

'Yeah. OK. As long as I don't have to force the door.'

Karen limped over to the van. The pain in her side was subsiding but she hoped she wouldn't be peeing blood from a damaged kidney. Her wrist was agony and she propped up the injured arm with her other hand. She was relieved to find the key to the van's back door was still in the lock, and as she turned it, she called out.

'Police. I'm opening the door.'

A dishevelled individual, smelling of vomit and with blood running down the side of his head, tumbled out, a terrified look on his face.

'He hit me. Locked me up. I thought he was going to kill me. Who are you?'

'DC Karen Groves, sir. And my colleague DC Trevor Blake is guarding a prisoner over there. Is that the man who assaulted you?'

'Yes. That's him. I'm Gavin Ward. Environment Agency. I came to inspect the place and he wouldn't let me. I said I'd come back with the police and he knocked me over as I was leaving. He took my phone and wallet. He's obviously up to something.'

'We had a similar reaction. He attacked me, too. We'll need a formal statement from you at some stage, but as it looks like we'll be sharing an ambulance, you can give me some details on the way. Can you walk OK?'

'I'm pretty shaky. We don't normally get this sort of reaction when we come to check a permit. I'll just sit down for a bit.'

Karen guided Gavin to an old oil drum that served as a makeshift, if dirty, seat. She nursed her damaged wrist, longing for pain relief and counting down the seconds before the ambulance arrived. Five minutes later a marked police car pulled into the yard, followed by Jack Vaughan in his own vehicle. A white van bearing the logo 'Laverty's Industrial Refrigeration' pulled onto the site but immediately turned round and left when it drew level with the police car. The ambulance appeared a minute later. Before climbing into it she gave Jack a brief account of what had happened.

'Mr Ward, here, works for the Environment Agency and was assaulted and shoved in a van. He was trying to inspect the place. The suspect refused to let us look around, and when we heard Mr Ward banging inside the van, he attacked us. We managed to handcuff him, as you can see, but he seems to have broken my wrist. Can I go and get it fixed, now? Please?'

'Yes. Of course. Let me know what happens at the hospital. If you can't write up proper notes, can you dictate a full account into your phone? I'll get the site sealed and a couple of PCs to stand guard overnight. We'll take a proper look in the morning.'

'Will do. Oh, that pipe over there. That's what he hit me with.'

Jack grimaced. 'A narrow escape then. Off you go.'

He helped Karen into the ambulance while a paramedic did the same with Gavin. Karen cursed as the ambulance drove over the rutted track leading out of the scrapyard, with every jolt sending a flash of pain through her wrist. A shitty end to a shitty day, she thought. The only bright spot in her whole week was knowing that Valentina Malenka was dead.

The black Mercedes SUV cruised past the scrapyard for the second time in twenty minutes.

'The cops are still there,' said the driver. 'They look like they'll be there all night.'

'Are they armed?' asked his passenger.

'No. This is UK. Only special cops carry guns.'

'Good,' said the other, thumbing cartridges into a pump action shotgun, an illegal but highly useful weapon.

'What the fuck are you doing?'

'Taking out the cops. Then we get the goods and take them to the other site.'

'Don't be stupid. This isn't Tirana. You can't declare war on the cops.'

'But there's over ten thousand euros worth, there. Artan will fucking kill us.'

'It's Guzim who'll meet with an accident. And so will you if you draw any more attention to us. Put that fucking thing away. We can't do anything more until the cops have gone. Maybe they won't find everything. Come on. Nothing more we can do.'

The SUV glided away, leaving the two officers on overnight duty oblivious to their narrow escape.

Chapter Fifty-Three

Day 30

'OK, EVERYBODY,'

Emma raised her voice to be heard over the hubbub in the incident room. 'As some of you know there was an incident at a scrapyard yesterday where Karen and Trevor went to check for stolen catalytic converters. An officer from the Environment Agency was assaulted and locked in a van, and the same attacker broke Karen's wrist. She's OK, but will be off until tomorrow. When she comes back she'll be on desk duties for a while, so be nice to her.

'We've arrested the person in charge of the scrappie on assault and false imprisonment charges. An Albanian named Guzim Marku, according to his driver's licence. He's saying nothing and is clearly not the boss of the racket. He'll probably get bail, but we'll keep an eye on him.

'So, we need to search the yard and office. Mel, I want you to go through any paperwork you can find. We need information on where they send their scrap, who they buy it from, the names of employees and the details of any vehicles they operate. I suspect it will all look above board, but we have to explore every avenue. If there's too much to go through, seize it and bring it back to the station. Get someone to help you carry it if your shoulder's still hurting. There's a couple of PCs guarding the scene.

'Trevor, go and look around the yard for these converters. We've got some photos of what they look like, and Phil, from the police garage, has agreed to go along to help you spot them. You will need hard hats and steel-toed boots. The site could be dangerous, so don't go pulling at piles of scrap in case they fall on you. Don't take any risks, please. Understand?'

'Yes, guv,' replied Trevor.

'When Jack gives you the nod, off you go. I've got a meeting with the DCI later on to discuss Inheritance, so the rest of you, keep working on that please. If anyone's found something new, let me know. You'd better come with me, Jack. I might need some moral support.'

Mel sat in the scrapyard office leafing through invoices and receipts. Many were illegible, deliberately so, she suspected. Bored, she decided to take a break from the stuffy atmosphere and get some fresh air. She would see if Trevor and Phil had found anything of interest, although, with her shoulder still healing, she wasn't about to start shifting lumps of metal.

Stepping out of the cabin, she saw her colleagues peering at a pile of scrapped cars that must have been at least ten metres high. As she did so a movement caught her eye. The jib of the crane that had, presumably, piled the cars on top of each other started to turn. Alerted to the noise, Phil and Trevor looked up, but they couldn't see the machine's movement. Mel could, and she realised that it was about to topple the pile of cars on top of the police officers.

'Run. Left, left, left,' she yelled.

Phil looked confused but Trevor obeyed. He grabbed his colleague and pulled him in the direction Mel had shouted. A terrible grinding sound drowned out the noise of the crane, and the stack began to fall. Mel stood horrified as tens of tonnes of steel slid towards her colleagues. Trevor stumbled, and Phil tripped over him as the carcass of an ancient Volvo hurtled past them, slamming bonnet-first into the ground with a crash that Mel could feel twenty metres away. It teetered and the back end tipped slowly backwards until it came to rest on the base of the stack, covering the two officers. A fraction of a second later a Toyota bounced off the back of the Volvo, closely followed by a Fiesta.

Realising there was nothing she could do for Trevor and Phil, Mel phoned for an ambulance and the fire service. She ran round the side of the office and headed for the crane. Lengths of twisted steel rebars, odd sections of pipe and a selection of girders blocked her path. Before she could get anywhere near the crane, she saw the cabin open and a figure drop to the ground. On seeing Mel, he ran towards the back of the site and climbed swiftly over the chain-link fence, disappearing from view. Mel had no hope of chasing him but she did manage to take a short video on her phone.

With a sick feeling in her stomach, she picked her way over the metal debris towards her colleagues. What sort of mess would she find? Should she wait for someone to stabilise the stack of cars before she went any closer? Obviously, the sensible approach. Fuck it, she thought. If there was any chance of them surviving, she would have to look. So she tiptoed towards the remains of the Volvo, flinching at any sound that could indicate that metal was moving again. The air was filled with dust and rust particles that made her cough. Her heart jumped when she heard a faint voice from under the car. Trevor's.

'Help. Help. Get us out of here. Are you there, Mel?'

'Yes. Yes. I'm here, mate. Are you hurt? How's Phil?'

Trevor coughed. 'I'm all right, I think. Probably a sprained ankle. Phil's knocked out but I can feel him breathing. We're trapped by something.'

'Well, don't struggle in case you bring the whole lot down on you. I've called Fire and Rescue. They're on the way. Christ, mate, I thought you were both dead.'

'Yeah. Whatever this car is, it protected us from the others.'

'It's an old Volvo. Built like a tank.'

'That's what I want for our next car. Especially with a kid on the way.'

Mel kept chatting to Trevor while they waited for the fire engines, fearful that his injuries were worse than he realised. Phil regained consciousness at one point and threw up over the two trapped men. He seemed confused and couldn't say where it hurt. Mel realised that he was concussed and used her radio to check that the ambulance was on its way.

When the first fire engine arrived, closely followed by an ambulance, the Senior Fire Officer ordered Mel away, so she could only watch from a distance. While paramedics administered oxygen to Trevor and Phil, the fire officers assessed the site and worked out a rescue plan.

'It's a tricky one, this,' said the SFO. 'We're going to have to be a bit unorthodox.'

First off, they positioned the basket of a turntable ladder over the Volvo, in case anything else fell off the stack. Then they used hydraulic shears to cut away part of the car. As they did so, it made a groaning sound and the frame began to move. A few seconds later it stabilised again and they were able to ease Phil through the gap on a body board. Trevor managed to crawl through without assistance, dragging his injured ankle behind him. Both casualties had minor cuts and scratches and were filthy, with torn clothes and streaks of oil on exposed skin. Bruises would, no doubt, develop later. Phil was stretchered off to the ambulance while Trevor was supported by a paramedic to the same vehicle.

'You're a jinx, Mel Cotton,' Trevor called. 'Last time we nearly got burned to death and now I was nearly flattened. I want another partner in future,' he joked.

'Ah, you love me really,' she laughed. 'I'll drop by the hospital when the boss and the SOCOs have arrived.'

She waved at her departing colleague and turned back to the office. She had already notified the DI of the attempted murder and she was slightly nervous that someone would come back for her, despite the uniformed presence. The attacker didn't know that Trevor and Phil were still alive and she guessed that Emma would want to keep it that way. These were not petty thieves, they were serious criminals, prepared to murder police officers. When she thought how close it had been, she shivered. Another of her nine lives almost lost? She knew what Jack would say.

Chapter Fifty-Four

Day 31

'TREVOR'S FINE,' began Emma, once the team had settled down for the morning briefing. 'His ankle isn't broken and he'll be back in the office this afternoon. Phil wasn't so lucky. He got concussion and a cracked shoulder blade. He'll be off work for a few days and only doing light tasks for a while. Mel's warning undoubtedly saved both their lives.'

Mel looked slightly embarrassed.

'Did you get anything from the office, Mel?' continued Emma.

'Not much, guv. Most of the documents were hard to read and some were in a foreign language, possibly Albanian. I found the environmental permit, which had the name Artan Delvina on it, presumably the site owner. I've put in a request to the Environment Agency for a list of any other sites he, or his company Delvina Recycling, operates. We're getting material brought back to the station for examination, with the help of a translator. Once we get the names of any employees, we can run PNC checks on them.

'OK. Thanks. I've arranged for someone from the Health and Safety Executive to help us search the site safely. They're understaffed, but provided no factories blow up or collapse in the meantime, a Ms Moira Brook will meet Martin, and a couple of uniforms, there at two o'clock. There must be something hidden there. Something worth killing for.

'Now, we need to look at vehicles. There's some CCTV at a builders' merchants a few hundred metres along the road from the scrap yard. It's a cul-de-sac, which means anything going to or from the site should be picked up. There's also ANPR on the main road. Addy and Martin – can you get hold of the CCTV recordings and go through them and cross-check with ANPR? We need to know where vehicles leaving the site go. Draw on some civilian support if you need to.'

'Yes, guv.'

'Mel, can you follow up on the owner and his company? Check what Companies House, HMRC and DVLA know about them. Give Addy the reg numbers of any vehicles they own.

'What we need, folks, is a picture of how this scrap yard operates and anything going on that looks out of the ordinary. Jack – can you talk to any informants we have who might know something? The National Crime Agency may have picked up a whisper about Albanian, or other foreign, organised crime groups operating in this area. Give them a ring.

'Right. The attack on Trevor and Phil has pushed this one up the agenda, but don't forget we still have a serial poisoner and Valentina's murderer to catch. Get to it!'

Emma left the incident room and headed to the DCI's office to brief him on developments.

'DC Groves? This is Gavin Ward, Environment Agency.' Karen, desperate for a couple of paracetamol, had answered her phone reluctantly.

'Hello, Mr Ward. How are you? How can I help?'

'Fine thanks. How's your wrist?'

'Mending, thank you. What can I do for you?'

'It's just something that occurred to me, when I had a chance to think about what happened at the Delvina yard.'

'Yes. Go on.'

'Do you remember a white van that pulled into the yard then drove away without stopping? It looked as though the driver had spotted the police car.'

'Vaguely. I was concentrating on my wrist at the time.'

'Well, we had a tip-off that the scrapyard was dealing in illicit HCFCs, which was one of the reasons I wanted to inspect them.'

'What are HCFCs when they're at home?'

'Powerful greenhouse gases. They were used in industrial refrigeration equipment but are now banned because they heat up the atmosphere. There's a black market in them, though.'

'Where do they come from?'

'They are made in Ukraine and come into the rest of Europe through Romania, mostly. Organised crime gangs sell them to refrigeration companies who don't want the expense of changing their kit to use safer alternatives. I wonder whether I could gain access to the site to look for these gases.'

'At the moment, it's a crime scene, so we can't let you on site I'm afraid. But tell me what to look for and I'll ask the team to keep an eye open.'

'OK. Thank you.' Ward reeled off a list of chemical names and numbers.

'Right,' said Karen. 'I'll let you know if we find anything.'

'Thank you, DC Groves. I hope your wrist gets better soon.'

'Thank you, Mr Ward.' Karen hung up and went to brief Jack on Gavin Ward's call.

Chapter Fifty-Five

'What's up, Sally? You look pissed off.'

Mel put her plate of egg and chips on the canteen table and sat down opposite PC Erskine, who was toying with a salad.

'It's Nicky Mallett. She tried to top herself again last night. The third time this month. It's so fucking depressing.'

'What's the matter with her?' asked Mel, shovelling down her food.

'She's got a shedload of mental health problems. Mainly depression, I think. She can't get the help she needs and the drugs don't work for her. We're in touch with the community mental health team, who are supposed to support her, but half of them are off with Covid and they're incredibly overloaded. She took a swing at Reg the other night, but he's not taking it further. He's a great cop, but none of us is trained in mental health. We're having to do other people's jobs as well as our own and it's making me sick. Some of the lads say she's got PITA syndrome.'

'What's that?'

'Pain in the arse syndrome. They've no time for her and have no idea what to do.'

'I sympathise with you. I really do. But at least you care. A copper who doesn't give a shit about people shouldn't be in the job. You can tell those lads that if I hear them saying that about a vulnerable person I'll personally twist their bollocks until they scream. Look, come out for a drink one evening. It might cheer you up. It's a long time since we trained together and there's a lot of catching up to do. And if you're lucky I'll tell you where Tyrone Johnson hid three wraps of coke and four nine-millimetre cartridges.'

Sally giggled. 'OK, Mel, you're on. I'm on nights for the next few days, but sometime next week would be great.'

Mel smiled as she got up, carrying her empty plate. But inside she wondered, not for the first time, what had happened to the Job.

Guzim Marku left the Magistrates Court and thanked the solicitor who had argued successfully that he should be given bail. He was forced to surrender his passport, but that was not a problem. He had another, and this time tomorrow, he would be at his brother's flat in Elbasan, well out of the reach of Mexton police. The tag on his leg was a nuisance, but he would be on his way long before anyone realised he had cut it off. He was about to hire a taxi when he saw a familiar black SUV waiting by the kerb. 'Good,' he thought. 'I'll be at the airport in a couple of hours.' He climbed in the back.

'Take me to the airport but call at my flat first. I need to pick some things up.'

The bulky man in the passenger seat grinned.

'No flat. No airport. You have appointment.'

Chapter Fifty-Six

Day 32

'Right. Settle down, please.'

Emma's voice cut through the racket in the incident room, and discussions of last night's football results tailed off abruptly.

'What have we got on traffic from the scrapyard?' she asked.

'It's very patchy, guv,' replied Addy. 'The CCTV from the builders' merchants down the road only covers the previous month, but we've been able to track about four hundred vehicle movements, using the recordings plus ANPR on the main road. We're looking mainly at trucks and vans, and most of them are operated by licensed waste carriers. A couple of small garages seem to take scrap to the site, but they look legit.

'Most of the activity goes on between seven in the morning and four in the afternoon, but on a few occasions, a white van with false plates has approached the site in the early hours of the morning, leaving an hour or so later and heading eastwards along the main road. Usually, a black SUV followed it. I did some cross-checking, and the times are just after reported thefts of catalytic converters in the Mexton area.

'Anything else?'

'Well, it looks like they switched the plates on it for each journey, always with those from scrapped vehicles.'

'Good stuff, Addy. Well done. Anything else, anyone?'

Martin spoke up. 'I talked to Mr Ward from the Environment Agency, who explained a bit about how these sites work. Once the scrap is sorted into different types of metal it's consolidated into lorry loads and goes to steelworks or similar industrial sites. Fluids such as oil and fuel are collected and sent for incineration, while plastics are dispatched for recycling where possible, Anything that can't be used gets sent to landfill. So, most of the vehicles leaving the site, apart from those that have just dropped off scrap, are large trucks, not small vans.

'They're obviously up to summat,' Emma said. 'Any idea where the van and the SUV go?'

'Not for certain,' Martin replied. 'But Delvina Recycling owns a warehouse a mile or so in the direction the van usually takes. It offers reclaimed car parts for sale, and I went along, asking if they had a second-hand clutch for my sports car, but there was very little in the way of stock there. I think it's a front.'

Emma looked sceptical. 'The van could quite legitimately be carrying usable car parts, couldn't it?'

'Yes, but why piss about with phoney plates? And why move them at night, with a Chelsea tractor apparently riding shotgun?'

'I take your point. So, you're thinking that the van takes the stolen cats to the warehouse, where they're dismantled and the valuable metals are sorted for shipping off to a dodgy smelter somewhere?'

'That's my theory.'

'It's certainly possible, but not enough for a warrant to search the warehouse. But why would they take them to a warehouse rather than doing the job at the scrapyards?'

'If all they are doing is, ostensibly, selling car parts, they wouldn't be inspected by the Environment Agency's waste enforcement people, not that they've got enough staff to inspect everyone. It reduces the risk of detection. Also, Delvina Recycling has a couple of other scrapyards in the area. Maybe they collect stolen cats as well. Processing them in a central, uninspected, location makes some sort of sense.'

'OK. Thanks, Martin. I'll see if we can set up some surveillance on the warehouse. How about staff and vehicles, Mel?'

'The company owns a couple of vans and a recovery truck, which they use to transport written-off vehicles. The SUV Martin mentioned is registered to them as well and insured for any employee to drive. According to HMRC, Delvina Recycling employs fifteen people in all. The firm's records suggest that about half of them are Albanians, who probably settled here in the late 1990s. I don't think that's enough staff to run three scrap yards, a warehouse and their central office. They must be paying other people, cash in hand. The boss is Artan Delvina, also Albanian.'

'Thanks, Mel. Can you run their names past the NCA? See if any of them are suspected of involvement with any of the Albanian gangs?'

'Will do. I've already checked the PNC, and a few of them have convictions for drunkenness, assault and driving offences, but nothing really serious.'

'OK. So far, investigating these buggers has given Karen a broken wrist and nearly killed Trevor and Phil. And who knows what would have happened to Gavin Ward if Karen and Trevor hadn't turned up when they did? I think we need a chat with Mr Delvina. Addy – you're about the only one on the team who hasn't been injured. We'll call on him at his office this afternoon.'

Chapter Fifty-Seven

Emma and Addy parked outside a depressing concrete building that served as the headquarters of Delvina Recycling. They pushed open a smeary glass door and approached a dilapidated counter, fitted with a yellowing plastic screen, presenting their warrant cards to a pinched-faced receptionist with dyed blonde hair and eyebrow piercings.

'Police. We're here to see Mr Delvina.'

'He's not here.'

Her initially friendly expression shut down like a sprung rat trap.

'Funny that,' replied Emma. 'The BMW in the car park is his, we believe. Why don't you try his office line?'

The receptionist scowled, thought for a moment, and dialled a number, turning away from the detectives and whispering when the phone was answered. She turned back.

'Mr Delvina can spare you five minutes. Please wait in there.'

She pointed to a small side office, equipped with a desk and a couple of chairs. They were joined two minutes later by a florid, stocky man with bulging biceps distorting the cut of his jacket and a hostile expression on his face.

'What you want? I have important meeting. No time to waste talking to police.'

'It's about a number of offences committed at one of your sites, Mr Delvina,' Emma said, pleasantly.

'What offences? I know nothing about them. We have permits. We pay VAT. What you talking about?'

'Well, false imprisonment, assaulting an emergency worker and a member of the public, attempted murder, handling stolen goods. They'll do for starters.'

Delvina shrugged.

'We had a bad manager. He may have done some of this. Nothing to do with me. I fired him. He's gone back to Albania.'

'I'm surprised to hear that, Mr Delvina, as he surrendered his passport as a condition of bail. We would like to interview you, under caution, at the police station. You can come with us willingly or we can arrest you. Which is it to be?'

Delvina muttered something undoubtedly rude under his breath.

'OK. I come with you. I will ring my lawyer.'

He called a number on his mobile phone and spat a stream of Albanian into it.

'We go in your car.'

As Emma got into the unmarked police car, with Addy driving and Delvina in the back, she felt unsettled. This is too easy, she thought. Surely, he would have put up more resistance?

'Blue light, it, please, Addy. I'm not happy. Get us back to the nick as quick as you can.'

Addy nodded and switched on the siren and hidden lights. The car jerked as he put his foot down, the acceleration pushing his passengers back into their seats.

Emma's fears were confirmed when a skip lorry suddenly pulled out in front of them as they approached the main road into town. She saw Delvina shift sideways on his seat, and a second later, a black SUV, emerging from a side road, smashed into the side of the police car, sending it spinning. The airbags deployed with deafening bangs, stunning her and slamming her head back against the headrest. Her ears were ringing and she was dimly aware of someone forcing open the ruined rear door. And through her confusion she heard the unmistakeable sounds of two shotgun blasts.

Chapter Fifty-Eight

'ISN'T that our friend Guzim Marku?' called Trevor. 'Only it's hard to tell with his face in that state.'

He peered at the body lying on a patch of waste ground, on the outskirts of Mexton, while Jack conferred with a paramedic.

'I think you're right,' Jack replied, as the paramedic packed away her gear and returned to the ambulance car.

'Someone's given him a right going over and it looks like he's been stabbed. I bet he regretted getting bail. Death's confirmed and this is a crime scene. I'll call the DI and ask her to send the SOCOs and a couple of uniforms. Get some tape from the car, would you, and we'll set up a cordon.'

While Trevor strung tape between a series of bushes and small trees, limping slightly, Jack phoned Emma's mobile. No answer. Cursing, he phoned the station and demanded to speak to DCI Farlowe.

'We've got a suspicious death, sir. One of the Albanian gang, it seems. I've tried to contact DI Thorpe but she's not answering. Do you want to attend?'

'I'm sorry to tell you, Jack, that DI Thorpe and DC

Adeyemo have just been involved in an RTC. They were bringing Artan Delvina back for questioning when they were rammed by another vehicle, a black SUV. Delvina was spirited away in the SUV and Emma's car was shot up to prevent them following.'

'How are they?'

'Both will be taken to hospital when an ambulance turns up, but it doesn't look as though they're seriously hurt. DC Adeyemo was able to give a lucid account of the incident. He managed to get the registration number of the attacking vehicle. We're following it through ANPR and the helicopter has been scrambled. We'll get these bastards.'

Jack realised that the DCI was furious, despite his calm manner, as he almost never swore.

'Thank you, sir. I'll hold the fort here at the crime scene until the SOCOs and uniforms arrive, then I'll call in at the hospital, if that's OK.'

'Yes. That's fine. I'll be the SIO on this murder but I don't need to attend the scene, at least not yet.'

Jack sat fuming in the car while Trevor finished setting up the cordon. His thoughts, which mainly concerned what he'd like to do to the thugs who attacked his colleagues, were interrupted by the roaring of a vehicle engine approaching. A black SUV, with a damaged front end, hurtled past.

'It's them,' he thought, starting the car and pulling off the waste ground on to the road.

'Stay here, Trevor,' he yelled.

The SUV was a couple of hundred metres ahead, heading away from town. Jack put his foot down and caught up with his quarry just as it was turning onto the A-road. It sped up as the driver realised he was being followed. Jack kept pace, thirty metres behind. He radioed the station and kept up a running commentary.

'In pursuit of suspects in black SUV, reg number Whisky

eight eight one Charlie Alpha Juliet, heading along Camberton Road at speed. Please confirm vehicle involved in RTC with DI Thorpe.'

'Identity confirmed. Exercise extreme caution. Occupants armed. Bird directed to your location.'

'Roger that. Approaching Camberton village. Oh fuck. Pedestrian struck by SUV on crossing on high street. Send ambulance.'

'Ambulance on its way. For Christ's sake be careful.'

'Taking third exit at Crosshills Roundabout. Little traffic on road. Heading into open country. Stuck behind waste truck emerged from landfill site. Shit.'

The screech of Jack's tyres as he slowed down was clearly audible over the Airwave.

'Now clear. Hang on. Target vehicle slowing down. Shiiiit.'

The bang of a gunshot and the sound of smashing glass was the last thing the control officer heard from Jack's Airwave.

Chapter Fifty-Nine

JACK STAGGERED from the police car and swore at the SUV's receding tail lights. The moment he saw a figure leaning out the vehicle's nearside window, aiming a shotgun at him, he had slammed on his brakes and started to swerve. This, he realised, probably saved his life, because much of the charge bypassed the car, while the rest hit the windscreen on the passenger side, wrecking it. A few pellets penetrated the glass and smashed into his Airwave, on the dashboard, destroying it. In swerving, he had crossed the centre line and ended up in a ditch on the wrong side of the road. The airbags hadn't inflated and he wasn't injured, but the car needed rescuing. Sitting in a mobile phone dead spot, with no radio, all Jack could do was wait for someone to stop and summon help. His only consolation was the sight of the police helicopter speeding in the direction of the SUV.

Within ten minutes, several police vehicles, with blues and twos going and led by an Armed Response Vehicle, swept past, following directions from the helicopter. Someone must have radioed the Road Policing Unit, thought Jack, as, shortly after, a traffic car pulled in beside Jack's disabled vehicle.

'DS Jack Vaughan,' he greeted the driver. 'Can you give me a lift back to Mexton nick? My windscreen's been shot out and I need to arrange recovery. SOCOs will need to collect the shot.'

'Course, Sarge. Are you hurt? Do you need medical attention?'

'No. Just pissed off.'

'OK. We'll put some cones and signs around this and get it taken back to the garage. Any other vehicles involved?'

'Yeah. A black SUV that the helicopter and an ARV are chasing. A passenger fired the shot to stop me following. I swerved and the charge hit the near side. That's how I ended up on the wrong side of the road.'

'Looks like a lucky escape. Good job there was nothing coming towards you.'

'Yep. I'll worry about that later. We're a DI down and I need to get back.'

Five minutes later Jack was on his way back to Mexton. As soon as he got a signal, he phoned the DCI to explain what had happened.

'How are DI Thorpe and Addy?' was his first question.

'Mild concussion in both cases,' replied Farlowe. 'They should be back at work tomorrow. The suspects only shot out the car tyres to prevent pursuit. Presumably they drew the line at murdering police officers.'

'I'm not so sure, boss. They aimed at me and it wasn't meant to be a warning shot. Marku would have killed Karen at the scrapyard, as well. What's the situation now?'

'They've been tracked to an isolated farm building. It's in the hands of the AFOs now. Chief Inspector Gary Callaghan is the Tactical Firearms Commander and I'm running our side of things. We hope to arrest them without shots being fired, but we know they're ruthless and desperate.'

'Right, boss. I should be back in half an hour or so.'

Chapter Sixty

The icy glare of half a dozen spotlights picked out the farmhouse, its pale walls gleaming like icing on a Christmas cake. The beam from the helicopter, which hovered at a prudent height above the roof, played on the rear of the building, guiding two AFOs, through the deep shadows cast by the lights, into a position where they could cover the back door. Three men had been seen by the helicopter crew running from the black SUV into the building and none had been seen leaving. The only sounds were the clatter of the chopper's rotors and the hum of the generators powering the spotlights.

The firearms unit had been in position since night began to fall. AFOs, with carbines and pistols, covered the windows and doors, while an officer with a rifle took cover behind a police car. The helicopter moved further away so the gang could hear the Operational Firearms Commander, Sergeant Terry Carter.

'Armed Police. Come to the door with your hands on your heads,' he shouted, through a megaphone. 'Leave any weapons behind. Do exactly as you are told by the officers who are waiting.'

Carter's demands were met by a blast from a shotgun, its barrels pushed through the letterbox and hastily withdrawn after firing. The unaimed shot hit nobody but peppered the police cars with pellets. Carter radioed Chief inspector Callaghan and briefed him on the situation.

'They're still in the farmhouse and have discharged a weapon, believed a shotgun, through the letter box. No injuries. No other weapons seen or discharged. We need to make contact before the negotiator arrives. Can you confirm if there's a landline we can call in on?'

'Stand by, we'll see what we can find out. Is there anything else you need?'

'An intrusive surveillance so we can use the laser mike that's on its way would be useful,' replied Carter. 'And an Albanian interpreter.'

He ended the call just as Bob Meredith, the hostage negotiator, parked his Ford Fiesta behind the row of police cars. Bob shook hands with Callaghan, who explained the situation, and picked up the megaphone.

'Hello, Artan. I'm Bob and I'm here to help so nobody gets hurt. I need to talk to you and we are trying to set up a phone link, so bear with us.'

His words were met by 'Fuck off,' plus a few phrases in Albanian that, presumably, had a similar meaning

---

An hour later, recording equipment and a laser microphone had been set up, the laser beam bouncing off a window pane and converting the faint vibrations of the glass back into speech. The conversation was in Albanian, but Milana Dunford, the interpreter sitting in a police car out of sight of the farmhouse, rapidly translated it into English. The men inside the house were clearly arguing. It seemed as though one was determined to stay there, while the other two wanted to give themselves up. A landline was identified, but despite Bob's attempts to establish communication, no-one answered the phone.

There was the sound of a scuffle and curses, and slowly the door opened. Two men walked out cautiously, their hands in the air and no weapons visible.

The lead AFO shouted, 'Armed police. Put your hands on your heads and walk slowly towards me.' Before the two men could get three metres, a voice screamed, 'Tradhtarët,' and two shotgun blasts rang out, the flashes drowned out by the spotlights. Both men collapsed, blood pouring from wounds in their backs, and the third man appeared in the doorway, firing a handgun towards the police vehicles. A single shot from a rifle, hitting him square in the chest, knocked him down and destroyed his heart. He died a few seconds later.

'Traitors. He called them traitors,' whispered Milana Dunford, shaking as she pulled off her headphones. She hadn't seen the carnage but she knew what had happened.

'Come on, love. Let's get you a cuppa,' said a PC, leading the terrified interpreter to a nearby police van, knowing that what Milana really needed was a strong drink. Callaghan phoned Farlowe with the grim news as the firearms officers cleared the house and made safe the gang's weapons.

Chapter Sixty-One

Day 33

'As some of you know,' began DCI Farlowe at the morning briefing, 'several of our colleagues had dangerous encounters with the Albanian gang yesterday. DI Thorpe and DC Adeyemo were deliberately rammed and their vehicle immobilised with a shotgun. DS Vaughan was also shot at and nearly killed. DI Thorpe has mild concussion. She will be back tomorrow and I'm glad to see Addy and Jack back at work unharmed today.'

The team applauded.

'Tragically,' continued Farlowe, 'the day ended with a double murder and a provoked shooting, which the media will, no doubt, call suicide by cop,'

'But why, guv?' asked Addy. 'Unless we could prove conspiracy all we had him on was handling stolen goods and, maybe, money laundering. He denied any involvement in the assaults and attempted murder.'

'That's right,' added Martin. 'It doesn't make a lot of

sense. Delvina would have got about five years, tops, and been out in less than three. And why shoot his underlings?'

'Perhaps he thought they'd betrayed him by surrendering,' suggested Mel. 'Apparently, he shouted "traitors" at them in Albanian before he fired.'

'We thought he was the big man,' said Jack. 'But suppose he was part of a bigger operation and feared reprisals for getting caught. These Albanian gangs don't look kindly on mistakes, especially when they cost them a lot of money. A clean death from a gunshot could be better than something really nasty happening to him inside. There's a lot of Albanians in British prisons.'

'Good point,' agreed Farlowe.

'But we still don't know who tried to kill Trev and Phil, do we?' said Martin.

'No. Maybe we never will,' replied Farlowe. 'Unfortunately, Mel's video was too blurred to be useful. The scrapyard seems abandoned, and I wouldn't be surprised if the Albanians working there have gone back home or moved on to another town. Some of them were probably here illegally.

'So far, we've recovered about eight thousand pounds' worth of stolen converters and couple of grand's worth of HCFCs. There could be more, but it's not safe to search further without specialist equipment. We'll keep it sealed until someone takes it over. We did a warrant on the warehouse and found another cache of cats plus a pistol. We're still looking at the other scrapyards. It's a slow process.

'Now. We've still got work to do. Have we found out where the metals go yet?'

'Some progress, guv,' said Trevor. 'From the documents we found in the offices, it seems that Delvina Recycling regularly sends smallish loads of scrap to a recycling plant in the Netherlands. The type of metal isn't specified, but I spoke to the Dutch police, who have suspicions about the site. They think the owners handle stolen precious metals. Nothing's been proven, but they think it's dodgy. I've been in touch with the Environment Agency's international waste shipments people in Warrington, who told me that this type of scrap is a green list waste, so they don't need a permit, or have to notify anyone, when they export it to the EU.'

'Something's worrying me, guv,' said Jack. 'As Addy and Martin pointed out, the offences committed at the scrapyard were not that serious, but the villains were prepared to murder police officers and Gavin Ward to prevent discovery. Unless they are completely psychotic, there must be something more going on, surely?'

His colleagues nodded.

'I tend to agree, Jack,' replied Farlowe. 'I have a Teams meeting with some people from the National Crime Agency later today. They're in touch with Interpol. I'll ask them if they know anything more about Delvina's associates, here and abroad. I'll tell them what's happened and mention Jack's idea. DI Thorpe should be back tomorrow and she'll let you know the outcome. Now, is there any progress on the Malenka murder?'

'SOCOs found some fibres clutched in one of her hands,' reported Jack. 'The lab says they come from an expensive, dark blue coat of some kind, probably cashmere. It's possible the victim grabbed her assailant as she was stabbed. No use without a suspect, but something to bear in mind. More interesting, however, is a silver Golf the traffic unit spotted, parked near a bus stop on the outskirts of town. The fingerprint unit found Valentina's prints all over it, so it's reasonable to assume it was hers. It's registered to a Sophie Hancock at a false address. We also found a burner phone hidden under one of the seats. I've asked Trevor to find the vehicle on ANPR, which may give us some idea of where Valentina lived and also how it got there.'

'So do we think the killer took it, dumped it at the bus stop and rode back into town?' asked the DCI.

'It's possible,' Jack replied. 'Though why he or she would bother is a puzzle. Mel's looking at CCTV records from the buses using that stop, from the time of the killing to the last service that night. There's only a couple of late services, so it shouldn't take long.'

'I thought the buses shut down about eleven?' queried Martin.

'Most do,' said Jack. 'But the Council pays for a few late-night buses in an attempt to cut down drink-driving. It seems to help, because most of the passengers on them are pissed. The drivers hate being rostered to drive them.'

'I'm not surprised. I'd rather walk than be surrounded by a couple of dozen rat-arsed, maskless, drinkers for several miles.'

Several of Martin's colleagues chuckled.

'We seem to have made some progress, then,' said Farlowe, ignoring Martin's remark. 'I'll hold a separate briefing on Operation Inheritance when DI Thorpe returns. Thank you, everyone. Carry on.'

Chapter Sixty-Two

HALF-WAY THROUGH THE AFTERNOON, Trevor knocked on DCI Farlowe's office door.

'Something interesting, boss,' he began, when told to enter. 'I've followed the Golf on CCTV and ANPR from a parking bay three hundred metres from the murder scene to the road served by the bus stop, at around eleven thirty. Nothing special so far, but we can ask for witnesses who may have seen someone following her from the car park towards Castle Street.'

'Is that all?' asked Farlowe, impatiently.

'No, boss. The car came into town at around ten thirty from a different direction. I've managed to trace its route back to the Highchester road. And I've found several other journeys into and out of town along that road over the past couple of weeks.'

'And?'

'Four miles along the Highchester road is the lane leading to the cottage that burned down during the night of the murder. I asked the tech guys at the police garage if there were any journeys recorded on the satnav, but it had been wiped. But, anyway, my guess is that the cottage is Valentina's. The killer found her address from the satnav, and drove out there to set fire to the cottage, collecting the accelerant and candle on the way. He or she returned later, in a different vehicle, to check the job was done.'

'That's highly possible, Trevor. Good work. So, we need ANPR data on all vehicles on the Highchester road between the estimated time of the killing and sunrise.'

'I'm working on it, boss. I'll have something by tomorrow's briefing.'

'Good man.'

When Trevor had left, DCI Farlowe fiddled with his cufflinks and lined up the pens on his desk with the edge of his laptop. He poured himself some green tea from a porcelain teapot, carefully wiped up a droplet that had spilled onto his desktop and considered the situation. Much as he deplored murder in principle, he didn't regret Valentina Malenka's death. She had brought it upon herself. He certainly wouldn't share his views with his colleagues. Likewise, the poisoner's victims were no great loss to society, but the failure to catch their killer reflected badly on the force as a whole and himself in particular. Was it time to seek outside help? He hoped not, but realised that it might be forced upon him if there was no progress soon. And that would be humiliating.

Amar cradled the Mossberg Shockwave pump-action shotgun as Mirjet drove the silver saloon slowly along The Drove and turned left into East Quay.

'It's along here. Not far,' he said, in Albanian.

As Rivers House, the Environment Agency's Bridgwater offices, came into view, he worked the weapon's action and wound down his window. Mirjet stopped the car to let a white van with the Agency's logo emerge from the EA car park, then he drove in. He pulled up outside the doors and arranged the car so that Amar could get a clear shot, with his foot holding the clutch down and the vehicle in reverse gear. Six shotgun blasts rang out in the space of five seconds as Amar fired, pumped and fired. Glass shattered as the entrance doors and an adjacent office window were destroyed. They could barely hear the screams from the building above the ringing in their ears. Mirjet dropped the clutch and the car screamed out of the side road in reverse, the stink of burning rubber adding to the smell of gunsmoke. It juddered as Mirjet slammed it into first gear and roared off down the road, narrowly missing a lorry emerging from a builders' merchants.

Fifteen minutes later, after changing the number plates in a quiet side road, the two gangsters were motoring sedately along the M5, heading back to Mexton.

'Nice job, Amar. Teach those bastards to fuck with us,' grinned Mirjet.

'Yeah. Just like the old days in Tirana,' his colleague laughed, stroking the still-warm barrel of the shotgun. 'Maybe we can do the cops as well? I'd like that.'

'Sure you would. But that's down to the boss. And he's seriously pissed off with what's happened.'

Chapter Sixty-Three

Day 34

'FIRST OFF,' said Emma, once welcoming noises in the briefing room had subsided, 'We've had a call from Gavin Ward, the Environment Agency guy. His office was shot up yesterday by a couple of goons with a shotgun.'

'It's getting like the bloody wild west,' said Jack, breaking a shocked silence.

'No-one was hurt, fortunately,' continued Emma, 'but there was a lot of damage done to the building, inside and out. Thousands of pounds worth of external glass was shattered and a vehicle in the car park was also hit. The shooters got away. I've been on to the Avon and Somerset force, who are looking at CCTV, but they think they must have changed plates somewhere in the business park where it happened.'

'So, we're thinking Albanians, again, are we?' asked Mel.

'I reckon so. The NCA did suggest that there were more of them in play. This could be reprisals for shutting down the cat racket. So, you all need to be extra careful in your working and home lives, especially those of you who were directly involved. There is a risk that they'll target police officers, too. Don't forget we never found the crane operator who tried to kill Trevor and Phil.'

'Can we get anything more from the NCA?' asked Martin.

'I've asked them to send someone down to give us a briefing, but they can't do that at the moment. They've too many people off sick with Covid. They think they can do a Teams session next week, and I reckon we should go for that, as those people working from home can see it as well.'

'Good idea,' said Jack. 'I'm sure we don't really know what we're up against.'

'Right. I'll ask them to set it up.'

Mel sipped her coffee, barely noticing the taste. Be extra careful. That was a fucking joke. Four times someone had tried to kill her in the past few years, and, once, she had been set up on a phoney drugs charge. How much more careful could she be? Sometimes she envied Tom his cushy job in computer crime, where the villains were all in cyberspace, and incapable of strangling, poisoning or decapitating him. She realised she could be headstrong, but, equally, she knew her dad was proud of what she had achieved.

Remembering the sword attack brought her out in a cold sweat. Perhaps it had affected her more than she realised. Maybe she should take up the offer of counselling. It couldn't do any harm, and Emma had assured her it wasn't a sign of weakness. She poured the rest of her coffee away and stepped out of the stuffy police station, seeking some fresh air. Finding a quiet corner of the car park, she pulled out her phone and dialled the number of the counselling service. Engaged. She dialled again. Still engaged. 'Shit,' she thought. 'I'll try later. Maybe.'

Chapter Sixty-Four

Just as Emma got back to her office after the briefing, Dr Durbridge telephoned her.

'Good morning, DI Thorpe. I think we've solved the puzzle of the suicidal priest. He was tripping, in the common parlance.'

'Pardon? He was seen running, not falling.'

'Yes, but he was high on LSD. I couldn't find anything organically wrong with him at the PM. Death, as you probably guessed, was the result of a massive head trauma. But his behaviour seemed odd. There was some alcohol in his blood, although not much, and he didn't have a brain tumour that could have made him act strangely. So, I thought about hallucinogens and other mind-altering drugs, prompted in part by the reported smile on his face. I sent off samples and the lab found a significant quantity of LSD in his system. His sense of reality would have been grossly distorted and he wouldn't have known what he was doing.'

'You mean like those kids in the sixties who jumped off buildings thinking they could fly? Did he feel invincible?'

'I think most of those stories are apocryphal, and of course, I can't say what was going through his mind at the time. But he may simply have not noticed the traffic, or anything else about his surroundings.'

'Bloody hell. I can't believe he would have taken that deliberately.'

'If he was a regular user, we might get some evidence from hair analysis. It's not very reliable for LSD, though, so it's probably not worth bothering with. I'll get my full report to you tomorrow.'

'Thank you very much, Doctor. Much appreciated.'

Emma made a couple of phone calls, then called the team together.

'It looks like Father McKenzie was high on LSD when he died. He wouldn't have known what he was doing.'

A stunned silence settled around the room.

'You mean he was a secret hippie?' suggested Mel.

'Highly unlikely,' replied Emma. 'I've spoken to his housekeeper and the bishop, and there have never been any suggestions of illegal drug use. He liked a drink, but wasn't an alcoholic, and he hadn't seemed depressed. He wasn't on medication, apart from blood pressure tablets. So, it looks like someone gave him the drug without his knowledge.'

'Why would anyone do that?' asked Addy. 'Some kind of joke?'

'Not a very funny one, in the end. I don't think it was meant to kill him. It takes a lot of LSD to do that. But it was probably meant to disorientate and distress him.'

'Just a thought, guv,' began Jack, tentatively. 'Back in the sixties people used to take LSD – "acid" – to "see God". All that Timothy Leary nonsense. Could somebody have wanted him to have a "religious experience"?'

'I suppose that's possible. Difficult to prove, though. Anyway, I've talked to DCI Farlowe and he wants me to run this one. We're calling it Operation Lucy for the moment.'

Jack grinned and Emma looked at him quizzically.

'We've no reason to suppose it's the same person who's killing people with poison,' she continued, 'but we must keep an open mind and bring it in to Inheritance if need be. So, Jack, can you get some folks to search the church and Father McKenzie's home for any traces of drugs? There was some wine in his stomach when he died, so that could be how he took it. Trevor, can you look more deeply into Father McKenzie? Get a full career history and ask around in his previous parishes. Check social media, too. I reckon the bishop wasn't telling me everything, so there's something to find, I'm sure. I'll go and see him again and tell him what the PM found. Now, what have we got on the Malenka murder? The DCI has briefed me on what you found yesterday.'

'We've got some more CCTV for the area near where Valentina was found, although there was nothing covering the alley itself,' reported Trevor. 'There wasn't much traffic about at that time of night, and the CCTV didn't pick up all the number plates. Those we've checked look all above board, but we'll contact the drivers and ask them if they saw anything. There was one odd one. A vintage saloon picked up on Castle Street. The number plate light was very faint so we couldn't make out the reg. Martin – you like old cars, don't you? What do you think this make is?'

Martin peered at Trevor's screen, then stood up, slowly and thoughtfully.

'It's an Alvis. You can tell by the large headlights. And take a look at the rear car park.'

Trevor and Emma pushed a dusty vertical blind aside,

disturbing the slumber of several small spiders, and peered out of the window.

'Oh shit,' said Trevor. 'That's it. Or one very like it. Whose is it?'

'I'm afraid it's the DCI's,' replied Martin. 'I asked him about it once. He inherited it from his father and it's his pride and joy. He only uses it for work when his BMW is off the road. It must be the same one. They're really rare and the chances of there being two in a place like Mexton are minute. So, what do we do now?'

'I'll go and have a word with him,' said Emma. 'I'll ask him if he saw anything. He could be a useful witness.'

'There is one more thing, guv,' interjected Mel. 'Before the murder, there were a few calls from the phone found in Valentina's car to another burner in the general area of the nick, and vice versa.'

'What are you saying?'

'Nothing. But it would be nice to know what the DCI was doing near the crime scene at that time of night.'

'I can't exactly interrogate him, but I'll ask him discreetly. Surely, he's not a suspect? His reputation is spotless.'

'I know. But it wouldn't be the first time that Valentina's blackmailed a police officer. Just saying.'

'Well, keep your suspicions to yourself for the moment,' frowned Emma.

On her way to Farlowe's office, Emma stopped at Karen's desk.

'Are you OK, lass?' she asked. 'Only you look a bit pale. Are you sure you didn't come back to work too soon?

Karen seemed uncomfortable.

'It's all right, guv. My wrist's playing up.' She fiddled with the cast. 'I'll be glad when I can type with both hands again. I'm better off working than moping at home.'

'Well don't forget we'll arrange some physiotherapy for you when the fracture's healed.'

'Yes, thanks, boss,' she replied, turning back to her computer.

Chapter Sixty-Five

'HAVE YOU GOT A MOMENT?' asked Emma, knocking on DCI Farlowe's door.

'Yes. Come in. I've been meaning to have a word with you. Where are we with the catalytic converters case, now?'

'Pretty much finished. We're waiting for the inquests on the dead Albanians, but we're not looking for anyone else. We found stolen cats at two more scrapyards owned by Delvina Recycling, eventually, and the Border Force intercepted a load of them headed for the Netherlands.'

'What does the NCA say about it?'

'They were pleased that we shut this end of the operation down but pointed out that it was probably part of a much larger network of criminal activity, spread out across the country. Certainly, Delvina was afraid of someone, otherwise he wouldn't have got himself shot. There may well be other things, like sex trafficking and drugs, going on in Mexton, which associates of Delvina are running. We've found no links so far, but we're looking when we have the time.

'Disturbingly, the NCA did suggest that there is a real risk they could strike back at us, so I've warned the folks involved in the case to be extra vigilant. Gavin Ward's office in Somerset was shot up yesterday, we think as a reprisal for his work on the scrapyard. Fortunately, there were no casualties. Also, we found some of those HCFCs at Laverty's Industrial Refrigeration, so that was a useful result for him. He's retiring from the Environment Agency soon. Apparently, the job isn't the same as when he joined, and they have nowhere near the number of staff they need to do it properly, because of government cutbacks.'

'Can't say I blame him,' said Farlowe. 'It's the same everywhere. OK. Keep me informed and check in with the NCA from time to time, in case they hear of anything else happening on our patch.'

'Of course.'

'One other thing. The Chief Super phoned half an hour ago. He's talking about bringing in a senior officer from another force to review the poisonings case. I'm resisting that for the moment, but you need to be aware it could happen. We need to make some progress on this, and quickly. It would be humiliating if someone else took over, and that Pike woman would have a field day.'

'I quite agree we need results, but we've not exactly been sitting on our hands,' Emma replied, tartly. 'We've had three DCs injured, Valentina Malenka's murder and these bloody Albanians to deal with. The Covid situation hasn't helped either, with people off sick. Briefing a stranger would waste valuable time when we could be chasing down the killers.'

'I know. I know. But I mentioned it just to make you aware. I hope it won't come to that. Was there anything else?'

'Can I ask you something?' Emma spoke hesitantly.

'Go ahead,' replied Farlowe, looking slightly puzzled.

'We've got the CCTV back from the night Valentina Malenka was killed. There's a car on it that looks very like your Alvis. Were you, by any chance, in the area that evening?'

'Ah. Yes.'

Farlowe drummed his fingers on his immaculately organised desk and looked slightly embarrassed.

'I should have mentioned it sooner. I was driving down Castle Street at about eleven thirty. I didn't speak up because I hadn't seen anything relevant. I'd left a meeting at the Lodge rather late and I was taking advantage of the empty roads to give the car a bit of a run. She needs a bit of exercise from time to time.'

He gave a short laugh.

'Was that all?'

'Yes. Thank you. That's fine. I'll put a note in the Murder Book.'

Emma left the room looking thoughtful. She realised how little she knew about her boss. He had transferred to Mexton from the Met and had a good reputation, everyone said. He had never told anyone how he got the scar on his face, but Emma wondered whether it had anything to do with the Queen's Gallantry Medal that she knew he held. He never joined the rest of the team in the pub, but his manner was more reserved than unfriendly. Although a bit obsessed with neatness and tidiness, he was easy enough to work with, but Emma still harboured a slight resentment over his appointment to DCI instead of her.

Chapter Sixty-Six

'OK, FOLKS,' said Emma, placing a tray of drinks on the pub table.

'Just to cheer us up, there's a game we used to play in Sheffield CID. I want you each to suggest a new offence the government should create. As daft as you like, just for fun.'

Four of her colleagues, assembled in the Cat and Cushion, looked thoughtful. Jack spoke first.

'Using the word detox in connection with diets, health supplements and spurious cures.'

'Why's that, Jack?' asked Mel, tucking a stray blonde hair back into her ponytail.

'Because if you've got a functioning liver and kidneys, they do the job. You don't need to spend a fortune on pointless crap. If you've actually been poisoned with mercury or something, you need a hospital not a lifestyle guru.'

'Interesting idea,' said Emma. 'Who's next?'

'Using a petrol-driven leaf blower within fifty metres of an occupied dwelling,' said Trevor, with vehemence. 'The bloke next door is driving us mad with one of those infernal machines cos the twat's too lazy to use a broom. God knows how we'll manage when the baby arrives.'

The others nodded in agreement.

'How about driving while wearing a hat?' suggested Martin, mischievously.

'What's wrong with that?' asked Emma, somewhat incredulously.

'Well, in my experience, old men who wear flat caps drive too slowly and wander all over the road, while young men in baseball caps drive aggressively and too fast, especially if their caps are on backwards.'

This suggestion provoked chuckles from his colleagues.

'I've got a motoring one, too,' said Mel. 'Fitting any device to a car to deliberately increase the noise it makes. It's back to arrogant young men, again, isn't it?'

Martin grinned in agreement.

'How about you, guv?'

'Well, we had quite a few ideas in Sheffield. My boss was keen to make it illegal to play that Christmas song '*Mistletoe and wine*', by a celibate teetotaller, in public. A wildlife fan wanted to make it unlawful to animate African meerkats with Russian accents. Bans on various tunes played over the phone while you're kept waiting were mooted, but the consensus was that half the Cabinet at the time should be prosecuted for impersonating human beings. But don't tell the *Messenger* I said that.'

The others laughed.

'Just to be serious for a moment,' continued Emma. 'We're getting increasing pressure from above to make progress on the poisoner, and there's talk of getting someone in from another force to review us. The DCI's resisting it, but things could get a bit political.'

Jack snorted. 'A lot of bloody good that would do. We don't need the distraction. The last external bloke we had, from the Met, turned out to be a complete tosser and nearly lost some important evidence.'

'Jessop, you mean,' said Mel, and Jack nodded.

'Anyway,' said Emma. 'I want you to know that I have complete faith in the team and I really appreciate how hard you're all working. I'm particularly grateful to those of you who've been hurt and returned to duty quickly. I know it must have been difficult. We'll get this bugger, I know it. Please pass my words on to Addy and Karen. Now, whose round is it? Mine's a pint of Theakston's.'

Karen's mood had lightened once Valentina was out of the way, and the burning of her blackmailer's cottage had reassured her that the compromising video had been destroyed. She knew that there was nothing on Valentina's person when she died. But when the pain in her wrist woke her in the early hours of the morning, a thought struck her. What if Valentina had a cloud account? Could anyone get access to it? The thought murdered sleep and she wondered, once again, whether she should leave the police and find a nice, safe job on civvy street. One where mad Albanians wouldn't break her wrist with steel pipes.

Chapter Sixty-Seven

Day 35

'THANK you for seeing me again, Your Grace,' said Emma, now using the correct mode of address, as a young priest ushered her into the bishop's study.

'I'm afraid I have some puzzling news,' she continued.

'Please sit down,' replied the bishop, a frown crossing his face.

'It would appear that Father McKenzie was under the influence of LSD when he was killed. In common parlance, he was tripping.'

Bishop Donovan looked aghast.

'I can't believe it. Are you sure?'

'I'm afraid the toxicology is clear. He had ingested a large dose and was probably hallucinating when he ran out of the church. Most likely, he didn't see the van.'

'Well, I can assure you that Father McKenzie had never been suspected of using drugs.'

'We don't think he was. There were no illegal substances in his home or at the church. We believe that someone gave the drug to him, possibly in communion wine, with intent to cause harm.'

'That's appalling. Do you have any suspects?'

'I'm afraid not, which is why I wanted to talk to you. Can you think of anyone he'd fallen out with during his career? Any complaints, rumours or conflicts? I got the impression, when we spoke last, that there was something you were unwilling to speak about.'

The bishop looked slightly embarrassed and hesitated a few moments before speaking.

'Father McKenzie was a devout and honest man who discharged his duties diligently. There has never been any hint of his being involved in the scandals that have beset the Holy Church in recent years. But.'

'But?' prompted Emma.

'If anything, he could be a little too strict, concentrating more on condemning sin than forgiving it. He once refused to marry two young people who shared the same address, and when he was attached to a local school in his previous parish, a few families, four, I think, complained that he had made their children feel worthless. Hardly grounds for murder, surely?'

'We don't believe the attacker intended to kill Father McKenzie. He probably just meant to frighten him. When we catch him, though, he will be charged with murder or manslaughter.'

'May God forgive him. Is there anything I can do to help?'

'Yes, please. Can you find out the names of the people you mentioned – the couple and the children he picked on? Perhaps one of them bore a grudge. We need to eliminate them from our enquiries. Apart from that, if anything else occurs to you, please let me know.'

'I will, Detective Inspector. I will.'

Bishop Donovan showed Emma out with a thoughtful expression on his face.

'There is something, Detective Inspector,' he said, just as Emma was leaving. 'I don't know if it's relevant, but a bottle of communion wine disappeared from St Benedict's on the day Father McKenzie passed away. I was informed by the deacon, but we didn't think it was worth reporting it to the police.'

'Thank you, Your Grace. That could well be significant. Good bye.'

'At last,' thought Emma, 'we may get a suspect. But will it lead to the Mexton Borgia?'

Chapter Sixty-Eight

When Emma returned to the station, she called Jack over.

'I've just spoken to the bishop. He mentioned the theft of a bottle of communion wine from the church the day Father McKenzie died, which tends to support the suggestion that the LSD was in it. So, we need to talk to the altar boys, the deacon and anyone else who could have had access to the wine during the time between the previous Mass and the last one Father McKenzie officiated at. We also need to know where the wine is normally kept and how secure it is. Bishop Donovan is sending me a list of people who may have had a grudge against the priest and I'll pass it on to you. We need to TIE these individuals as soon as possible. Can you organise this lot while I bring the DCI up to speed?'

'Sure, Emma. I'll send Mel to the church. It's probably the safest place for her. She can check for any CCTV as well.'

'Thanks, Jack.'

Something was still niggling Mel about the get well card from Valentina. It wasn't the card itself, but something someone had said. But what and who? It was when she was renewing her car insurance that it came to her. She chose to have her no-claims bonus protected, and it was the word 'protected' that rang the bell. Karen had said she was protected but refused to explain what she meant. Surely she wasn't working for Valentina? As far as she could tell, Karen was a diligent and honest young officer, with no suggestions of misconduct attached to her. She would keep her suspicions to herself until she had had a quiet word with Karen. She didn't want to malign an innocent colleague, and there could be a perfectly reasonable explanation for the remark. She really hoped there would be. She would ask Tom's advice when she got home. And she still had her suspicions about the DCI.

'Dad, can I ask you something sensitive?'

'Course you can, love,' Mel's father replied. 'What's bothering you?'

'If I suspected that a senior officer was guilty of a serious offence, what should I do about it?'

There was a silence on the line for a few moments, then the former DCI spoke.

'Officially, you should raise it with your line manager – DS Vaughan, isn't it?'

'Yes. But I'm worried he thinks I'm too impetuous and might dismiss my concerns out of hand.'

'Well how much evidence have you got? And who are we talking about, anyway?'

'It's the DCI. Colin Farlowe. His car was seen in the vicinity of the site where Marnie Draycott, now known as Valentina Malenka, was killed. The timings matched up, too.

There were calls between her and someone near the station on several occasions. Valentina was a known blackmailer of police officers, so that gives us motive and opportunity. We haven't recovered the murder weapon, but it was clearly used by someone familiar with stabbings. If it was anyone else, we would bring them in for interview, arresting them if necessary.'

'Does anyone else share your suspicions?'

'Tom agrees with me and I think Martin sympathises. I haven't really discussed it with the others.'

'Perhaps you could have an informal chat with DS Vaughan and DI Thorpe. She impressed me when I worked with her and she's got a lot of common sense. In the meantime, I know a few people still serving in the Met. I'll ask them what they know about your DCI. But please be careful. A false accusation would blight your whole career.'

'Will do, Dad. Thanks a lot.'

'Bye, love.'

Mel ended the call with mixed feelings. She knew her dad was right. A detective constable with only a couple of years in CID should be extremely cautious when accusing a chief inspector of murder. But she was sure there was something strange about the man and she couldn't quite work out what. Of course, being a bit odd wasn't grounds for suspicion, but she found it hard to dismiss her gut instinct. She would follow her dad's advice and talk to Jack and Emma, preparing for the meeting thoroughly and choosing her words carefully. After all, it was reasonable to present evidence and raise her concerns. Wasn't it?

Chapter Sixty-Nine

Day 36

THE INCIDENT ROOM was unusually hot, as summer sunlight streamed through the grimy windows, highlighting the dust propelled into the air by an array of desk fans, which only managed to move warm air around, noisily, rather than cooling the room.

'Right. We've got some CCTV from the last bus into town on the night of the murder,' began Emma, raising her voice slightly. 'This figure got on the bus one stop up the route from where the victim's car was found. As you can see, the images are not great and the individual is wearing a puffa jacket, a baseball cap pulled down over their face and a scarf. The bus was full of drunks returning from someone's stag night, and no-one was in a fit state to describe our person of interest. We think he or she got off when the crowd of pissheads left the bus and we've no CCTV after that.'

'So, we're looking for a person of either sex, possibly thin, possibly plump, hair colour and style unknown, height about average. Bloody great,' said Jack.

'Yeah. Fits just about anyone in this room,' Mel commented.

'Oh shit.'

A voice came from the back of the incident room and the team turned to see Karen furiously wiping a stain from the front of her trousers.'

'Sorry, guv. Spilt my bloody coffee.'

'Are you OK, Karen?' asked Mel, handing her a tissue. 'You look a bit pale.'

'It's all right. Up late wondering what to do about my mum. I really needed that coffee.'

'I'll get you another one when the guv's finished,' Mel whispered. Karen smiled uncertainly.

'When you two are ready,' Emma called, sharply, 'I'll continue.'

The two detectives sat down, looking apologetic.

'So far, we have no motive for the murder. It was made to look like a robbery, but whoever did it missed a valuable chain and pendant round the victim's neck and an expensive watch.'

'Guv,' said Mel. 'When she was in Mexton before, using the name Marnie Draycott, she was running a blackmail racket. One of her victims was a senior police officer and there were other prominent members of society in her clutches, we believe. Could she be back at her old game?'

'It's a thought. Are you suggesting someone in the Job killed her?'

'No, no, guv. But if it wasn't a random killing someone could have lured her to a meeting, and it wouldn't be some scrote from the Eastside. It would have to have been someone respectable.'

'Good point, Mel. So how do we find out who she was blackmailing, given her cottage was burned to the ground?'

'The cloud?' suggested Trevor.

'If we had her email address or user name, maybe. But we

haven't. There was no landline so she must have used 5G for all her internet access,' replied Jack.

'Good thought. Amira's looking at the burner phone and the tech in Valentina's car,' said Emma. 'We're keeping our fingers crossed. Now, do we have anything on this bloody poisoner?'

'We've reached a dead end, I'm afraid,' said Jack. 'Marvin Lambton's mother rings us every couple of days to ask if we've found out who killed her son. I'm sure she doesn't realise what the little shit was up to. She's threatened to go to the papers, but I've managed to persuade her that it would do more harm than good, diverting resources and wasting time.

'Let's hope she doesn't,' said Emma. 'Jenny Pike would love that.'

Emma closed the briefing with a frown on her face and a sick feeling in her stomach. How many more people would be poisoned before they caught this maniac? she asked herself. And she had no answer to the question.

Chapter Seventy

'CHRIST, Mel, you're going out on a limb again.'

'Hang on, Jack. Hear her out,' said Emma, thoughtfully.

Jack scowled.

'It's just that we've got evidence that puts him near the locus and he could be one of Valentina's blackmail victims,' said Mel. 'I checked with the ANPR data, and his Alvis was also on the Highchester road that night. He would know how to stab someone effectively and he wears a dark blue cashmere overcoat that could match the fibres in Valentina's hand.'

'It's very flimsy.' said Emma. 'I agree that, if it was anyone else, we'd pull him in. But I've spoken to DCI Farlowe and he has a reasonable explanation for why he was in the area and driving his car late at night. The fact that Valentina has blackmailed other police officers doesn't mean that she had a hold over our boss. I've not heard a bad word against him. Obviously, I don't have access to his service record, but there's been no gossip on the grapevine.'

'Yes, my dad hasn't heard anything bad, and he has asked around,' conceded Mel. 'So what should we do?'

'Well, I can't authorise you to investigate a senior officer,' said Emma, slowly, 'and there's not enough to involve the IOPC.'

Jack nodded, vigorously.

'I suppose you can keep your eyes open and tell me if anything else comes up. If we find out he really was being blackmailed, we could take it further. But not now. Sorry, lass. Full marks for initiative, though,' Emma added.

Mel left Emma's office, disappointed and angry. She realised that the evidence against Farlowe was thin, but she had hoped for more support. She wouldn't leave things as they stood. If Farlowe was guilty, she would make damn sure he was caught. And sod Jack and Emma.

'Did we get anything from the Father McKenzie interviews?' asked Emma, when the team convened after lunch.

'We've tracked down the couple he wouldn't marry,' replied Karen. 'They live in Basingstoke, have three children and appear to bear no grudge against the priest. They were on holiday in the Lake District when Father McKenzie died.'

'I've looked into the children he humiliated at school,' said Addy. 'Those I managed to track down don't appear to bear him any ill will. Two have abandoned their faith, one has become a priest and there's one unaccounted for. A Matthew Condon. I'm still trying to find him.'

'OK. Thanks. Keep at it.'

'Guv,' said Martin. 'Something's occurred to me. We're assuming that one of Martina's blackmail victims killed her. But could someone else have a motive? Someone from her past, maybe?'

'It's a thought,' said Emma. 'What do you reckon, Mel?'

'Most of the Maldobourne gang are either dead or inside,' she replied. 'As far as we know, there are no relatives or associates who would bear a grudge. She contributed to the deaths of two of them, but they had no families we could find. One of them had a wife, but she left the country and vanished years ago. I suppose a previous contact, from her days in London, could have come after her, but how would they know that Valentina Malenka was Marnie Draycott? Do you want me to look into it?'

'Yes, please. Work with Martin. You both had a personal investment in the case. But don't spend too much time on it.'

'Yes, boss,' they responded.

Chapter Seventy-One

Day 37

TREVOR STRAIGHTENED UP, rubbed his stiff neck, switched off his computer and went in search of fresh air and coffee. Amira had managed to find Valentina Malenka's cloud login details, using information on her car's satnav system and a powerful hacking program, but it fell to Trevor to examine the material stored there. After three hours he was heartily sick of seeing people, some of whom were in the public eye, indulging in threesomes, cocaine and bondage. A few of the videos were truly sickening and he would pass the details on to Cathy Merritt in the Child Protection Unit. Most of the others would provide little scope for prosecution, but could ruin the participants' lives if they were ever published.

Twenty minutes later, duly refreshed and carrying a packet of biscuits, he returned to the stuffy viewing suite and switched the computer back on. The first image he examined showed a well-built, long-haired man apparently snorting cocaine from a young woman's bare breasts. Yet another one, thought Trevor, but when the man turned towards the –

presumably hidden – camera and grinned as the drug took effect, Trevor nearly dropped the remains of his coffee. It couldn't be him, could it? Surely not. He pulled out his phone and dialled.

'Guv. Can you come down to the viewing suite? I've found something.'

DI Thorpe pursed her lips and looked again at the frozen image on Trevor's screen. Perhaps Mel was right, she thought. This could be the evidence we need. She was stunned to see that the man indulging in erotic drug-taking was clearly a younger Colin Farlowe.

'OK, Trevor. This is game changing. Mel may have told you that she suspected the DCI of murdering Valentina Malenka, although I told her to keep her suspicions to herself.'

'First I've heard of it, guv,' interrupted Trevor.

Emma looked slightly relieved.

'Anyway, although she thought that the boss could have been blackmailed, there was no evidence. Until now. So, what I need you to do is email this sequence to me as an encrypted file. Carry on looking at the rest and don't, I repeat, don't tell anyone what you found. I'll work out what to do with it and let you know the result.'

'Right you are, boss. I'll do it straight away.'

'Thanks, lad. Well done.'

When Emma had left, Trevor turned back to his screen. He sent the video file to Emma as instructed and returned to searching through the crimes and misdemeanours of Valentina's victims. By the time he got to the last half dozen, his eyes were stinging and his concentration was flagging. He skipped through them briskly and didn't recognise the young woman bent over an office desk being screwed by the older man standing behind her.

Trevor picked up his half-finished packet of ginger nuts, packed away his notes and laptop, and returned to the main office. Just in case, he locked the laptop and notes away, and left for the evening. His immediate need was for a long shower, to wash away the smell of the viewing room and the generally sordid feeling engendered by the sleazy video show. Then an evening in with his wife and a couple of bottles of beer.

Chapter Seventy-Two

'I've been poisoned,' said Jenny Pike, glaring at Mel for keeping her waiting in reception for half an hour.

'What with? Gin?' replied Mel, signing her in and steering her though the door towards an interview room.

'No. It's not funny. Mercury. It's been affecting my brain. Look, I know I've not been very friendly towards the police and I don't blame you for hating me. But someone put mercury in my car deliberately and my doctor suggested I get my hair analysed. It's been going on for months.'

At this, Mel's expression changed from cynicism to concern.

'We don't hate you, Ms Pike. But some people find your coverage less than responsible and a hindrance to our work. But if you have evidence that someone is trying to harm you with mercury, we will, of course, investigate. Can you tell me what's been happening and when it started? I'll record you, if I may.'

'OK. Thanks.' Jenny pulled a sheaf of papers from her bag. 'I'd been feeing weird for some time. Nervous, depressed, irritable and headachey. It wasn't so bad at the weekends, but when I was at work, driving around, it got worse.

'A couple of weeks ago, I scraped my car and the guy in the garage found this in the footwell.'

Jenny placed a small jar containing a teaspoonful of silvery liquid on the table between them.

'It's mercury. He didn't manage to collect all of it, but he did clean the car OK. I Googled mercury and found it can cause the symptoms I had. The GP agreed and said I should get my hair analysed as it will show a record of exposure to poisons and drugs. This is the lab report. For four months I was exposed to excessive levels of this stuff and it was making me mad. As a hatter.'

'So, who do you think is behind it? Who have you upset recently?'

'I cover the crime beat, as you know, and some villains might be annoyed. I'm not exactly bringing down the Mafia, though. The last big story was about catalytic converter thefts. My editor was targeted and his car was written off.'

'Yes, I remember the headline. "*Police inaction lets cats out of the bag.*" Not very helpful, was it?'

Jenny looked sheepish.

'Sorry. But we do have to sell papers.'

Mel kept her thoughts to herself.

'OK. We'll certainly treat this as a crime. I'll write up what you've said as a formal statement for you to sign. I'll hang on to this.'

She slipped the jar of mercury into an evidence bag.

'Can I have copies of your hair tests? I need to know when you first started to feel unwell and who could have had access to your car around that time. Also, can you draw up a list of anyone who might have a grudge against you? Please don't quote me, but catalytic converter theft is big business and some nasty people are involved.'

Jenny looked frightened and handed over the lab reports.

'Thanks. I appreciate this. I'll get you the list by tomorrow morning. I'll come in and sign the statement.'

'Good. And in future, Ms Pike, I suggest you think carefully about who you annoy.'

Jenny nodded, avoiding Mel's eye, and gathered up her things.

'Typical,' thought Mel. 'Slag us off mercilessly until you need us. Then we're your bestie. But could this be linked to Operation Inheritance? It's poison, after all, although not a fatal dose. The guv and the DCI need to know.'

Mel reported on her interview with Jenny Pike to Emma.

'What do you think, guv? Another case for Inheritance?'

'I suppose it's possible, although it doesn't look as though the poison was intended to kill. Unless the poisoner hoped Jenny would have a fatal RTC, which seems unlikely.'

'Perhaps he or she was just trying to scare her. Becoming more subtle instead of going for murder.'

'That's pretty similar to Father McKenzie's death. No-one could have predicted that giving him LSD would end up in his death. We thought it was a prank by someone he had upset in a previous job, but perhaps it's our serial poisoner. We'd better look a little deeper into Father McKenzie's history. I take it someone ran a PNC check?'

Mel nodded. 'Nothing came up.'

'OK. Can you concentrate on the Jenny Pike case, then, and give us something at the next briefing? I'll let the DCI know.'

''Yes, guv. Will do.'

Chapter Seventy-Three

Day 38

AT THE CLOSE of the editorial meeting Jenny asked to speak, hoping that what she had to say would restore her colleagues' faith in her.

'Firstly, I must apologise for being such a cow these past few months. I know I can be a bit stroppy when I'm on the scent of a scoop, but this was out of order. The truth is, I was being poisoned.'

Her colleagues looked incredulous.

'What with?' asked the editor.

'Someone put mercury in my car and I was breathing it in for months. It fucks up your brain and makes you nervy, irritable and difficult. So, sorry, but it wasn't all my fault.'

'But who would do such a thing?' asked Ricky, 'and why?'

'Well, the cops think it was someone I pissed off with my writing. Possibly these scrotes who've been nicking catalytic converters.'

'And are you feeling better?'

'Yes, thanks, Ricky. The stuff's been removed from the car

and the doctor said there should be no lasting damage. I wasn't exposed for long enough.

Jenny's colleagues looked relieved.

'So,' Jenny continued, 'I've got to draw up a list of people who might bear a grudge. Any suggestions gratefully received. And you should get yourself checked for mercury exposure, Ricky. You were in my car a lot.'

Ricky nodded.

'You could put the police at the top of the list,' suggested George, the letters editor, apparently attempting to lighten the mood.

'There's no need to apologise, Jenny,' said the editor. 'It clearly wasn't your fault. How can we help? Do you want to move off crime?'

Jenny sighed. 'I suppose we'd better be on the lookout for suspicious packages, hate mail and so on. I spoke to DC Cotton and she's taking it seriously, although the police aren't my greatest fans. But there's no way I'm giving up reporting crime. It's my lifeblood.'

'OK. We'll keep this under review. But be careful. Journalism can be a dangerous profession. You know what happened to those writers in Northern Ireland and Malta.'

Jenny shuddered. As she left the meeting, both Ricky and Marilyn, the health and society correspondent, offered to help with her work or just with coffee and a chat. She smiled gratefully and thought she might take up the offer of coffee. But nobody was going to muscle in on her crime patch.

Chapter Seventy-Four

'WHAT CAN I do for you, Emma?' asked Detective Superintendent Gorman, ushering her to a chair. 'Any progress with this serial poisoner?'

'Some, sir, but that's not why I wanted to see you. I'm afraid to say that some material has come to light that could implicate DCI Farlowe in the murder of Valentina Malenka.'

Gorman looked shocked.

'What is this material?'

'Firstly, he admits driving his car in the vicinity of the murder scene at around the time she was killed and also on the main road near her cottage. Secondly, someone has been making calls to, and receiving calls from, Valentina's burner phone, close to this station. Now, DC Cotton had mentioned this to me and I advised her to keep quiet about her suspicions. But DC Blake found this video on Valentina's cloud site.'

She opened her laptop and played the film.

'As you can see, it looks like the DCI, earlier in his career, was indulging in illegal drug use. I think he may have been blackmailed, and this provides a motive for murder.'

The DSup smiled, stood up and checked that his office door was closed.

'That's very clever of your team, Emma, but they're wrong.'

'How come?' she asked, the thought of a cover-up worming itself into a corner of her mind. 'Surely it's worth looking into?'

'This is for your ears only,' replied Gorman, 'although you had better explain it to DCs Cotton and Blake, swearing them to secrecy. That video was taken when Colin Farlowe was a detective sergeant in the Met, working under cover. Liaising with a supergrass, he infiltrated a major drugs gang, and his efforts led to around 120 years in jail sentences and the recovery of a million pounds worth of Class A. He tried to leave just before the arrest but one of the gang sussed him and went for him with a knife, slashing him from temple to chin. Hence his scar. He got the QGM for his efforts but he was off work for months. Oh, and the powder on that girl's chest was icing sugar. Apparently.'

'So he didn't know about the video?'

'Yes, he did. The woman approached him recently, demanding regular payments for her silence. He reported this to me at once and we decided to play her along for a while. We hoped that she would let something slip that could lead to an arrest. Unfortunately, she was killed before that happened. We kept it between ourselves because Valentina indicated that she had another source in the police who would report to her if he deviated from her instructions. We thought that was probably a bluff, but we didn't want to take the chance.'

'Well, I must say I'm relieved, sir. I hated the thought of a colleague being a murderer. I'll tell the others in confidence. I take it you won't mention this to DCI Farlowe?'

'No. There's no need, though he might be slightly amused. Thank you for coming to me. And do redouble your efforts on this Mexton Borgia, or whatever the press is calling him. People are getting nervous.'

'Yes, sir. Thank you.'

Emma left Gorman's office and went in search of coffee, her feelings of relief diluted slightly by the fact that they were no nearer to catching Valentina's murderer. If it wasn't the DCI, who else could it be? Another police officer? They would have to go through the list of people Trevor had identified from the recovered videos and start interviewing. She knew it wouldn't be easy, as staff were still going off sick with Covid and suspects would be similarly unavailable, so they would have to focus their resources more precisely. At least the cat thefts were sorted out, although there was plenty of paperwork still to complete. Just as long as the poisoner didn't strike again.

Chapter Seventy-Five

Day 39

'CAN I speak to DC Mel Cotton?' asked the worried-looking young man, standing at the reception counter. 'I think someone's tried to poison me.'

The civilian receptionist looked sceptical.

'And why would you think that, sir?'

'Because there's something wrong with my vegetables. And a colleague of mine, Jenny Pike, was poisoned with mercury. Please, I need to speak to DC Cotton.'

'Can I have your name, please?'

'Marriott. Ricky Marriott. I work for the *Mexton Messenger*.'

'Take a seat then please, Mr Marriott. I'll see if DC Cotton is available.'

Ricky sat on the hard plastic chair indicated and fidgeted, obviously unwilling to wait. He stood up and started pacing around the station foyer until Mel appeared, signed him in and led him to an interview room in the depths of the station.

'I'm afraid I can't offer you a drink, Mr Marriott,' she apologised. 'Covid precautions, you know. I just need a quick word with my sergeant and I'll be with you.'

Ricky scowled and sat down to wait while Mel conferred with Jack.

Five minutes later, Mel returned and sat opposite Ricky, a plastic screen between them.

'So. Tell me why you think someone tried to poison you. My colleague mentioned something about vegetables?'

'I get a delivery of organic veg every two weeks. Yesterday's arrived as normal, although they weren't packed as neatly as usual. At the bottom was this plastic bag.'

He fumbled in his pocket and pulled out a clear bag with a handful of plant material in it.

'The label says "Complimentary flat-leaved parsley", but it didn't look quite right and it didn't smell like the herb either. I phoned the supplier and they said it didn't come from them. They haven't stocked it for weeks.'

'So, what do you think it is?'

'I took a picture and emailed it to my aunt. She's a keen gardener. She said they look like Larkspur leaves and that they're poisonous. You spoke to my colleague, Jenny, when she had mercury poisoning, so I came to you. Is someone out to get the *Messenger*?'

'I shouldn't think so, Mr Marriott. As you are aware, there have been other poisonings in the Mexton area, although there are no obvious links between them and the attack on Ms Pike, or yourself. Have you written anything about these poisonings that could have inflamed the perpetrator?'

Ricky scowled.

'No. Jenny gets all the crime stuff. I chip in a few bits of research now and again but it all goes under her byline.'

'OK. Let me collect a few details. I'll need the name of the veg box supplier and an idea of when it was delivered.'

'It's a local firm called Mexton Organics. They normally deliver at about four in the afternoon. I've a plastic box beside the doorstep where they leave it as I'm usually out. It arrived yesterday.'

'We'll need your fingerprints. Obviously, they will be on the plastic bag but I'll send it for examination to check for anyone else's, as well as DNA. Do you mind if I take a cheek swab of your DNA for elimination purposes? I promise you it will be destroyed once the case is concluded.'

Ricky looked slightly nervous, but agreed. Once she had taken the sample, and arranged for him to be fingerprinted on his way out, Mel continued.

'I'll need your address and contact details, please. We'll talk to your neighbours and look for any CCTV cameras in the area. Somebody might have seen someone fiddling with the box after it was delivered. In the meantime, I'll get a botanist to look at the leaves to confirm your aunt's identification. Is there anything else I can help you with?'

'No. That's fine. Thank you. I guess I'd better be careful what I eat from now on.' He laughed uncertainly.

'That would be a good idea, Mr Marriott. Just in case this is a real attempt to poison you. Here's my card. Please contact me if you can think of anything that might help us, or if anything else suspicious happens.'

'I will. Thank you.'

Chapter Seventy-Six

'WHAT DO YOU THINK, JACK?' asked Mel when she had filled him in on Ricky's interview.

'Well it's the first time there's been an obvious link between two targets. Did you give him any details of the other cases?'

'He did ask, but he's a reporter and he works with Jenny Pike. I wouldn't dream of it. He seemed worried about the possible threat, but I caught an undertone of arrogance. Perhaps you need that to be a journalist. Something occurred to me, though. The poisoner, if it's the same person, didn't try very hard to kill Marriott, and we don't know whether his attack on Pike was intended to be lethal.'

'And?'

'Nothing, really. Perhaps he's losing his touch.'

'Could be, I suppose. Well, write it up and let the DCI know. I'll ask for some uniforms to go door-to-door and look for CCTV. We've got enough on our plate in CID at the moment.'

Mel collected a coffee on the way to her desk.

'Who was that waiting for you in the foyer?' asked Martin, as she sat down.

'Ricky Marriott. A journalist on the *Messenger*. Someone's tried to poison him, or so he thinks. Why?'

'I've seen him around somewhere. Possibly at the gym. Didn't know his name. What's the story?'

'Someone put some leaves, which he believes are from a poisonous plant, in his organic veg box. I'm sending them for identification, and uniforms are doing door-to-door. I'll raise it at the DCI's Inheritance review tomorrow morning.'

How are you getting on identifying the people in the videos, Trev?' asked Emma.

'Just about complete, guv. Apart from the paedophiles, we've got four TV personalities, two MPs, one of whom is now deceased, a magistrate, a bishop, three senior civil servants, a couple of local councillors, half a dozen famous sports personalities, the head of a local charity, five notable business people and about a dozen I couldn't recognise. Most are live action videos, but there are some still images of documents as well. Possible evidence of financial crimes, I suppose, but I don't understand what they refer to.'

'Any other police officers?'

'Not that I saw.'

'OK. It looks as though Valentina was bluffing about another source. I don't want these names and faces up on the wall in the incident room where everyone can see them. Someone's bound to gossip or let something slip. We don't even know how many of them are being blackmailed.'

She thought for a moment.

'Can you give them code letters or numbers that we can use to refer to them? Then, would you set up interview schedules, starting with those fit enough to stab someone? Divide the work between two teams – you and Martin, and Mel and Addy. Give the others a brief outline of why we want to speak to the suspects, but only those on their lists. We need to know if they knew Valentina and where they were at the time of her murder. Let me know which of them are outside our area and I'll notify the forces concerned, out of courtesy.'

'OK, boss. What about the nonces?'

'Arrange to sit in on the interviews when they're pulled in and ask the questions. I'll clear it with Cathy Merritt's boss.'

'Right. I'm on it.'

'Thanks, Trevor. Well done, lad.'

Trevor smiled and turned back to his computer, reaching for a custard cream.

Chapter Seventy-Seven

Day 40

'THERE's a gentleman here to see you, DI Thorpe,' the civilian receptionist said, when Emma answered her phone, as soon as she arrived in her office.

'Did he say what it was about? Can't a DC deal with it?'

'He said he killed Father McKenzie. He insisted on talking to the officer in charge.'

'OK. I'll be down. Two minutes.'

Emma collected Martin as she rushed through the office and headed for the stairs.

'A killer or a timewaster,' said Martin. 'What's the odds?'

'About evens,' replied Emma. 'He won't be the first to confess to someone else's crime.'

The two detectives led the visitor into an interview room.

'My name is Matthew Condon. You need to arrest me,' he said.

'Oh, yes, Mr Condon. We've been trying to get in touch with you. Given what you've said to the receptionist, this will be a recorded interview under caution. Do you want a solicitor?'

'No. I don't. It's fine.'

Emma switched on the recording, recited the caution and invited Matthew to speak.

'I was at a Catholic school,' he began, 'and Father McKenzie was the school priest. He preached regularly there and also held religious instruction classes. He was vicious. He told us we were all sinners and were going to hell. He picked on me especially, because my mum was divorced and remarried in a civil ceremony. She still had her faith and wasn't allowed to go to church, but she wanted me to be raised a Catholic and so did my step-dad, which is why I went to St. Joseph's.'

Tears began to form in Matthew's eyes and Martin pushed a box of tissues towards him.

'I mean, Jesus was supposed to be all about love and forgiveness. Father McKenzie had as much forgiveness as a shotgun. I was only seven, for goodness sake. So, I was doing worse and worse at school. I started wetting the bed. I couldn't sleep. Eventually I told my parents what had been going on and they moved me to a different school, but not without writing formal letters of complaint to the headteacher and the diocese. They were fobbed off and Father McKenzie continued at the school.'

'Can you tell us what happened at St Benedict's?' asked Emma, gently.

'I only moved to Mexton recently, for a new job. I was walking past the church one afternoon and I saw Father McKenzie's name on the noticeboard. I was nearly sick in the gutter. When I got home, I realised that something had been gnawing at me for all these years. I wanted revenge. I know we're supposed to forgive people who harm us, but I just couldn't.'

'So, you decided to kill him?'

'No. No. I just wanted to frighten him or something. I'd read this book about the sixties. I'm a history fan. In it the author talked about hippies finding God through LSD and other drugs. I thought if Father McKenzie took some LSD it might give him a better idea of what God was about. So, I got some from a man in a pub and put it in a bottle of communion wine. I slipped in while the church was being cleaned, delivering some flowers. I never meant him to die, I promise you. I'll swear on the Bible.'

'OK, Mr Condon, I must stop you there,' interrupted Emma. 'I'm arresting you on suspicion of manslaughter and supplying a Class A drug. I strongly urge you to consult a solicitor. Martin, will you take Mr Condon to the custody sergeant please?'

Matthew broke down sobbing as Martin led him out of the room.

When Matthew's interview resumed, Emma repeated the caution and again recommended that a solicitor be consulted. Matthew declined. He reiterated his previous statement, almost verbatim, this time maintaining his composure.

'How did you know only Father McKenzie would take the LSD?' asked Martinl.

'I had been to Mass there previously, to make sure it was him. Only he drank the wine. Covid regulations, I think. I didn't take communion in case he recognised me.

'On the day I killed him, I hid in the church after the service and watched him meditate. He had this beatific smile on his face. It's working, I thought. Then he rushed out of the church and I heard the crash. My first thought was to run but I couldn't move. When I realised that my fingerprints would be on the wine bottle, I grabbed it and ran out the back entrance. I threw it in the river. I couldn't think of what else to do.'

'So why did you come to us?' asked Emma.

'I haven't been able to sleep ever since, with these dreadful deeds on my conscience. I went to confession at my own church and the priest advised me to come to you. I think if I'm punished, I'll be able to rest. Until I face a more exacting judgement.'

'Thank you for coming in, Mr Condon,' said Emma. 'DC Cotton will escort you back to the cells and I will consult the Crown Prosecution Service about the most appropriate charges.' She terminated the interview and switched off the recording equipment.

Martin led a wordless and unresisting Matthew Condon out of the room while Emma sat back in the cracked plastic chair, stretched her back and ran her hands through her hair. 'Morality's such a strange thing,' she thought. 'Thank God I'm not religious.'

Chapter Seventy-Eight

Day 41

'Good morning, ladies and gentlemen.' DCI Farlowe's voice cut through the hubbub and the room fell quiet.

'The purpose of this review is to draw together everything we know about the poisonings in Mexton and identify what we've done, and what we should be doing, to catch this poisoner. I do not want these discussions mentioned outside this room. I particularly do not want any more publicity in the local paper, unless we need their help in apprehending a suspect, not least because two of their journalists may have been targeted. Any questions?'

No-one answered and the DCI continued, summarising the main features of each case.

'Now,' he said, 'What's new since our last review? We'll start with the paedophile, Gordon Howell. Martin, I think you were focussing on this one.'

'Yes, guv. The assistant in the bakery who sold him the baklava remembered someone bumping into him just outside the shop, which we knew from CCTV. She said the person was fairly tall and was wearing a silvery puffa jacket over green or blue trousers, but she couldn't describe his face.

'Very observant of her,' commented Farlowe.

'Yes, guv. Apparently, her brother has a similar jacket and she thought it might be him. She couldn't provide anything else in the way of a description.'

'Pity,' said Farlowe. 'Anything else?'

'Not really, guv. There were no death threats against him that we know of and he lived a quiet life. He shouldn't have been anywhere near a children's playground. A local dealer saw him talking to someone in a paramedic's uniform who helped him into a dark van on the afternoon he disappeared. The dealer didn't get the number, but the letters were LSD. There are no dark vans with those letters in the reg number, although there's a legitimate white one in the West Country, so the plates were fake. We know the paramedic was phoney. Howell was accessing unlawful sites on his laptop, but apart from that, there was nothing electronic of relevance. Another parent came forward to say she had seen him on the bench, and didn't like the way he looked at her daughter, but no-one saw him anywhere else in the park.'

'Thank you, Martin. Who's going to update us on the photographer, Marvin Lambton?'

Mel spoke up.

'We've spoken to his fellow students, tutors, friends and family. No-one seems to have known what he was up to with the non-consensual nude photos, least of all his mother, who keeps phoning us for updates. His tutors said he had a talent for portrait photographs and was diligent with his course work. Two more women have come forward since our appeal and told us Lambton had tried to blackmail them into having sex, using photos of them swimming naked in a local lake, but they told him where to go. His laptop was full of images like that.

'We tried to trace the chemicals used to produce the cyanide gas, but the batch numbers had been scratched off. We have no witnesses, no forensics and no leads from the photographs in Lambton's darkroom. There was nothing useful on his social media either.'

'OK. Now, the bodybuilder, Gary Foreman?'

'Nobody saw the poisoner putting the fake package from the supplements company through his door or rummaging through his bins to get his details,' said Trevor. 'The packaging was forensically clean. An appeal for drivers with dashcam footage has yielded nothing.'

'How about the builder, Terry Barwell?'

Addy replied.

'There are no Deadly Nightshade plants growing wild anywhere near his premises, according to the experts we spoke to. We know that he made a habit of fleecing vulnerable customers. We found some more paperwork for jobs that seemed to be overpriced and contacted the homeowners concerned. They were aggrieved, but none of them seemed credible suspects. Most were elderly and couldn't have got him onto the roof. The only forensics of any use was some fresh blood on a ladder that may or may not have come from the killer. The DNA profile is not on the database. A cyclist said she was nearly knocked off her bike by a dark van in that area, around eleven o'clock on the morning Barwell died, but she didn't get the number or a good look at the driver. She thought it was a man. There's no ANPR on the road in question.'

'That's a pity. That's the second time a dark van has turned up. I don't suppose it had any distinguishing features, such as a logo or obvious damage?'

'Fraid not, guv. She wasn't even sure whether it was black or dark blue.'

'The drunk driver, Stephen Brown?'

Farlowe was sounding increasingly frustrated. Martin replied.

'We don't know where the poisoned whisky came from, but a dog walker thought he saw someone stop a dark-coloured van up the road from Brown's place and carry a package towards his house. He couldn't identify the make and didn't get the reg number. No description of the driver and no forensics.'

'And the carer, Sharon Cattrall?'

'There's no forensics, but door-to-door enquiries turned up a neighbour who mentioned seeing a paramedic in the street,' said Mel. 'We've spoken again to Sharon's employers and also to other people she's cared for. Most seemed happy with the care she provided, although two thought she might have taken cash but couldn't prove it. We didn't discover any vengeful relatives. Her workmates didn't know her very well, but had no complaints about her.'

'What about those two lads on the Eastside, to round off this dismal catalogue?'

'No witnesses, no forensics,' responded Karen. 'Mind you, we wouldn't expect much from that estate.'

'Right. Thank you,' said Farlowe, his disappointment obvious. 'So, in summary, we've got eight fatal poisonings with no credible witnesses, no forensics and no electronic evidence of any use. The only real leads we've got are a dark van and a phoney paramedic putting Gordon Howell in the back of a van. It's not good enough.

'We've got some news on Father McKenzie, which is small comfort. I understand we have someone in custody.'

''Yes', replied Emma. 'Matthew Condon came into the station and confessed to putting LSD in the communion wine. Apparently, Father McKenzie made his life a misery when he was at school and he's harboured a grudge ever since. He didn't mean to kill him, but he's been charged with murder and supplying Class A, nonetheless. It may end up as manslaughter. It was nothing to do with our serial poisoner.'

'Well, that's something, anyway,' said Farlowe, grudgingly. 'I've been looking at the attempts on Pike and Marriott. In the earlier cases, the poisoner intended to kill and was successful. He's clearly efficient, which makes me wonder if a different person targeted the journalists. I think we'll consider them separately for the moment. Emma – can you handle that, please? Keep me informed of progress. We'll bring them back into Operation Inheritance if we get any evidence to suggest they're linked.'

'Yes, boss. I'll hold a separate briefing later. So, what do we do now?'

'Review everything we've got, please. Prioritise that van. Review CCTV footage, although a criminal this smart will probably have changed the plates several times. And track down that paramedic. I also think a reconstruction of one or more of the murders could be helpful. We need more information from the public. A drug dealer and a few sightings of a van, aren't enough. Someone else must have seen something, surely. It's a pity *Crimewatch* isn't still running, but we could, maybe, persuade local TV to show something. Any suggestions?'

'Most of the poisonings took place indoors, didn't they?' said Mel. 'So, there's only Gordon Howell and Sharon Cattrall who were seen outside at the relevant times. We could go with them, I suppose, though I doubt many people would want to help us catch whoever killed Howell. The person pretending to be him would probably have stones thrown at him.'

'Well, it is worth a try. Have a chat with the media liaison unit, Emma, and see what they think. We really need to make progress on this before anyone else gets killed. That's all. Thank you.'

Farlowe left the incident room, leaving a team of disgruntled detectives behind.

'It isn't as if we've been putting our feet up,' grumbled Martin. 'We've practically been working round the clock, and we've had the other murder and the catalyst thefts to deal with.'

'I know,' replied Emma. 'But he's feeling the heat from above as well as from the press. Now get your coffees and we'll review the journalists.'

Chapter Seventy-Nine

'So, what have we got on the Marriott case?' asked Emma. 'The lab confirmed that the leaves were Larkspur – poisonous, but not in the same class as strychnine. You can get Larkspur in garden centres: it's not rare or exotic.'

'We've not got much,' replied Karen. 'Uniform found nothing when they went door-to-door, and there were no fingerprints on the bag of leaves. SOCOs swabbed it for DNA, but they said there's likely to be several different sources, including the contents of the veg box.'

'So the guilty party is a cabbage,' laughed Mel.

Karen gave her dirty look.

'No, Mel. He had some organic beef as well, and it wasn't a cow that killed him. They can separate the sources, but it complicates things. Anyway, Marriott has a doorbell camera, which, unfortunately, wasn't working properly all that day. None of the neighbours has private CCTV or doorbells covering Marriott's place. So, we've no images of the box arriving or being tampered with afterwards.'

'Did you get anything from the delivery driver, Martin?' asked Emma.

'Nothing useful. It was the same bloke as usual and he didn't see anyone hanging around. He delivers to two other houses in that street, so he would probably have noticed. He's sure the produce was packed neatly in the box when he dropped it off.'

'OK, thanks. Trev, can you put out an appeal on social media for any motorists with dashcam footage, who drove down Marriott's street during the relevant time, to come forward? See if you can get a sign or placard put up as well. You never know, someone's tech might have picked up something.'

'On it, guv.'

'We also need to build up a picture of Ricky Marriott, from friends, colleagues and anyone else he might know. I assume we've asked him if anything threatening has turned up on his social media?'

Jack nodded.

'Look into his past. Previous jobs where he might have upset someone. Failed relationships. You know the drill.'

The assembled detectives groaned as Emma added to their, already heavy, workload. She ignored them and continued.

'Right. How about Ms Pike's poisoning?'

'Nothing, boss,' replied Mel. 'The mercury would have been put in her car shortly before she started feeling the effects. It doesn't cause symptoms immediately, but they build up. You can't buy it without a licence, but it's been used in thermometers, scientific instruments, some barometers and old-style ding-dong doorbells. The lab said you'd need quite a few thermometers to produce a dangerous amount like this, though. Her hair analysis confirmed she'd been exposed for about four months.'

'Have you come across anyone with a motive yet?'

'She's pretty unpopular with most of us, but I can't

imagine a serving police officer would do something like this. We're planning to interview her colleagues next, and that should give us some idea of how other people felt about her. One thing, though.' Mel paused.

'Come on, lass, don't keep us in suspense.'

'She did write a long article about the catalytic converter thefts, which could have annoyed some of our Albanian friends. They have access to metals. Maybe mercury?'

'Possibly,' mused Emma, 'But it's a bit subtle and not very effective as a warning to back off. I'd expect them to attack her in the street or ram her car, then threaten her verbally. Worth bearing in mind, though.

'So, we've got a lot of work to do talking to friends and colleagues of Jenny Pike and Ricky Marriott. We need to find out where Jenny leaves her car overnight and whether anyone could get access to it. Could it have been tampered with during the day? Has anyone else at the *Messenger* had any threats or unexplained illnesses? We'll need to talk to both victims again, perhaps after we've spoken to the other people. Has Ricky Marriott pissed off a gardener who might hold a grudge? Did Jenny Pike annoy an astrologer who was trying to take some kind of planetary revenge? Look again for threats on social media – Amira can give Trevor a hand. I'll leave you to divvy up the jobs, Jack. I'm going for a walk to clear my head. And we need a session in the pub very soon.'

Emma sat on the sofa, her head leaning on her husband's shoulder and a rapidly emptying glass of wine in her hand, feeling totally overwhelmed. He massaged her neck gently, feeling the tension slowly dissipate.

'OK,' said Mike. 'Sum up the job in three words.'

'How about "Fucking ridiculous"? I only need two.'

Then the flood gates opened.

'We're drowning at the moment. We've got a serial poisoner running around town, killing people without leaving us any useful evidence. The press is hounding us, despite the fact we are trying to find out who attempted to poison a couple of journalists. Maybe the same poisoner. Maybe not. We've got the murder of a blackmailer to deal with and no real suspects. We had that business with the Albanians and the dodgy scrapyard, which could have got three officers killed, as well as my concussion and Jack being shot at. We had a priest poisoned with LSD, although the person who did it has now confessed, and there's the usual stream of less dramatic crimes that we have to deal with.'

Emma drew breath and continued.

'I've got a great team working their arses off, and the DCI isn't bad, although he has other stuff to do as well. But officers are off sick with this bloody virus, many of us are showing signs of serious stress, and we never had enough officers in the first place because of police cuts. We have detectives and civilian support staff working from home because of Covid precautions, which is better than nothing, but it's always best to have people in the office. We are so close to fucking collapsing.'

'Do you want to move back to Sheffield?' asked Mike, stroking her hair.

'No, no. I'm sure it's just as bad there, although I doubt they've got such a cunning bastard to deal with as our poisoner. We'll get through it, I suppose. We usually do.'

'Well, I have absolute faith in you, pet. Now, how about I run you a hot bath and bring you a large glass of Glenmorangie? Then an early night?'

Emma kissed him.

'You're a lifesaver. I'd like nothing better.'

Chapter Eighty

'So, when are you two tying the knot?' asked Sally Erskine, as they sat in the Cat and Cushion, a bottle of wine and two glasses in front of them.

'When this Covid business calms down, I guess,' replied Mel, ruefully. 'We had a date but we had to cancel, and it's a bit risky setting up another one, only to pull out at the last minute. How about you?'

'I've got a partner. Helen. A nurse. No marriage plans yet but we get along really well. I don't see much of her at the moment as she's always working. They're haemorrhaging hospital staff, either with Covid or stress. She's not had it, thank goodness, but many of her colleagues have. Two died.'

The two women continued chatting about work and life for a while, before Mel changed the subject.

'What's this Nicky Mallett business?'

'She's a nice woman with terrible mental health problems. She's forty and was married for several years, but her husband was abusive, they lost a child and split up. She became increasingly ill, got into debt and was homeless for a while.

She's had fuck-all help from Social Services and the county mental health action team – inaction, more like it. She wanders the streets at night making half-hearted attempts to kill herself, like walking onto a level crossing or driving into a wall. We get called out to pick her up and take her either to hospital or a place of safety under Section 136 of the Mental Health Act. She can get a bit stroppy, but most of us are used to her.'

'Shit. That's tragic. Is she dangerous?'

'Only to herself. She sees things. Last time I came across her, she'd developed a fear of paramedics. She claimed she saw one set a tripwire across a gateway and a young woman fell over it. She saw him give her a drink and remove the string or whatever later.'

Mel nearly spilled her drink.

'Was that in Rose Street, by any chance?'

'Yes, it was. She was walking back from her GP surgery and stopped to rest, sitting on a wall. Why?'

'Then she's the first witness we've got to the poisoner actually killing someone. That was Sharon Cattrall and the drink contained a lethal dose of nicotine. Shit! Is she reliable?'

'Well, she's not stupid and can be very lucid at times. The fear of paramedics may be irrational, but if she said she saw those things happening then she possibly did.'

'Could she testify or give us a statement?'

'I seriously doubt it. She wouldn't cope with a formal situation like that. I can have a friendly word with her next time I see her, if you like.'

'Yes please! Anything you can get in the way of a description could help us catch the bastard, even if we can't use it in court.'

'I'll do what I can. Another drink?'

'Better not. I'm in early tomorrow. But you and Helen

must come over for a meal once things settle down. As long as you don't mind parrots.'

'I'll eat anything. But isn't Tom vegetarian?'

'Idiot! You sound just like the Sally I knew at police training college. It's been great to see you. Just like being single ladies again. Bye.'

They decided against hugging and went their separate ways, Mel with a spring in her step. A possible witness to a paramedic committing murder, she mused. Perhaps they were getting somewhere at last.

As Mel left the pub to walk back home, she noticed someone leaning against a car, apparently watching her. She shivered, remembering how she was once followed home by a gunman. But this individual looked familiar, so she decided to challenge him. Stepping briskly towards him, her warrant card at the ready, she was about to speak when he turned so that the light from a street lamp fell on his face. Then she recognised him.

'Good evening, Mr Marriott,' she said, 'What brings you here?'

'Hello, DC Cotton. Oh, the beer, really. They serve a good pint. I often meet contacts here as well. And you? Are you sleuthing?'

His manner set Mel's nerves on edge, but she replied politely.

'No. An off-duty drink. In case you're asking, I'm afraid we haven't got far with your possible attempted poisoning, but we are working on it.'

'I'm sure you are. I did see you and was going to come over and ask, but you've saved me the trouble. I must be off. Good night, DC Cotton.'

'Good night, Mr Marriott. Mind how you go.'

Mel pulled her jacket tighter as she started walking. Had it got colder or did the chill come from meeting Marriott? She glanced over her shoulder to check that he wasn't following her and, just to be on the safe side, took a roundabout way home.

Chapter Eighty-One

Day 42

'We may have a lead, at last,' said Emma, raising her voice against the banging coming from the ventilation system, as engineers attempted to fix it. 'We have a possible witness who saw a paramedic give Sharon Cattrall a drink after she fell over in the street. The witness claimed the man set a trip-wire and removed it after Sharon fell over it. She told PC Erskine, who mentioned it to Mel. Unfortunately, she's unable to give us a statement or testify. She's very fragile.'

'That's three cases where a paramedic seems to have been involved,' said Mel. 'Stacey Bannister said she was comforted by an ambulanceman, after she bought the morning after pill. Sharon Cattrall was given a drink by a paramedic, who may have set up a tripwire to make her fall, and it's odd how quickly he was on the scene, by the way. A witness saw Gordon Howell being helped into a van by someone in a paramedic's uniform, and there were fibres on his body that could have come from that type of clothing.'

'Yes, but that's only three cases out of eight, ten if you count the journalists,' Addy said. 'And why wouldn't a paramedic try to comfort an upset girl? The witness could have been wrong about the tripwire, and the paramedic could have come along just by chance, although I agree the timing is suspicious. In the Howell case we know it wasn't a real paramedic.'

'True, but people working in the ambulance service would hear about cases where people escaped justice. They talk among themselves and will know police officers who would discuss them.'

'It's a thought, Mel,' mused Emma. 'Tomorrow, someone needs to contact the ambulance NHS trust and find out which of their paramedics were off duty or off sick at the times of the murders. We also need to check with industrial clothing suppliers to find out if anyone's bought a uniform recently. Can you sort this, Jack?'

Jack nodded.

'Did we get anything from CCTV in the pharmacy where Stacey bought the pill? She said he was standing behind her, didn't she?'

'Nothing useful, guv,' replied Mel. 'The person standing behind Stacey had a hat pulled down over his eyes and a Covid mask on. He made no purchases and left when she did.'

'Did it look as though he followed her in?'

'No. I don't think so.'

'That must have been him,' said Emma, running her hands through her hair in frustration. 'I suppose he heard her buying the pill and followed her out of the pharmacy when he saw how upset she was. She trusted him because she thought he was a paramedic.'

The others nodded their agreement.

'Might be worth checking CCTV to see if there were any

ambulance cars in the area when Marriott's veg was delivered, just in case the poisonings are linked,' suggested Martin.

'Good point. If anything turns up, we could ask to see satnav records for the cars,' replied Emma. 'I'm leaning towards the view that all the sightings are of a fake paramedic. Our killer. So, crack on, and those of you involved in the reconstructions liaise with the media relations unit, please.'

'How many more times have we got to do this?' grumbled Mel. 'I'm getting a cold bum.'

She had spent an hour outside Mrs Morrison's house, dressed in clothes like Sharon Cattrall's, pretending to trip over and sitting on the ground. Martin, dressed in a paramedic's uniform, repeatedly set up a tripwire and plied her with fruit juice. The TV cameras had long gone, with vague promises of a feature on tonight's local news, but DCI Farlowe had insisted they should repeat the performance numerous times, leading up to the point at which the request for a welfare check was made.

'Once more, with feeling,' chuckled Martin, who didn't have to sit on wet stone flags, slippery with drizzly rain. Mel scowled.

Passers-by looked at the scene with puzzlement, read the associated signs asking for information, and moved on without offering anything other than comments like 'You look like you could do with a cuppa, love.'

Outside the entrance to the park there was rather more public interest, mainly from people waving placards calling for sex offenders to be jailed for longer, castrated, deported, hanged and various combinations of these options. The TV companies, happy to record the mayhem, had declined to take part in the attempted reconstruction, which was called off after half an hour.

Chapter Eighty-Two

'COME ON, folks. Sup up and get the grey cells working,' said Emma, as they sat in 'Incident Room B', the corner of the Cat and Cushion where they habitually met, after a day's solid but largely unproductive work.

'There must be something we've missed. The bugger must have made a mistake, somewhere.'

'It doesn't look like it,' replied Jack. 'The poisons are all different and we can't trace where they came from. There's no forensics worth anything, apart from a drop of blood on a ladder with no DNA match, direct or familial, and no CCTV of any use. We don't have a vehicle reg number or any useful witnesses. That reconstruction was a complete waste of time.'

'Yes, I know,' said Emma. 'No-one saw anything, apart from a woman calling herself Mrs Dorothy Trellis, who said she saw Elvis talking to Sharon Cattrall, and a tinfoil-hat merchant called Andy, who swore she'd been attacked by aliens working for the CIA.'

'We've looked everywhere for connections,' continued Jack, 'but the only link between the victims is that Foreman did some work for Barwell. It's not someone bumping off former bullying schoolmates, like in the thrillers.'

He buried his face disconsolately in his pint and took a large swig.

'You look pensive, Mel,' said Emma.

'Yes, guv. I'm sure the journalists weren't attacked by the same person. I agree with Mr Farlowe. Our poisoner has been extremely efficient up to now. As far as we know, he's never missed a target. It's just niggling me, that's all. At least we know he didn't kill Father McKenzie.'

'OK, Mel. Let it niggle, and if you come up with any bright ideas, please talk to me first,' said Jack. 'We don't want you accusing the DSup now the DCI is off your hook.'

The others laughed. Mel flushed.

'Come on, Jack. I didn't actually accuse Mr Farlowe of being the poisoner. I just pointed out that he seems to know a lot about poisons and there was some circumstantial stuff. He would obviously know about people escaping justice and he hates them. Also, he's out of the office at meetings a lot. It wasn't really serious.'

'OK. OK. Just teasing. Anyway, I'd better be off. My pub quiz starts in half an hour.'

'Well don't hit anyone this time,' grinned Mel. 'Just teasing.'

So what are you working on at the moment, love?' asked Mel, as she passed Tom a plate of vegetable curry. 'Anything you can talk about?'

'Nothing top secret. We're focussing on bitcoin frauds, dodgy investment schemes, that sort of thing, at the moment. It sounds pretty dull, but the bad guys make millions out of these scams. They're ingenious bastards, and tracking them down is quite a challenge. Keeps the little grey cells busy, anyway.'

Mel laughed.

'You haven't got the moustache for Poirot. Where are these shits based?'

'Funny you should mention that. Most are overseas, but we've tracked down a couple of computers in the Mexton area that seem to be involved. We're still gathering intel, but it looks like we could do a warrant fairly soon. I suspect they are fairly minor players, but people are getting hurt, so it's worth pursuing them. These things tend to grow, so taking them out early is useful.'

'Any links to organised crime, or is it just a couple of amateurs?'

'Hard to tell at the moment. They're pretty sophisticated, so we don't think it's schoolkids.'

'Emma suspects there's an OCG developing in Mexton, so let me know if it looks like there's a connection.'

'Will do. Are there any more poppadoms?'

Chapter Eighty-Three

STEFAN PAWESKI WAS proud of his heritage. His grandfather was one of the 145 Polish pilots who had fought courageously in the Battle of Britain. His father had been born in the UK, carving out a successful career as a teacher, but Stefan himself had rebelled against formal education and gone into business. He now owned a chain of five Mexton Mini-Marts, which provided him with a comfortable income. He considered himself both Polish and British and couldn't understand why people had turned against him in the run-up to Brexit and afterwards.

He hated the graffiti urging him to go home, the occasional brick through one of his shop windows and the inevitable increase in his insurance premiums. But there was no way he was going to live in Poland, with its burgeoning right-wing nationalism.

He was working in one of his shops shortly before closing time, filling in for an absent manager and generally keeping an eye on things, when a thick-set, muscular man came in and demanded to see 'the boss'.

'That's me,' replied Stefan. 'Can I help you?'

'You have to pay tax to stay in business,' said the man, holding a cap up so it blocked the view of the CCTV camera above the counter.

'What are you talking about? I pay VAT and business tax. And you don't look like an accountant. Who are you?'

'I work for people who can make sure you stay in business or go out of business. Your choice. We look after your health. Make sure you don't have accident. You will pay us. Ten percent of your takings. Starting today.'

Stefan looked at him incredulously.

'Like fuck I will. I've stood up to racist bullies on the streets. My grandad fought for this country. I'm not frightened by some shitty little gangster. Now piss off.'

With some difficulty, and full of rage, he pushed the man out of the shop and closed the door behind him. 'Was that wise?' he asked himself. The guy looked eastern European but he certainly wasn't Polish. Russian? Ukrainian? Albanian? No matter. He wouldn't be intimidated and would contact the police at the first chance he got.

Stefan locked up the shop at ten o'clock as usual and walked around the back of the building to the small car park. He cursed when he saw the four flat tyres on his car, and in his fury, he didn't notice the two men who crept up behind him. But he did notice the fist that smashed into his side, setting his kidney on fire, and he certainly felt the baseball bat that slammed into the side of his head, knocking him unconscious. He didn't feel the rest of the damage: the broken ribs, the flattened nose and the dislocated shoulder, until he woke up in hospital to find a nurse and a police officer by the side of his bed.

Chapter Eighty-Four

Day 43

'Mr Paweski? I'm Detective Constable Melanie Cotton,' said Mel, the following morning, when the doctor had agreed Stefan could talk to her.

'Have you any idea who attacked you? The doctors say you are lucky to be alive.'

'They got me from behind. Bastards. I think I know who they were.'

'Who?'

'Before, a man came into my shop. He told me I must pay money to people to stay in business. It would make sure I didn't have an accident.'

Stefan's voice was slow and drowsy, because of the morphine being pumped into his arm, Mel assumed.

'Can you describe this person.?'

'He was not English. He spoke like a Russian or an Albanian. Not Polish.'

'Would you be able to help an artist make an e-fit of him?'

'I can do better. He hid from the main CCTV, but he

didn't notice the hidden camera covering the till. Money was disappearing and I didn't tell anyone else. The film is on my laptop.'

'That's brilliant, Mr Paweski. When can I see it?'

'Take shop key...in stockroom...tired now.'

Stefan's voice tailed away as he succumbed to the opiate. Mel stood up, stretching her cramped legs and brushing biscuit crumbs from her jumper. On her way out she passed the nurses' station and spotted a vase full of spectacular red and yellow flowers.

'They're nice,' she said, to the nurse working at a computer.

'Yes. Someone left them for Mr Paweski. There was an odd note, though. It said "Enjoy the fire lilies". I thought "Get well soon" would have been more appropriate.'

Mel shivered. Could that be a threat of arson?

'Did you see who left them?'

'Briefly. Medium height. Stocky. He had a cap on his head and a Covid facemask so I couldn't see his face. Why? Is it important?'

'It could be. Look, can you make sure he has no visitors who aren't family? And phone the police if anyone suspicious turns up. He could be in danger. I'll try to get a PC to stand guard but we're really short staffed.'

'So are we,' replied the nurse. 'But I'll let the hospital security guys know.'

'Thank you. I'll come back tomorrow and have another chat with him.'

Mel smiled and walked slowly down the corridor, her thoughts much bleaker than her expression. A protection racket, escalating rapidly from a beating to a firebombing? This was nasty. Could it be connected with the Albanian cat thieves they had just disrupted? She would raise it with the DI when she got back to the station.

Mel, Jack and Emma sat in the incident room, fresh coffees in front of them, discussing the attack on Stefan. His laptop was on the table, open and displaying a blurred image.

'What makes you think it's linked to the cat thieves, Mel?' asked Emma.

'Stefan said the man who threatened him sounded Russian or Albanian, but he couldn't be sure.'

'OK. But there's loads of Eastern Europeans living in Mexton, even after Brexit,' said Jack. 'There's a sizeable Polish community that's been here since the war, for a start.'

'Agreed,' replied Mel, 'but he was sure that the man wasn't Polish. Also, the NCA told the boss that the Albanian gang was probably involved in other unpleasantness such as drugs, people trafficking and protection. Surely it's a possibility? I know we've cleared up the cat thefts, but maybe we've only cut one head off the hydra.'

'All right,' said Emma. 'What do you suggest we do about it? We haven't got the resources to mount a full-scale investigation. We're stretched as it is, with people off sick and all these murders.'

'I think they'll try again,' said Mel, thoughtfully. 'The flame lilies they sent to the hospital were clearly a threat to burn the shop down. Could we set a trap? I could pose as a shop worker and we would be able to get them on the shop's CCTV.'

'Oh gawd,' moaned Jack. 'I feel another life-threatening situation coming on. How many lives have you got left, Mel?'

Mel ignored him.

'It shouldn't be dangerous and it's better than sitting on my arse in the rain. We'd have a couple of burly uniforms in the stock room who would rush out when I give a signal. An unmarked car would cut off any escape attempt. No problem at all.'

'I appreciate your enthusiasm, Mel,' said Emma, 'But they would never try to threaten an employee. They would go for the owner. The basic idea is sound, though I'm not sure about the shop cameras. Apart from anything else, the images on Stefan's laptop are pretty useless. If we could set something up with Stefan when he's out of hospital, it might work. Can you talk to him and see what he thinks?'

'OK, guv. I'll suggest I pose as his daughter or niece and work alongside him. He's got fair hair and so have I, so it would look credible.'

'I'll think about that. Let me know what he says.'

The meeting broke up with Mel looking cheerful, Jack looking worried and Emma agreeing to put the idea to DCI Farlowe.

Chapter Eighty-Five

Day 44

'Hi, Stefan. How are you feeling? You're looking much better.'

Stefan, now sitting up in bed with fewer leads and tubes attached to him than when Mel last visited him, grunted.

'Not so bad. They say there's no brain damage. I'll be out soon, I think.'

'When you're ready, I'll need to take a formal statement from you, but there's something else I'd like to talk to you about. How we can get the men who did this to you.'

'If they come back, I will deal with them. I have friends who don't fuck about. They'll sort them out properly.'

'I'm sure you do, Stefan, but we can't have people taking the law into their own hands. Your friends could end up in jail for assault.'

Stefan looked disgruntled. 'What do you have in mind?'

'We're sure they will come back, when you're out of hospital, probably threatening to burn your shop down if you don't pay. We would like to be in the shop when they do, so we can arrest them.'

'They will know you're police. They won't talk to you.'

'I will be next to you at the counter. You can say I'm a relative. My colleagues will hide in the stockroom and there will be more outside. We'll record what they say and we'll give you some suggestions about what you should say to them. What do you think of the idea?'

'I think you're crazy. But it might work, I guess. I will think about it.'

Chapter Eighty-Six

'I THINK there's something a bit dodgy about our Mr Marriott,' said Mel, blowing on her coffee to cool it.

'What do you mean?' asked Jack.

'Well, although he seems to be the victim of an attempted poisoning, he's obviously not been affected.'

'So? Maybe he was just lucky.'

'Perhaps. But it's a bit odd that his doorbell camera should be malfunctioning on the very day the poisoned veg was delivered.'

'S'pose so. But tech does go wrong. The trouble we've been having with our broadband since we switched to a new provider, you wouldn't believe. Anything else?'

'He would have easy access to Jenny Pike's car. He used to drive it until Jenny got her licence back but then started using his own. He could have dropped the mercury in it before he switched.'

'Why would he do that?'

'Well Jenny isn't exactly likeable, but what if it's more than that? What if he wants her job?'

'Why do you think that?'

'He's got a driven look about him. When I interviewed him, he seemed fascinated by how things worked at the station. At one point he asked me if he could contact me for information before Jenny got it.'

'I take it you told him where to go.' Jack looked stern.

'Course I did. But the PC who called to collect the veg box for forensics noticed a couple of shelves in his lounge full of true crime books and autobiographies of pathologists and forensic scientists.'

'But that doesn't make him a poisoner, Mel. My dad's probably got most of the same books. He's interested in crime but wouldn't hurt a fly. I can see Marriott might want to shunt Jenny Pike out of the way, but poisoning her is a bit extreme, isn't it? Are you saying he's copying our serial killer?'

'More than that. He could be that killer.'

'Oh, come on. That's really going out on a limb.'

'Stay with me. We're looking for someone who knew what the victims had done or been suspected of doing. He would probably have sat in on court proceedings and would undoubtedly have picked up things from Jenny. As a reporter, he could ask people questions without attracting suspicion, even about cases that didn't get as far as court. Someone would be bound to let things slip, over a few pints or with some kind of financial inducement. So, he would know a lot of stuff that never found its way into print or onto social media.'

'OK, Sherlock. You've obviously switched your target from the DCI to Ricky Marriott. But why the hell should he do this? And how would he know what to do? They don't teach you to extract poison from plants, and murder people, on journalism courses.'

'That is a gap,' Mel admitted. 'But I've got an idea.'

She fished out her phone and dialled.

'Trev, can you do me a favour?'

There was a resigned grunt from the other end.

'Can you find out Ricky Marriott's education and employment records from Facebook or somewhere? I need to find out what he did before he started working for the *Messenger*.'

Another grunt.

'Thanks, Trev. You're a real gem.'

She turned back to Jack.

'That could answer your second point. As to motive, maybe he's got a strong sense of justice or something nasty happened in his childhood. I don't know. I'm not much good at this profiling stuff. I just try to put the evidence together. There's one other thing.' Mel looked triumphant.

'Go on, then.'

'We've got his DNA. And we can compare it with the DNA in the blood found on Terry Barwell's ladder. We know it wasn't Barwell's, so it's probably the killer's.'

Jack frowned. 'Sorry, Mel, but we can't.'

'Why the fuck not?'

'Because he gave a voluntary sample so we could eliminate any DNA of his on the plastic bag or in the veg box. It was specifically for use in investigating his suspected poisoning. We're not allowed to use it in a different investigation. It's PACE, I'm afraid.

'Oh fuck. Is there any way round that?'

'No. Not unless he's arrested for an offence. He obviously hasn't been so far, as his DNA isn't on the database.'

'Well, we'll just have to nick him for something, then, won't we?'

Mel slammed her cup down and stormed out, leaving Jack to mop up the spilled coffee.

Chapter Eighty-Seven

Day 45

STEFAN RETURNED to the shop with his ribs strapped up and his arm in a sling. His nose was still swollen, and a spectacular bruise, fading from purple to greenish-yellow, covered much of his face. Katya, the woman who usually ran the shop, made a terrific fuss of him, telling him he should be in bed and offering to fetch him coffee approximately every half hour. As arranged with the police, he sent her home two hours before the ten o'clock closing time, and as soon as she left, Mel slipped into the shop through the back entrance. With her hair tied back, and a lilac-coloured nylon tabard over her clothes, she made a convincing shop assistant.

By nine o'clock, Mel was bored. She'd learned how to use the till, take payments from customers and top up their electricity and gas accounts. She staffed the counter while Stefan sorted out stock and paperwork, alert for anyone suspicious. Four times she refused to serve cider or cigarettes to people clearly under age, and, once, she sent a fourteen-year-old away when he tried to buy a lottery ticket. She must have a word with Stefan about age restrictions.

The time dragged, with few other incidents of interest, and Mel swore to herself that she would never work in a shop. Just as the store was about to close, two men entered the shop, hats pulled down over their eyes and scarves covering the lower halves of their faces.

'Yes?' she queried, with a non-specific Eastern European accent.

'Give me matches and get the boss,' replied the taller of the two. 'Tell him Amar is back. Then fuck off.'

'Stefan,' she called. 'Someone wants to talk to you.'

She handed over a box of Swan Vestas to the man, whose companion ostentatiously placed two green petrol containers by the door, and busied herself tidying shelves in the tinned goods aisle, a few metres from the counter but still within earshot.

Stefan emerged from the stock room at the rear of the shop and stalked angrily to the counter.

'What do you want? I told you, piss off. I have friends. They are looking for you.'

'Fuck your friends. You pay tax. It is now fifteen percent because of the inconvenience. You don't pay, you lose your shop. Mirjet,' he called. 'Show him.'

Mirjet unscrewed the lid from one of the petrol containers and carefully poured fuel over a display of newspapers and the floor in front of it. Amar picked up a handful of lottery tickets and set fire to them, moving towards the papers.

'You pay now?' he sneered.

'Now! Now!' shouted Mel into the Airwave, which she had concealed under her tabard.

Two PCs rushed from the stockroom and grabbed Mirjet as an unmarked police car, its blue lights flashing behind the grille, pulled up in front of the shop, blocking the door.

Mel pulled out her warrant card, shouted 'Police!' and barged into Amar, knocking him backwards. Pain shot through her damaged shoulder. The flaming tickets dropped from his hand and he tried to kick them towards the newspaper stand, but Mel stamped on his foot. He threw a punch at her, cursing in a language she didn't recognise. She ducked and aimed her pepper spray, catching him full in the face. Amar jerked backwards, giving her the chance to grab a bottle of water from a display. She wrenched the top off and poured its contents over the burning debris, which a draught from the back of the shop was propelling towards the petrol.

Amar flailed and kicked, yelling and swearing, his eyes streaming and his face burning. He knocked down a display of sweets, which scattered confectionery over the shop floor. As Mel tried to handcuff him, she slipped on a packet of Maltesers and crashed to the ground. Amar kicked wildly at her, catching her a glancing blow above the eye, which cut her skin. She swore and leapt up, wiping the blood from her eyes, and grabbed his arm. Her shoulder still hurt but she swept his legs from under him with a ju-jitsu move. He hit the floor and one of the PCs sat on his chest while Mel cuffed his hands in front of him.

'Don't, Stefan,' she shouted, as the furious shopkeeper advanced on their prisoner, a baseball bat raised to strike.

'If you hit him, we'll have to arrest you.'

Stefan lowered the weapon reluctantly and spat on Amar instead.

'You tell your boss if his punks come here again they will have me to deal with. Not the nice friendly British police.'

He turned away in disgust and started shovelling the petrol-soaked papers out of the door, now propped open to disperse the fumes from the fuel.

'Here,' Mel said, handing Amar a carton of yogurt and a paper towel.

'Wipe your face with this. It should help. And you owe Mr Paweski seventy pence for the yogurt.'

Half an hour later, the two Albanians, cautioned and arrested on suspicion of assault and conspiracy to commit arson, were being processed by the custody sergeant. Mel drove home wearing the Grateful Dead T-shirt that Mexton CID officers wore when they had bled over their clothes in the line of duty. A couple of Steristrips closed the cut on her forehead, which was swollen but no longer bleeding. Her head ached, her shoulder was sore and, although she was desperately tired, she knew she wouldn't sleep tonight. Perhaps she really should apply to join Tom's unit. But she realised this was idle musing. She would be bored within a week, missing the excitement of helping to track down murderers and gangsters.

Kreshnik poured himself a large glass of rakia and let the fruited spirit warm his throat while he reviewed the disaster at the Mini-Mart. Those morons had gone too far and got themselves arrested as a result. They were told to increase the threats in stages, not go straight to torching the place, and now they would pay for it in the courts. That was on top of shooting up the Environment Agency office, a few hundred metres from a police station. He hadn't authorised it, and it was stupid, but at least the police hadn't arrested them for that, and he knew they wouldn't talk. He hadn't decided whether he would order an additional punishment for them, but that could wait until later. The shopkeeper would pay, though. It might have been a small sum involved, but there were principles and reputations at stake.

In the meantime, he was worried that he would be in trouble with the bosses back home for employing such idiots. He was warned, when the police broke up the catalytic converter operation, that he must make no more mistakes, but at least he could remedy this one, in time. He would hold off on the protection business for a while, until the publicity died down, and start it up again with some more reliable operatives. For the time being, the drugs, the girls and the cyberscams should make enough money to keep his superiors happy. It was a shame that Mexton was such a shithole, he complained to himself. Markets were limited and he could be making much more money in a big city like London or Birmingham. But locals and other nationalities had too much influence there and the group couldn't afford to go to war with them.

Time for relaxation, he thought, clearing some space on his desk. He pressed the intercom. 'Send in Ilyena. Tell her to leave her clothes outside.'

Chapter Eighty-Eight

Day 46

WORD of what happened had already reached the office when Mel came into work. A chorus of 'Hey, it's Fireman Samantha' greeted her and someone hummed the *Fireman Sam* theme tune. She grinned and went in search of coffee.

'Well done, Mel,' said Emma, 'Karen and Addy will interview that pair this morning when their brief arrives. Feel free to...'

Emma was interrupted by Jack storming into the office.

'Look at this. The fucking *Messenger*. That bloody woman deserves to be poisoned,' he raged, brandishing the offending newspaper. The *Mexton Messenger's* article was typical Jenny Pike.

The Mexton Messenger

The Mexton Borgia still at large!

Police are at a loss as a deadly poisoner stalks the streets of

Mexton. So far eight people have died at the hands of this cowardly killer. How many more will suffer agonising deaths before our hopeless police force catches him? Keen photography student Marvin Lambton, his promising career cut short by cyanide. Well-known local builder Terry Barwell, killed by a poisoned pie. Sharon Cattrall, devoted care worker, slain by nicotine. These are just three of the victims of this hellish killer.

DCI Colin Farlowe told the Messenger *that the police are following several leads, but it seems they are no nearer to making an arrest than when the first victim, a paedophile school caretaker, was found. Even the* Messenger's *fearless reporters have been attacked.*

Are we safe? The Messenger *wants to know. Can we trust what we eat? Is it time for the police to call for help from Scotland Yard? Local MP Christopher Tarley certainly thinks so. He has called the police operation 'woefully inadequate' and accused them of spending too much time chasing people for violations of the Covid regulations instead of hunting murderers.*

The Messenger *will shortly be announcing a reward for anyone who helps bring this toxic torturer to justice. (More details of the victims and the poisons used on pages 5&6).*

'Yes, I know, Jack', said Emma, wearily. 'I suppose a reward might help flush someone out of the woodwork, but she really enjoys spreading panic. She did it with that bomb factory. We're doing our best to find out who poisoned her, but still she's having a go. And as to that MP, he's only complaining because he was fined for holding a garden party during lockdown. The benefits of a free press, I suppose.'

'You're not calling for censorship, surely?'

'No. But a bit of responsibility towards the public good, rather than the interests of the paper's owners, would be welcome.'

'In your dreams,' snorted Jack, hurling the paper at the waste bin and missing.

'She's gone too bloody far this time,' raged Ricky Marriott to himself. 'I did all the work on that feature, describing the poisons, the scrotes who died and their crimes, which she didn't even mention, and then she takes all the fucking credit. I don't even get a mention in the byline. She's never acknowledged the work I've done on all the other stories either. She's a scheming, self-serving, arrogant cow. And she's gonna pay. I'll have her job. I'll fucking make sure of it.'

Chapter Eighty-Nine

'So WHAT DID you get from the ambulance service, Trev?' asked Emma.

'Pretty much nothing, guv. They had no-one off duty on more than a couple of relevant occasions, and there's no-one on long-term sick leave, which is surprising, given the pressure they're under. No single individual seemed to be calling in sick for the day on the dates in question, either. They have a system for tracking ambulance movements, but I don't think there's much point asking for data. They're so busy that a driver nipping off for half an hour to poison someone would be noticed.'

'Right. Thanks. So, we're definitely looking for an impostor. Someone who wanders around in a paramedic's uniform either gathering information or dispensing vengeance. I did think that was a possibility.'

'I asked the ambulance trust if they had had any uniforms stolen,' said Trevor, 'but there were none missing. Any that are no longer wearable go to a textile recycling firm. I also checked the three fancy dress shops in town and they haven't hired out a paramedic's uniform since before Christmas.'

'Good thinking, Trev. Did you get anything from the workwear suppliers, Karen?'

'Two of the three firms in town don't stock paramedic uniforms as hospitals and ambulance operators normally provide them. Mexton Industrial Clothing used to, but someone bought their whole stock, six of them, a few months ago. There's no CCTV, but the guy on the counter remembers a tallish bloke with glasses and a Covid mask paying cash. He thought cash was a bit odd but said nothing to the purchaser, who, he remembered, spoke with a West Midlands accent.'

'Easy to mimic,' said Emma. 'That must be our man. There's no point looking at ANPR footage on roads around the store now, but if we get a suspect vehicle, it might be worth it. Karen, can you check whether any private CCTV owners near the site have any footage going back that far, and ask them to retain it? Probably a long shot.'

'Sure, boss.'

Chapter Ninety

Day 47

JENNY PIKE's article provoked a storm of activity on social and conventional media. A Facebook page purporting to come from the poisoner, listing the reasons the victims had been killed, was swiftly taken down at the request of the police, but not before its content had been circulated widely. It had received several thousand likes before it was removed. Jenny was asked for interviews by national and online media about the case, opportunities that she exploited avidly.

The story had gone viral on Twitter. Some posts criticised the police for lack of progress in finding the killer. Some wanted the killer to get away with it and others had ideas, often very bizarre, as to his identity. The NHS helpline and the town's pharmacists had their work cut out explaining to worried patients that there was no such thing as a generic antidote to poisons.

Instagram carried numerous photos and video clips of the poisonous plants mentioned in Jenny's article, and several contributors offered joke recipes for Belladonna pies. The usual racists blamed Muslim immigrants for the deaths, while others swore that aliens were responsible. Mexton became world famous on social media, and journalists from the national press phoned their stringers in the town for juicy titbits of information. Few were forthcoming.

The police, inundated by a tsunami of public anxiety, implored people to stay calm and report any suspicious activity. A separate 'poisons line' and email address were set up to prevent the normal communications channels from being overwhelmed.

Quick to profit from the situation, someone set up a 'Mexton Poisoner' website displaying images of the victims, where available, as well as variably accurate details of the poisons used. Merchandise available through the site included T-shirts and coffee mugs bearing the phrase 'Keep Calm and Swallow Poison', poison rings with hinged compartments for dropping toxins into drinks, and ball-point pens in the shape of syringes.

Mexton Sound, the local radio station, ran a phone-in where listeners were invited to contribute their views on the situation. Most were hostile to the police for their lack of success. Many were panicky, despite an interview with DCI Farlowe in the programme that preceded the phone-in, reassuring people that they weren't at risk and that the police were making the poisoner their number one priority. Several listeners accused their spouses of being the killer, but as they phoned in every week to accuse the same spouses of other crimes including terrorism, bank robbery and stealing the Crown jewels, they were screened out and never made it to air. More than a few callers blamed Covid vaccinations for the deaths, claiming that the police, in league with the pharmaceutical industry, were part of a huge cover-up.

None of this made the job of the police any easier, diverting effort from where it was most needed, and the whole team was feeling angry and frustrated.

Chapter Ninety-One

EMMA LOOKED surprised when Mike's car pulled up outside the station, just as she was about to leave.

'Hi, love. Is something wrong? I was going to cycle home.'

'No, nothing's wrong,' her husband replied. 'Put your bike in the back. We're going for a meal out of town. You deserve it.'

Emma smiled and complied, pleased at the prospect of getting away from Mexton for a while. She didn't actually dislike the place, but while she was there, she was constantly thinking about the job. She was delighted when, twenty minutes later, they arrived at the County Arms, their favourite country pub.

'You've been looking a bit frazzled lately, love,' Mike said, as he sipped an orange juice and Emma took a deep draught of her pint. 'Anything I can do to help?'

'Just be yourself. And do things like this.' Emma smiled fondly at him. 'This poisoner's got to us all. The bugger's like a bloody ghost. And these barmy Albanians are taking up a lot of time too, to say nothing of the Malenka murder. Honestly, it's been all go since we moved here. Not the quiet town I expected.'

'Do you regret it?'

'No. You've asked me that before. I'd rather be busy than bored. Anyway, that's enough shop talk.'

The couple spent the next couple of hours relaxing and chatting, enjoying the food and each other's company. As they left, Emma slipped her arm into Mike's.

'Thank you. I needed that.'

Two hours later, Emma started to feel ill. She just made it to the toilet in time before she was violently sick, bringing up the meal she had previously enjoyed. 'Oh fuck,' she thought. 'The bastard's got me. Is this arsenic? The stomach pain and vomiting seem like the symptoms. But how did he know where I was going and what I would eat?' After an hour or so, her stomach calmed down and she went back to bed, uncertain whether or not she should seek medical help. Mike persuaded her to phone the NHS helpline, and after an hour's wait, she was advised to monitor her symptoms and contact her GP in the morning if she didn't feel better. The operator told her to drink some water, and if she felt very much worse, to go to A&E.

Chapter Ninety-Two

Day 48

THE FOLLOWING MORNING, still at home, Emma felt considerably better but phoned her doctor just in case. She knew that you could appear to recover from the poisons in some lethal mushrooms, before relapsing and dying. The doctor thought for a moment, then asked what she had eaten the previous night.

'Mushroom soup, chicken risotto and strawberry cheesecake.'

'Where did you eat it?'

'The County Arms. Why?'

'Ah. You're the third patient of mine who's been taken ill in recent weeks after dining there. Unless they used some poisonous mushrooms in the soup, which I seriously doubt, my money is on the risotto. It sounds like *Bacillus cereus* food poisoning, from contaminated rice. It's short, nasty at the time, but the effects pass quickly once the stomach's empty. Drink fluids and eat a little when you feel able to. You should feel better later on today. If you don't, phone again. I'd better get on to the Environmental Health department. That place obviously needs checking.'

'Thank you, Doctor,' Emma said. 'That's reassuring. Apart from the bit about the mushrooms.'

She phoned Jack and asked him to run things for the day, then went back to bed for a couple of hours. She spent much of the afternoon researching the Death Cap mushroom and its lethal relatives, while Mike plied her with tea and diluted fruit juice. She recalled the quote from a toxicologist she'd read somewhere: 'All mushrooms are edible but some only once,' and shivered. Later, she put these morbid thoughts behind her and managed to do some work from home in the evening, determined to go back to work the following day.

Chapter Ninety-Three

'You'll love this, Mel,' said Trevor. 'I've dug into Marriott's history. He's got an honours degree from the Open University in English, psychology and other odds and ends, plus a Masters Degree in journalism from the University of the West of England, in Bristol.'

'So? Hardly ideal qualifications for a poisoner.'

'Yes, but before the OU he did almost a year of a pharmacy degree at another west country uni, but left before taking the exams. I managed to get hold of one of his tutors, who spoke to me off the record. Marriott was suspected of stealing drugs from the laboratory during practical sessions. They were things like atropine, physostigmine and digoxin, and although they weren't controlled under the Misuse of Drugs Act, they were all poisonous. There was no proof, but smallish quantities kept disappearing when he was around, and on one occasion, he was seen in the stores when he shouldn't have been. When challenged, he claimed he was looking for something and demonstrated that his pockets were empty.

'The university didn't want a scandal so didn't call the police, but they made it clear to Marriott that he would be unlikely to qualify as a pharmacist since they couldn't vouch for his honesty. And, one other thing. His step-mother killed his father after years of abuse. Hit him with an iron. She was originally convicted of murder but this was reduced to manslaughter on appeal and she was let out, having served two years. I suspect that gave him a jaundiced view of the criminal justice system as well. He campaigned hard for her release when she was first sent down.'

'Brilliant, Trev. We've got the bastard! I'll tell Jack.'

'Hold on. Hold on. All we've done is establish that he's probably got the knowledge and lab skills to extract poisons and use them on people. It's all circumstantial. There's nothing directly linking him with the crimes. We've got no grounds to pull him in, let alone charge him with anything.'

'Yes, but it's another jigsaw piece. It should be enough for Jack to let me go and have a chat with him. Rattle his cage a bit.'

'Well, good luck with that.'

When Mel brought the new information to Jack, he agreed it was useful but shared Trevor's view that it was still not enough. He let Mel arrange an interview with Marriott on the strict understanding that the meeting was on neutral ground and she didn't go alone. That was why she was sitting in the Ace of Spades café with Karen, waiting for Marriott to arrive.

'He's late,' whispered Karen. 'D'you think he's chickened out?'

At that point Marriott swept into the café and over to their table with a self-important air. He shook their hands with a near-aggressive grip and dropped his expensive jacket on a chair next to them.

'Can I get you ladies a coffee?' he asked, all charm and confidence.

'No thank you, Mr Marriott. We've already ordered,' replied Mel. 'But we'll wait for you to get one.'

Marriott asked at the counter for a flat white and then returned to the detectives' table.

'I believe you wanted to talk to me about Jenny's mercury incident?'

'Yes, we do,' replied Mel, pausing as a surly barista with a shaven head and an ecosystem of a beard plonked their coffees on the table and commanded them to 'Enjoy'.

'This is just an informal chat, you understand. We'd like a bit of background, if possible. What's Ms Pike like to work with?'

Marriott thought for a moment then responded.

'Driven, I would say. She'll stop at nothing to get a story. But only the big ones. She's not interested in the minor crimes. It has to be bombs, murderers and serial killers for her.'

'She's following this serial poisoner, I see,' said Karen.

'Yes. She's obsessed with him but is taking no notice of the crimes committed by his targets. They're all innocent victims, as far as she's concerned.'

'And you don't think so?'

Marriott shrugged.

'They're no loss, but murder's murder and I can't condone it, of course.'

Karen leaned forward, conspiratorially.

'Strictly off the record, you're not the only one who thinks that.'

Marriott smiled slightly. Mel looked at her sharply.

'Getting back to Jenny Pike,' she said. 'Does she have any enemies?'

'Well, she does put people's backs up, sometimes. A bit too full of herself. But I've never had a problem. I've learned a lot from her.'

'Do you want her job?'

Mel's bluntness made Marriott start.

'Well, one day, perhaps. I've only been with the paper a few months so I wouldn't be in the running if she left. I know she wants to move on to better things, eventually, so who knows? Anyway, I've got to get back to the office. I'll have to leave the coffee. Perhaps we could continue this conversation over a drink one evening? Strictly informally, as you say.'

'Probably not, as I need to spend more time with my fiancé,' said Mel.

Karen simply smiled.

'Well, thanks for your time, Mr Marriott,' said Mel. 'We'll keep you updated when we have anything on whoever tried to poison you.'

Mel wished him goodbye as they stood up. She didn't notice Karen brushing against Marriott and slipping her business card into his pocket as they left the café.

'So did you get anything useful from him?' asked Jack, when the two women returned to the station.

'He's a cocky sod and he's definitely sympathetic to what the poisoner's doing,' replied Mel.

'I agree,' said Karen. 'He claims to have no problem with Jenny Pike and said he wasn't after her job. His expression and body language seemed to say something different, though. He invited us out for a drink, which we declined.'

'Cheeky bastard,' snorted Jack. 'I'm sure it wasn't just the pleasure of your company he wanted. He's after inside information.'

'Well, you can be bloody sure neither of us would leak to an arrogant creep like that,' said Mel, indignantly. 'Anyway, who wouldn't want the pleasure of our company?' She grinned.

'I know, I know,' replied Jack, smiling. 'Just teasing.'

Chapter Ninety-Four

Karen fiddled with her bracelet as she waited for her date to arrive. She had dressed up, used make up, and tidied her curly dark hair for the first time in months. She reluctantly admitted to herself that she didn't look bad. Perhaps the dating scene wouldn't be too difficult after all, although she would keep quiet about her job. Some men were put off at the thought of going out with a police officer. After tonight, which was work, she would go fishing, she decided.

She knew the enterprise was risky, but she had to do something. With Valentina Malenka out of the way, she should have felt secure, but the video could still be out there, waiting to ruin her life. And the guilt hadn't gone away, magnified by the death of the two youths. This was her chance to make up for what she had done, and she wasn't going to blow it. She wondered whether she should have let someone know what she was doing, but realised that she would have been ordered to drop the idea.

'Hi Karen. Glad you could make it,' said Ricky Marriott, easing himself onto the bar stool next to her. He glanced at her half-empty glass of wine.

'Fancy another?'

'Yes, please,' she replied, smiling. 'Pinot grigio.'

'OK. There's a free table over there. Why don't you grab it and I'll bring the drinks over?'

Karen complied and arranged her coat on the back of her chair, ensuring she had ready access to the pepper spray in her pocket. She knew she shouldn't have it while she was off duty, but as she had broken so many rules already, this didn't trouble her conscience in the slightest.

'You're looking very nice tonight,' smiled Ricky, placing his pint and Karen's wine carefully on beer mats. 'I didn't know policewomen could look so pretty.'

Karen smiled and cringed inwardly.

'Thank you. Actually, we're not policewomen any more. We're all police officers.'

'I stand corrected. Will you let me off with a caution?'

'I suppose so,' Karen forced a laugh and raised her glass. 'Cheers.'

Ricky echoed the toast and settled down in his seat.

'So how close are you to catching this poisoner then?'

'Well, I shouldn't be telling you anything, but if you promise not to write anything until we've made an arrest, I can give you a couple of hints.'

'Promise. Word of honour.'

'OK. Well, we think he's a rogue paramedic. Someone who knew what the little shits he targeted had done and wanted to punish them.'

'Interesting. So you're interviewing all paramedics in Mexton, are you?'

'Yes. It's a long job. The only thing is we don't know why he would target Jenny Pike, or you.'

Marriott appeared to think for a moment.

'Well Jenny did run a piece a few months ago, criticising the response times of the ambulance service. She got a photo of an ambulance crew drinking tea by a roadside van and slagged them off for not dealing with patients. Poor sods had been working for seven hours solid and this was the first break they'd had. We had to print an apology.'

'That's really helpful, Ricky. We'll prioritise talking to the crew involved. Then there's that priest.'

Marriott looked confused.

'What priest?'

'Father McKenzie at St. Benedict's. We initially thought he might have committed suicide. Jenny wrote about it. It seems he was poisoned with LSD and didn't realise he was running into a busy road. A van hit him and he died.'

'Bloody hell. That's awful. Do you have any leads?'

'We're looking into people he may have upset, but we've had no luck so far,' she lied.

'Would you let me know when you've got something we can publish? It would be nice to get a story ahead of Lady Pike.'

'So, you're really not keen on her?'

'As I said. She's up herself. Gets all the credit for her stories even when I've done much of the research. I'd just like to see something under my byline for a change.'

'I'll see what I can do,' said Karen.

Marriott smiled.

'Your glass is empty. We could have another if you like, or get something to eat. Do you like Italian food?'

'Yes. Yes, I do.'

'Well, I make an splendid pasta carbonara, if you're interested. And I've plenty of wine. What do you reckon?'

Karen thought for a moment.

'Yes. I'd love that. I've left my car at the station, so we'll have to go in yours. I'll get a taxi later.'

'No problem at all. I'll help you with your coat.'

As they left the wine bar Karen wondered whether she

was being incredibly stupid. Nothing in his words or behaviour had seemed remotely threatening, or hinted at his guilt, although it was clear that he disliked Jenny Pike. Nevertheless, he remained the prime suspect as far as Karen and Mel were concerned. At least she had her pepper spray, and if things looked like becoming risky, she would make her excuses and leave.

The meal was excellent, as Marriott had promised, and his ground floor flat was warm and comfortable. As he cleared away the plates and went in search of ice cream for dessert, Karen asked where the loo was. On the way back, she spotted the half-open door of a utility room and peered in. She stood, paralysed, for a few seconds, when she saw an unmistakeable paramedic's uniform in a basket of wet washing. Reaching into her handbag, she pulled out her phone and accidentally took a burst of photos instead of the single shot she intended. 'Shit,' she thought. 'If he heard the noise, I'm dead.' But when she returned to the kitchen-diner, Ricky seemed just the same as when she had left him.

Chapter Ninety-Five

THE RAPID CLICKS from Karen's phone, in a silent moment between the clatter of plates, alerted Marriott and he looked out of the kitchen doorway. He just caught sight of Karen, reflected in a mirror in the hallway, as she retreated from the utility room, fumbling with her phone and putting it back in her handbag. Fuck, he thought. The uniform. And that sounded like photos being taken on a phone. He would have to act quickly.

'Ice cream's ready,' he called. 'And you must try some of this dessert wine.'

He poured two small glasses of sauternes, dosing one of them with ketamine and hoping that the sickly sweetness would disguise the taste of the drug. He put the drugged glass closer to him, and when he stood up to make coffee, he glanced surreptitiously back at Karen and saw her switch them. So she knew, the bitch.

'Cheers!' he said, prompting Karen to drain her glass.

He kept the conversation light for the next twenty minutes, chatting about crime, his and Karen's career aspirations and the likelihood of a further lockdown. He didn't believe that Covid was serious but Karen did, and just as the discussion was becoming heated, Karen's voice began to slur.

'It's a pity you saw that uniform,' Marriott said, his voice hard and his eyes flashing with anger. 'I've now got to do something about you. And killing a police officer is much riskier than cleansing the gene pool of the arseholes I've been dealing with. I'll just have to arrange an accident, I suppose.'

He thought for a moment, as Karen slumped into unconsciousness.

Removing all traces of his DNA from Karen would be all but impossible, he realised. But, as they had met before, and she had brushed against him, there was no reason why there shouldn't be traces on her clothing. As long as no-one examined his van or flat, he should be OK, and he would make damn sure he wouldn't be suspected. To make doubly sure, he put on some dark overalls, which he would dump in a recycling bin when he had finished with them. He wrestled his victim into her coat, removed the battery from her phone and placed it back in her bag, taking out her pepper spray for later disposal. He dangled the bag round her neck and switched off his own phone.

Leaving Karen sleeping, he walked briskly to his lockup and retrieved the dark van he often used for his cleansings, as he called them. He parked it in the lane that ran behind the building and entered his flat by the back door. Checking that no-one was about, he hoisted Karen's unresisting body over his shoulder in a fireman's lift and carried her through the garden into his van.

He knew the right spot, and within fifteen minutes, he pulled up in a layby alongside the Highchester road. He took Karen's phone, replaced the battery and stamped on it, picking up the pieces of the ruined item. Then it was a question of waiting, with the lights off and a balaclava covering his face. When Karen began to wake up, he moved. He lifted her out of the van and supported her to walk across the road. He stood beside an information board that described the features of the nature reserve behind them, partly hidden by bushes. It wasn't long before the sound of a fast-moving vehicle shattered the evening's calm. He put Karen's bag over her shoulder, threw the broken phone onto the tarmac and shoved Karen into the path of the speeding van. He smiled with satisfaction as it smashed into her, sending her flying onto the grass verge. She hit her head on a signpost before she fell and lay sprawled on the ground, like a starfish abandoned by the receding tide.

The van screeched to a halt. The driver climbed out and ran back to the scene of the collision. Marriott saw him bend over Karen's body and shout, 'Oh fuck, she's dead,' into his mobile phone. He then dashed back to his vehicle and sped off in the direction of Mexton.

Marriott expected the emergency services to arrive, assuming the van driver had the decency to call them. He was about to check on Karen, when he saw a car's headlights approaching, so he hid in the bushes and crossed back to his own van after the car had passed. He was sure he hadn't been seen pushing Karen out from behind the information board. It seemed certain that Karen was dead. No-one could have survived that impact. He couldn't hang around to make sure, so he drove slowly back home, having obscured his number plates with mud.

Chapter Ninety-Six

Roy Garnett felt sick and scared. He'd never killed anyone before. Should he phone for an ambulance? No, it was too late for that, and he couldn't use his phone as the call would be traced back to him. But what if the woman was still alive? He couldn't afford to stop and get involved. If the police tested him and found the cocaine in his system, they would never believe it wasn't his fault. And there was the dodgy gear in the van. Knock-off Rolexes and Gucci handbags. They mustn't find them, either. The boss said to ignore it and get any damage fixed at a discreet garage in the morning. As he hurried back towards Mexton, just keeping to the speed limit, his mind was in knots. He wanted to do the right thing, but he feared his boss's wrath and the prospect of another jail sentence.

A solution appeared when a telephone box came into view on the outskirts of town. Praying that it hadn't been converted into a library, or vandalised and turned into a public urinal, he pulled in and opened the door. It was still working. He dialled 999, put the sleeve of his jacket over the mouthpiece and told the operator that there was a dead woman beside the Highchester road, four miles south of Mexton. Then he wiped his fingerprints off everything he'd touched and ran back to his van, his conscience feeling a little easier.

PCs Sally Erskine and Reg Dawnay nearly missed Karen as they drove slowly along the road, their headlights on full beam. She was lying face down and her dark clothing failed to show up as the patrol car approached.

'Hang on, Reg, there's something by the verge,' called Sally. 'It looks like a handbag. Pull in.'

The car drew to a halt, red and blue lights flashing to warn approaching drivers. Reg and Sally climbed out, and within seconds, they spotted Karen. Sally reached her first and felt for a pulse in the blood-smeared neck.

'She's alive, Reg. But only just. Get an ambulance. Oh shit,' said Sally, as she carefully turned Karen over. 'It's Karen Groves.'

Apart from the faint carotid pulse, Karen showed no signs of life. Sally tried talking to her, assuring her that help was on its way, but there was no response. When the paramedics arrived, they offered no comments on Karen's prognosis, merely saying that it was a good job they'd arrived when they did and not a few minutes later. They fitted an oxygen mask to Karen's face and a neck collar to protect her upper spine, eased her onto a stretcher and slid her into the ambulance while Reg and Sally taped off the scene, setting out cones and warning signs along the road.

Chapter Ninety-Seven

Day 49

'We've got some bad news about Karen,' said Emma, sombrely, at the start of the morning briefing. 'She was involved in a hit-and-run on the Highchester road late last night. She's in a coma and the doctors have no idea when, or if, she'll wake up. Apart from a cracked pelvis, four smashed ribs, a broken arm and a fractured collarbone, she's got a serious head injury. There's no telling whether or not her brain is damaged at this stage.'

Mutterings of 'Oh fuck', 'Poor Karen' and similar greeted Emma's announcement.

'But what the bloody hell was she doing on the Highchester road at midnight, for Christ's sake?' fumed Emma, still feeling slightly rough.

No-one answered.

'What's more, they found alcohol and ketamine in her system. Has anyone heard of her taking drugs?'

The team shook their heads and Mel spoke up.

'I don't know her very well, guv, but that really doesn't

sound like her. She's not the clubbing sort. She could have been drugged.'

'But why?' asked Emma.

'I think it might be something to do with these photos she sent me,' Mel replied. 'I got them around eleven last night. 'They're pictures of a paramedic's uniform in a washing basket. Could she, somehow, have met the killer and challenged him? With near-fatal consequences?'

'You mean she was drugged and pushed into the road deliberately? It's possible, I suppose, but we can't ask her now and maybe we never will.'

The room fell quiet.

'Right, ideas, please. Who could she have been meeting? Mel, pass your phone to IT forensics and see if they can work out where the photo was taken. Trevor, track Karen's phone. It was found, crushed, on the road, but see where it was before that. Jack, can you organise interviews at the locations Trevor identifies – pubs, wine bars etcetera? Ask them for CCTV. Was anyone seen stumbling out of their premises, apparently drunk and supported by someone else? Look for familiar faces, as whoever drugged her would have been someone she trusted. It's a lot of work, I know, but we owe it to Karen.'

'Just a thought, boss,' said Mel. 'When we interviewed Ricky Marriott, he invited us out for a drink. Could Karen have taken him up on that without telling anyone? I still suspect him of poisoning Jenny Pike, if not the others.'

'It's possible, I suppose. Surely she would have told someone. She strikes me as being pretty level-headed and unlikely to do anything foolhardy.'

'Unlike some,' muttered Jack, but Emma didn't seem to hear.

'OK. Mel and Martin, have an informal chat with Mr Marriott. See if he met Karen last night. Perhaps gently probe where he was during the evening. Don't let him think he's a suspect.'

'Will do, guv,' replied Martin.

Ricky Marriott stepped briskly into the reception area at the *Mexton Messenger* and greeted the two police officers.

'Hello. I seem to be rather popular with the force these days. Have you brought me news about my would-be poisoner?'

'I'm afraid not, sir,' replied Martin. 'We wanted to talk to you about a different matter.'

'Oh? What's that?'

'It's about our colleague, DC Groves,' said Mel. 'You met her, with me, yesterday.'

'Of course. I remember. How can I help?'

'We're trying to trace her movements yesterday evening and we wondered whether you had seen her, by any chance.'

'No. I haven't.' He adopted a puzzled expression. 'I'm not sure why you are asking me.'

'Do you recall asking both of us out for a drink? Perhaps she took you up on that.'

'Alas, no. But the offer is still open if either of you is interested.'

A cheeky grin replaced his puzzlement as he looked directly at Mel.

'But why do you need to know? Is she missing, or something?'

'Why would you think that, Mr Marriott?' responded Martin.

'Well, tracing someone's movements usually means they are either missing or are suspected of a crime, doesn't it? And I'm sure it's not the latter. Has something happened?'

'We'll get to that in a moment,' said Mel. 'You wouldn't, by any chance, have seen her in a pub or bar last evening?'

'Well I visited a few. The Cat and Cushion, the White Rabbit and a couple of wine bars – The Mexton Grape and Freaking Merlot. Also that craft beer pub, Alestorm, and the biker bar Denim and Leather. I didn't come across her.'

'All right. Thank you. That's a lot of pubs, if you don't mind my saying so.'

'It's research, DC Cotton. I'm working on crime stories and I like to talk to local people. And I don't drive home. I haven't yet plucked up the courage to visit the Fife and Drum. I think I'd need a bodyguard.' He laughed nervously.

'Well, I'm sorry to tell you that DC Groves was involved in a vehicle collision last night and it looked as though she had been drinking. We would like to find out where and with whom.'

'Oh, I'm really sorry to hear that. Have you got who hit her?'

'Not yet. She is still in a coma, but if and when she wakes up, she may be able to tell us what happened.'

Marriott looked shocked.

'Will she wake up? Can they tell?'

'The doctors aren't saying anything publicly, I'm afraid, but I can tell you she was badly hurt.'

'That's dreadful. People drive so carelessly these days, don't they?'

Martin nodded and the two officers thanked him and took their leave. As soon as they left the paper's offices Mel exploded.

'The bastard knew. Did you see his face when I said she was still alive? He was shit-scared. And he asked who hit her, so he knew it wasn't a vehicle-on-vehicle collision.'

'I agree. We'll report back and start checking where he said he was yesterday. There's a photo on the paper's website we can take round the pubs to find out where he's been and whether anyone saw him with a woman resembling Karen. I'll get a photo of her off the system and find out how Trevor's got on with tracking her phone. We'd better put a guard on her hospital room in case whoever did this tries again.'

Chapter Ninety-Eight

Day 50

'Karen's still in a coma,' said Emma, the anger in her voice barely suppressed, when she called the team together, 'and we've put a guard on her hospital room. She hasn't made much progress, I'm afraid, but at least she hasn't got any worse. The doctors say she probably won't remember anything when she wakes up. If she wakes up. So, results, please. Where were those two on the night Karen was hit?'

'Marriott's story checks out, at least in part,' said Mel. 'Bar staff at most of the places he mentioned recalled seeing him, early in the evening, but not with a woman. He just chatted to staff and other drinkers for a while and then left. We looked at places close to the path Karen's phone took and there was one wine bar where staff recognised him from his photo. They said he met a woman but they didn't recognise Karen. I'm not surprised, since her official force photo is old, and she was wearing make-up and her hair was different when we found her. Their CCTV has been broken for several days, so we've no images of the two people there. Marriott did mention going to the wine bar, but denied seeing Karen when we spoke to him.'

'How about later on? And what about that photo from Karen?'

'We tracked her phone to a residential suburb south of the town centre,' replied Trevor. 'It's mainly flats and maisonettes, with hundreds of people within the area identified by the tracking data. But guess who owns a flat in one of the buildings there?'

'Ricky Marriott,' chorused several detectives.

'Exactly. And the photo was taken in the same general area. So can we go in and nick him?'

'Not just yet,' said Emma. 'There's one more piece of evidence we need. I'll get approval to track Marriott's phone. If we can show that its movements parallel Karen's phone's, we've got a much stronger case for his involvement in her assault. But we still don't have enough to link him with the poisonings.'

'Sod the poisonings,' said Jack, angrily. 'Karen's the priority at the moment.'

'I agree,' replied Emma, 'I'm not forgetting that. But we need to get him for the whole bloody lot at the same time.'

Jack grunted his agreement.

'Did we get any forensics, guv?' asked Martin,

'There were fibres on her coat, but they could have come from anywhere. No traces of anything from the vehicle that hit her. There were some shoe marks in mud beside the road, next to hers, but they were indistinct and had no unusual features. They did suggest that someone was with her, though. I can't imagine why she would be out there on her own, at that time of night, full of alcohol and ketamine.'

'Any luck with ANPR?' asked Jack.

'I've pulled up some records,' replied Trevor. 'There wasn't much traffic around the time Karen was found, and

I've been able to eliminate most of the drivers. There are two vehicles I'm still looking at. A small dark van with dirty number plates and another van, paler, registered to a company that doesn't seem to exist. The camera was about a mile from the scene on the Mexton side, and looking at the timings, the phone call was made just a few minutes after the pale van was picked up. So, I reckon that van driver made the call.'

'So why didn't the driver stop?'

'Well, either he hit Karen or was up to something and didn't want to speak to the police,' said Addy.

'Exactly. So we need to find that van,' said Emma. 'Can you do anything with the other one?'

'We can't enhance the photo of the dirty plates, I'm afraid,' replied Trevor. 'It's not like on the telly. But a mate of mine in Traffic reckons it's a Transit. The offside rear light wasn't working, which will help if we ever find a suspect vehicle.'

'OK. Thanks. I'll let the DCI know that we're treating this as attempted murder. Get to it, folks. I'll not have people attacking members of my team. Changing the subject,' Emma continued. 'How are we doing with Valentina's blackmail victims?'

'All but two have been interviewed: a councillor and the head of a local charity,' replied Trevor. 'Martin and I will take the councillor, and Mel and Addy will see the charity bloke. His office is just over the road. The suspected paedophiles have been arrested and I sat in on the interviews. One admitted he was being blackmailed by Valentina but has a solid alibi for the night of her murder. Everyone else we've spoken to denied knowing her or being blackmailed by anyone.'

'Unsurprising, I suppose. How about Valentina's past, Mel? Did you find anything there?'

'No, boss, not a thing. I thought it was a long shot.'

'Yes, but no stone unturned, lass. We had to look. OK. One other thing. The Environment Agency CCTV picked up an image of the shooter. It looks like one of the clowns who were threatening Stefan Paweski. It's not clear enough to charge him, but we'll get the SOCOs to seize their clothes and have them tested for gunshot residues. You never know. We might get something. They've not said anything in interview, though.'

'Too scared to speak, I expect,' said Martin.

'You're probably right. Thanks, guys,' Emma said, and closed the briefing.

Chapter Ninety-Nine

'We've had some luck with the pale van, guv,' said Trevor. 'An unmarked traffic patrol spotted it in Merchant Street and discreetly followed it to a lockup on the industrial estate. They didn't get a chance to see if it was damaged. I asked them to keep an eye on it, and it's still there.'

'OK,' said Emma, excitement building in her voice. 'Get round there and grab him. Take a couple of uniforms with you in case of bother. Ask him to come with you voluntarily, but if he won't, arrest the bugger. And blue light it in case he moves.'

'You bet,' replied Trevor, excited at the prospect of a fast journey with blues and twos going.

By the time they arrived at the lockup the light was fading and little was happening on the industrial estate. A van pulled out of a side road, and Trevor was about to signal it to stop when he realised the number plate and colour were wrong. Twenty seconds later the police car pulled up behind another van, this time with the correct registration. The flashing blue lights on the car cast an eerie glow on the rundown buildings as they swept over them, while two men in overalls, passing on the opposite side of the road, paid scant attention to yet another police vehicle outside the lockups.

'Open up, police,' shouted PC Halligan, banging on the door of the lockup nearest the van.

No-one answered and the PC repeated his call, warning that he would force an entry if necessary. A few seconds later, the door of the lockup made a grinding moan as it opened, and a stocky man in a hoodie and trackies glared defiantly at the police.

'What do you want? I was just going home for my tea.'

The man's West Midlands accent was distinctive.

'We won't keep you a moment, sir,' replied Trevor. 'Is this your van?'

'Yeah, what of it?'

'We'd like to ask you a few questions about it. Would you mind coming down to the station with us?'

'Do I have to? I ain't done anything.'

'Well, we could arrest you, but let's hope it won't come to that.'

'OK. If I must.' The man climbed into the back of the police car with obvious reluctance, perspiring and trembling slightly.

Interview room three was hot and stuffy, the temperature accentuating the smell of sweat, farts and smoke-saturated clothing. The arrested man gave his name as Roy Garnett, acknowledged the caution and declined the services of a solicitor. Trevor switched on the recording equipment and made the formal introduction, with Addy beside him.

'So what's this all about?' he asked. 'Is there something wrong with my van? I haven't been speeding. I can't afford to get another ticket. I've too many points already.'

'It's not that, Mr Garnett,' replied Trevor. 'Would you mind telling me where your van was two nights ago, at around twelve o'clock?'

'At the lock up. I don't use it at night.'

'And what do you use it for during the day?'

'Shifting stuff. Deliveries. Whatever people want moved.'

'OK. And do you let anyone else drive it?'

'No. Just me. Why?'

'You're sure you weren't driving it at the time I mentioned?'

'Course not. I was at home. Watching football on the telly.'

'Was anyone with you?'

'No. My girlfriend doesn't like footie. She was out with her mates.'

'Rather late, wasn't it? And what matches are on at that time of night?'

'She likes clubs. And I've got Sky Sports. What's this all about?'

'Well, the reason I'm asking is that your van seems to have been involved in a serious collision with a pedestrian. I noticed that part of the nearside wing of your van appears to have been resprayed very recently. Would you like to say anything about that?'

'Nothing to do with me, mate. I wasn't driving it. Someone must have borrowed it.'

'So are you saying that someone borrowed your van without your knowledge, hit someone, had it resprayed overnight and returned it to where they found it by the time you needed it for work the following day?'

'I'm not saying anything. I took a day off, so I wouldn't have noticed. All I'm saying is I wasn't driving, I didn't kill anyone and I don't know anything about a respray. All right?'

Garnett continued blustering until Trevor held up his hand to silence him.

'Mr Garnett, I didn't say anything about a death. What made you say that?'

'I...er...well...you wouldn't be questioning me if she was only injured.'

'She, Mr Garnett? I didn't mention the sex of the pedestrian.'

Garnett paled and said nothing.

'I'd like you to listen to this recording, if you would. It's a call to the emergency services made at twelve oh five a.m. the night before last. Listen carefully. The voice is muffled but it's quite distinctive.'

Trevor played an audio file on his laptop.

Garnett looked as though he was about to be sick when he heard a voice with a West Midlands accent reporting a 'dead woman' on the Highchester road.

'Do you accept that it's your voice on the recording, Mr Garnett?'

'Yes. Yes. It is,' he replied, his voice barely louder than a whisper. 'I'm sorry. I think I need a solicitor now.'

'Yes, Mr Garnett. I think you do. I'm arresting you on suspicion of careless driving, failing to stop after an accident and perverting the course of justice. If the pedestrian dies, you will also be arrested on suspicion of causing death by dangerous driving.'

Trevor repeated the caution while Garnett began to sob, then escorted him to the custody sergeant for processing.

Chapter One Hundred

Day 51

'Karen's woken up,' announced Emma as the team assembled for the morning briefing. 'She's still very woozy, but I managed to talk to her for a few minutes. She has absolutely no memory of being hit by the van or even going anywhere near the Highchester road. She can't say what she was doing during the evening but has a vague recollection of having a drink with someone. She couldn't say who. She emphasised that she would never take ketamine or any other recreational drugs.

'The doctor said she might regain some memories with time. He called it retrograde amnesia. It often happens with trauma, and he thinks it's a way of the brain protecting the mind from frightening memories. Anyway, we'll have to wait and see. She can have visitors but only one at a time, for short periods.'

'I'll pop in and see her this evening,' said Trevor. We'll have a whip-round for some flowers and chocolates or something.'

'Good lad.'

'It was Garnett who hit her,' Trevor continued. 'He thought she was dead but decided he should ring us just in case. A flicker of conscience, I suppose. He wouldn't say what he was doing at that time of night. "Just driving around" were his words, but we had a look in his lockup and found loads of, probably counterfeit, gear there. We'll question him about that later.'

'Did he say how the collision happened?' asked Emma.

'He said she just appeared in front of him. He started to swerve and she bounced off his wing and went flying onto the verge. He couldn't be sure, but he thought he saw someone behind her. No description, though.'

'That ties in with our thinking that she was pushed,' said Martin.

'He got a dent in the wing beaten out and resprayed the following morning. He said he couldn't remember where. Probably one of those dodgy garages near the Eastside.'

'OK. It doesn't sound deliberate and we can't tell if he was under the influence of drugs or alcohol. Bail him on the existing charges. Take someone from trading standards to have a look at the stuff in his lockup, then interview him again.'

'Will do, guv,' replied Trevor.

'We've now got authorisation to track Ricky Marriott's phone. Amira is doing it and comparing its movements to Karen's. If they match, we've got grounds for arrest.

DCI Farlowe looked grave when Emma knocked on his door.

'Come in, Emma, come in. Please sit down. I've got some bad news.'

'What's the matter? Is it Karen?'

'No. It's something else. I've had an email from the Chief Constable. He's requested help from Hants Police to catch this poisoner. A Detective Superintendent John Regan will be with us in a day or so. He'll review everything we've done and make suggestions for improvements. In other words, he'll take over.'

'Shit,' said Emma, forgetting that the DCI disapproved of swearing. 'We've actually got a decent lead. Ricky Marriott. Do we have to have this bloke poking around?'

'We've no choice, I'm afraid. Apparently, he's a highly experienced detective who led the inquiry into an outbreak of food tampering. Someone was putting rat poison in supermarket goods and demanding money to stop. A few people were taken slightly ill, and one of the supermarkets was about to cave in to his demands, when Mr Regan caught him.'

'So how long have we got?'

'A couple of days. I'll try and stall him but the Chief is insistent. I'm happy to authorise overtime if you need officers to work extra hours to catch this menace.'

'Thank you, sir. We are stretched, but I'll let the troops know.'

'What was it you wanted to see me about?'

'I've heard something from the NCA about the Albanians,' said Emma. 'They'd been watching Delvina for a while. He seems to have been part of a syndicate involved in gun running, trafficking young girls and drug importation. The cat thefts were just a sideline, albeit a profitable one. We passed on some of the documents we found in Delvina's office to the NCA and they've come back to us requesting a Teams meeting with us, the Drug Squad, Vice and Cybercrime. There is talk of a joint operation. Can you join in a Teams meeting later on today?'

'Of course. I'm in the office all afternoon. Let me know the details.'

'Thanks, boss. Will do.'

Emma left the DCI's office angry and frustrated. It never looked good, having someone from another force inspecting your work and taking over. Of course, a fresh pair of eyes could be useful, but the implication was that you weren't doing your job properly. An outsider solving the case, after the huge efforts made by her team, would be incredibly demoralising. She knew she shouldn't mind, as long as the killer was caught, but the idea of another force getting the credit rankled with her. At least they had a decent lead, and if it was Marriott, they could have him behind bars before DSup Regan arrived in Mexton.

Oktapod. That's what the bosses called it. The English would call it octopus – many arms reaching out to take what it wanted. Kreshnik was told to set it up in Mexton, a starting point from which its tentacles could spread to many towns in the south of England. It had started well, a gap in the drugs market appearing when the gang that had controlled much of the town was dismantled by the police over a year ago. The rising price of rare metals made catalytic converter thefts highly profitable, and supplying a couple of tonnes of HCFCs added to the income generated by the scrapyards. Computer scams were beginning to produce results, and the three brothels in town, supplied by women trafficked through Portsmouth, had been doing well.

Now, Kreshnik was worried. One of the houses had been raided by the police, and although no links to him and the rest of the organisation had been discovered, as far as he knew, there was always a risk that someone would talk. A recent shipment of cocaine had been intercepted by the Border Force, and this, on top of the collapse of the scrapyards, had meant a serious loss of income. He'd managed to convince his bosses that the protection scheme would be up and running soon, but he had no illusions about what would happen if anything else went wrong. Perhaps he should cut his losses and move on. But where would he go? Oktapod had a long reach and he had seen what happened to anyone foolish enough to cross them. He was glad he had set up an exit strategy. He'd put together some cash, documents and other essentials in a holdall. He hoped he would never have to use it, but it was there. Just in case.

Chapter One Hundred One

Day 52

'Good morning, everyone,' began Emma. 'Yesterday DCI Farlowe, myself, and several local colleagues spent a couple of hours discussing, with the NCA, the Albanian criminal gang that's been making a bloody nuisance of itself in recent months. The upshot is, we are planning a joint operation to take them down. We've identified several criminal activities that we can put a stop to and it's vital we act at each site simultaneously, so the suspects don't have a chance to bugger off. I know it's short notice, but we are worried that recent arrests may have spooked them. It happens tonight and we need some volunteers to take part.'

Emma introduced three visitors to the team.

'Now, you all know DC Tom Ferris, from cybercrime, and DS Derek Palmer from the drug squad. Can I introduce DS Idle from Vice? He's known as Petal, for obscure musical reasons,' she smiled, 'but his real name is Mark.'

Several officers chuckled.

'Why's that?' whispered Mel to Jack.

'Edelweiss. Idle vice. Dreary song from *The Sound of Music,*' he replied.

'Know-it-all,' sniffed Mel.

'When you're ready,' continued Emma, sharply. 'We are planning to do warrants at several premises in and around Mexton. Our team will be helping Tom to take down a cyber fraud operation, run from domestic premises on the outskirts of town. Over to you, Derek.'

'Thanks. I'll be co-ordinating an op on a warehouse where, we believe, Class A drugs are handled. It's on the industrial estate and we've been watching it for a while. Vehicles belonging to known dealers have been visiting it at odd hours, and the Border Force alerted us to a suspicious van that came through the channel tunnel yesterday. It was tracked to Mexton and appeared on an ANPR camera near the warehouse. This suggests they've had a recent delivery, so we don't want to hang about.'

'Thanks, Derek. Let us know how we can help. Mark – what are you planning?'

'Last week we rescued a number of trafficked young women from a brothel in central Mexton. From documents and electronic devices we found there, we identified two other premises that, we believe, are used for the same purposes. These are currently under observation, in the hope that we will be able to determine who is controlling them. We will go in at the same time as the other entries, with someone from the NCA Modern Slavery and Human Trafficking Unit who will help to look after the women's welfare. We will have translators on standby, although we don't, as yet, know what languages the women speak.'

'Thanks, Mark. So, we need a couple of volunteers to accompany Tom's unit. The rest of you, please focus on tracking Marriott. As most of you know, these Albanians are extremely dangerous. They tried to kill Trevor and Phil, shot up the Environment Agency and nearly burned down a shop. One of them murdered two of his own men and then made an AFO shoot him. Another man was beaten and stabbed to death, we think because he failed in a task. There will almost certainly be firearms in play, so we will have armed support in place at all the premises. Do not take any risks. No more heroes, please.

'It is vital that they don't get any advance warning, so please don't discuss these ops outside this room. We don't think they have a mole in the station, but we can't be a hundred percent certain. It's all happening at eleven tonight, so prepare yourselves. There will be a final briefing, for all officers taking part, at nine this evening. In the meantime, come and talk to one of us if you need anything more. Thank you.'

Chapter One Hundred Two

'Armed police! Come to the door with your hands on your heads. Leave any weapons behind and do exactly as you're told,' shouted the lead firearms officer, as the Big Door Key smashed the door open. No-one replied to the commands, repeated several times, so a firearms dog was sent in, provoking a stream of Albanian curses from an upstairs room. These were drowned out by the thunder of boots on the uncarpeted stairs as AFOs cleared the building, a small semi-detached house on the outskirts of town.

'Any weapons?' called Tom, as he cautiously entered the hall once the AFOs had declared the premises safe.

'No, you can come up,' an AFO replied. 'The suspects are in the back room.'

Mel and Tom followed the officer's directions and saw two young men prone on the floor, their hands cuffed behind them. An array of computer equipment sat on a couple of desks in front of a slightly open window, humming gently. Tom rushed towards it and cursed.

'The bastards are running delete programs.'

He shut the lids on two laptops and pulled the power cable out of the back of a desktop machine.

'With a bit of luck, we should be able to retrieve something. Hang on. There's one missing. Did you see them do anything with another laptop?' he asked an AFO, who shook his head. 'There's some leads and a space here, and this charger is warm.'

The two detectives searched the room, finding no other technology apart from a variety of mobile phones, which they bagged up for forensic examination. Just as they were about to leave, Tom looked again at the desks and peered at the window.

'Can you have a look beneath this window, Mel, in case they chucked something into the garden?'

'Yes, boss,' she replied, pretending to be sarcastic. Tom grinned.

A few minutes later, Mel pushed open a half-rotted wooden gate at the side of the house and switched on her phone's torch. The gate moved easily on oiled hinges, despite its derelict condition. Slightly suspicious, she pulled out her baton and moved forward, her senses alert for a threat. She heard a shrieking sound but quickly dismissed it as the call of a randy fox. Then a dark shape charged at her, knocking the phone from her hand. She almost fell but manged to lash out at her assailant, catching him on a knee with her baton as he rushed past. He stumbled and Mel threw herself at him in a crude rugby tackle, wincing as her shoulder hit the ground. He crashed forward, but his elbow caught Mel on the side of the head, temporarily stunning her and forcing her to let go. A flash of silver, as the moon appeared from behind a cloud, revealed a wiry man struggling to stand up, clutching a laptop under his left arm.

'Police!' shouted Mel, although she knew full well she had been identified as such. The man staggered to his feet and reached into his pocket, and she heard the click of a flick knife opening. Moonlight glinted on the blade as he drew back his right arm to thrust it at her face. Mel froze at the sight of the knife.

'Fuck off, police bitch,' he snarled.

The noise had attracted the attention of an AFO who was stowing his equipment away in the van. As he ran down the side of the house towards them, Mel forced herself to move and retrieved her baton from the ground. She smashed the end into her attacker's arms and shoulders, over and over again, screaming 'Bastard' with every blow, until he dropped the laptop and the knife. In a desperate, limping, run he headed away from the house, pulled over a couple of recycling bins to impede pursuit and scaled a low wall at the end of the garden. As Mel and the AFO reached the wall, they heard the staccato sound of a small motorbike starting up. Mel hauled herself onto the wall with one arm, but by the time she caught a glimpse of it, the bike was hurtling along a narrow lane, with no lights or number plate visible.

'Fuck this,' she swore, dropping to the ground and collapsing, trembling, onto a rusty garden bench. 'Thanks, mate,' she said to the AFO. 'Good job you came along. He was about to slash me.'

'No problem at all,' he replied. 'But you went a bit OTT with your baton, didn't you? Not that I saw anything.'

'Perhaps. But I've got a thing about blades since someone tried to take my head off with a sword.'

'Fair enough. Pity he got away, but at least you got that laptop.'

'Yeah. Tom will be pleased with that. But it would have

been nice to have collared him. God, I ache and my shoulder's burning. I must be getting too old for this shit.'

Mel walked wearily back towards the house, feeling ashamed that she had lost control. She'd never done that before, even when policing riots as a uniformed constable. Fuck. If the suspect complained, she could lose her job. It was way beyond reasonable force. And what would her dad think? She wouldn't be able to look him in the eye, ever again, if she was dismissed from the service.

She picked up the laptop, which seemed to have landed in a flowerbed, judging by the soil smeared over it, and slipped it into a plastic evidence bag. What was so important about this one, she wondered? Presumably the men upstairs had alerted someone to pick it up, as the gang couldn't afford to let it fall into police hands. He must have been local, as he got here bloody quick. It would be really interesting to see what Amira and her colleagues in computer forensics discovered. For now, she would give the machine to Tom. It was a pity she hadn't made her attacker bleed, she thought, or there might have been some forensics from the fight. Still, there might be something on the laptop or the knife. He hadn't been wearing gloves.

Chapter One Hundred Three

Day 53

'An excellent night's work,' said Emma at the morning briefing. 'Tom and Mel recovered a shedload of IT from their site, which Amira is working on as we speak. One of the laptops seemed to be particularly significant, so she's prioritising that. It's heavily encrypted but she'll manage to crack it, I'm sure. We have two suspects in custody and they aren't talking.

'Derek and his guys discovered several kilos of coke at the warehouse as well as quantities of ecstasy and benzos. There was a small amount of heroin, too. Five Makarov pistols and a hundred rounds of ammunition were found in a crate. Three men were arrested, still going "No comment", and their phones will be analysed when there's time. We also stopped one of the known local dealers, leaving the premises with cocaine in his van. He'll be charged with possession with intent to supply Class A.'

'How about the knocking shops?' someone asked.

'Eight women were rescued and are now being looked

after. They're from several different countries in Eastern Europe and don't speak much English, so getting statements from them will be a lengthy process. The NCA is helping. As to arrests, three men and two women were picked up and are being questioned by Mark's team. We'll be celebrating in the Cat and Cushion tonight, but now we've got work to do.'

The body of a young man, broken and bloody, lay at Kreshnik's feet. A simple task. Collect the laptop from the garden and bring it to him. But he'd failed, and been defeated, by a woman of all things. He spat on the body and kicked it again as his contempt boiled over. Beating Zelic to death, with fists, feet and a hammer, had given him some satisfaction, but he knew it wouldn't protect him from the wrath of Oktapod. They would hold him responsible, no matter who else he punished. The information on the laptop couldn't be more sensitive, and he knew his life in Mexton was over. One way or another.

Slipping out of the office, which the police hadn't yet found, he shrugged on an overcoat that hid much of the blood on his suit. He would wipe down the trousers and shoes later. Holding tight to a small holdall, containing his escape kit, he flagged down a passing taxi and asked the driver to take him to Gatwick Airport. He should have been suspicious when the driver didn't query the distance or quote an exorbitant fare. When he sat back in the car and heard the child locks click he realised his error. As the car pulled away a wiry man uncoiled himself from the passenger seat and aimed a pistol at his head. Nikolla. Oktapod's enforcer.

The smell of urine filled the car, masking the odours of sweat and uncleaned upholstery, as Kreshnik contemplated his fate and lost control of his bladder.

Chapter One Hundred Four

Nikolla was not a sadist. He didn't do his job because he particularly enjoyed inflicting pain or killing people. But he had a set of skills that ensured he got the work done and pleased his employers. Pleased employers paid him well, and that was the part he liked.

He had slipped into the country via a small airfield in Northamptonshire and would leave by an even smaller aerodrome in Somerset. He always travelled light and had no time for fancy instruments or obscure poisons. Military expertise, a knowledge of anatomy and some basic tools, available in any hardware store, enabled him to discharge all his duties, from discreet assassination to extracting information. Today, however, he was told to send a clear message, and that's what he would do. Emphatically.

Emma suited up, signed the log and ducked under the cordon tape with trepidation. The PC who called it in, commendably holding on to his breakfast until he had moved clear of the scene, had said it was unpleasant but declined to give details. Emma could see why. The flabby, naked body of a middle-aged, overweight man, skin pasty in the glare of the SOCOs' lights, was tied to one of the posts that supported the roof of the old barn. He had clearly been badly beaten and several of his fingers appeared to be broken. He was missing an ear and several teeth. The only thing preventing him from slumping on the floor was the thin-bladed chisel shoved through the side of his throat and embedded in the post. Bright trails of blood snaked down his shoulder and chest, like strawberry sauce on an ice cream, suggesting that the man hadn't been dead very long.

Emma shuddered and turned to Dr Durbridge, who had stepped up quietly beside her.

'What do you think, Doctor?' she asked.

'Nasty. Give me a minute to examine him,' he replied, brusquely.

Ten minutes later he spoke again. 'This is just a preliminary opinion, you understand, but he was tortured before he died. It was almost certainly the chisel that killed him. It looks as though the killer pushed it through the side of his neck, avoiding the spine and the major blood vessels. He was very skilled. The tool sliced into his trachea – windpipe – and cut other blood vessels that would have slowly haemorrhaged into his lungs. In effect, he drowned in his own blood. Of course, I may need to revise my view once I've opened him up, so don't quote me, please. But that looks the most likely cause of death.'

'Thank you doctor. As soon as the SOCOs have finished we'll get him to the mortuary. I'll take a quick look round and then go back to the office. Given this level of violence, I have a suspicion about who's behind it, but we do need to identify the body.'

'We have an update on the Albanian gang,' said Emma, when the team convened. 'The laptop Mel retrieved was pure gold dust. Amira was able to get into it and found details of all the gang's operations in Mexton and the surrounding areas, as well as plans for expansion to much of southern England. It's now with the NCA, who nearly wet themselves with glee when we handed it over. It seems that they were part of an international OCG called Oktapod – octopus to you and me – and the NCA will be sharing information with colleagues overseas. A real result, so well done, lass.'

Mel looked slightly embarrassed.

'It was Tom who spotted that something was missing,' she said. 'If he'd been two minutes slower, the bloke in the garden would have taken it away.'

'True, but you grabbed it. Anyway, there was also useful stuff on the other computers. They tried to delete it, but Amira managed to recover most of the material, including details of the various cyberscams, bitcoin frauds, potential victims and electronic money trails. Tom's colleagues will be in touch with some of the targeted people, when they have enough fit staff to do so.'

'What about the tortured guy?' asked Addy.

'We had no DNA or fingerprints on record, and there were no identifying documents at the scene, but we sent his prints to Interpol. They had a match. His name was Kreshnik Osmani. He had convictions in various countries for violence, drug trafficking and brothel keeping. He seems to have been the local head honcho for the gang. We are assuming that his bosses held him responsible for the collapse of the gang's activities in Mexton and, probably even more importantly, the loss of the laptop. Pictures of his body have already appeared on several social media platforms, presumably as a warning to others. They were taken down quickly but the message is out there. There were no useful forensics from the scene, and whoever did the job is, no doubt, long gone. We've contacted the NCA and will be liaising with them over a full investigation. They'll be sending a couple of people to help. Now, we need to focus on the poisoner and also interview the charity guy and that councillor.'

Chapter One Hundred Five

Councillor Howard Plessey, a florid man in a tweed jacket, check shirt and cavalry twill trousers, looked nervous as Martin and Trevor introduced themselves in the Town Hall foyer. He led them to an unoccupied side room, surreptitiously wiping sweat from his face, and motioned them to sit in a couple of scruffy plastic chairs that faced a chipped table. Sitting on the other side, he put on his best fake smile.

'How can I help you, officers?' he asked.

'Just a couple of questions, if you don't mind,' began Martin, adjusting his facemask. 'Do you know a woman called Valentina Malenka?'

A fleeting expression of panic flashed across Plessey's face.

'No. I don't think I do. Is she one of my constituents?'

'Not as far as I know, sir. She was murdered in the town centre a few weeks ago.'

'Oh dear. That's terrible. But why do you want to speak to me?'

'Your name came up during the course of our investigation,' replied Trevor. 'We recovered some computer files belonging to Ms Malenka and you featured in them.'

'What sort of files?'

'Copies of documents that look like planning applications. You are on the planning committee, aren't you?'

Plessey nodded, apparently unable to speak.

'There is also some video footage of you, with a couple of scantily clad young women, possibly at a nightclub or party. Can you tell us if anything in that material could leave you open to blackmail?'

Plessey had gone pale, the drops of sweat on his face standing out like jewels on a slab of raw pastry.

'I've done nothing wrong, I swear. It's just that some of the things there could be...er...misinterpreted.'

'Misinterpreted? In what way?' asked Martin, his voice neutral.

'That party. It was to celebrate the opening of a new health club. I supported the planning application in committee, so the developer invited me. The girls were very friendly. That's all. But my wife is a deacon at our local church, and if she saw the pictures she might jump to the wrong conclusion.'

'Ah. I see. And if we looked into the granting of the planning consent, would we find anything irregular?'

'N...no. No. Of course not.'

'So can you categorically state that Valentina Malenka was not blackmailing you?'

'No. I mean yes. As I said, I didn't know the woman.'

'Right. Thank you, sir. One more thing. Where were you on the night of the seventeenth of last month, between ten p.m. and two a.m.?'

Plessey looked shifty.

'Er. Out driving, I think. I may have gone for a drink. I can't remember. It was weeks ago. We've been really busy here, with Covid absences, and I can't keep track of everything I do.'

A tone of defiance pushed through his nervousness.

'Can anyone confirm this? Just for elimination purposes, you understand.'

'I shouldn't think so. Well, possibly. I don't know.'

'Perhaps you would let us know when you come up with something,' said Trevor, as the two officers stood up to leave. 'Here's my card. Thank you for your time.'

'Well, what do you think, Trev?' asked Martin, as they climbed into the police car.

'He's hiding something. No doubt about it. I'm sure the scenes in that video weren't as innocent as he claimed, and I'll bet he took a backhander to steer that planning application through. Not our job to investigate at the moment, though. Whether or not Valentina had got round to blackmailing him, your guess is as good as mine. But could he be a murderer, do you think?'

'Anyone could be, if the stakes are high enough,' said Martin, emphatically. 'He seemed a bit weedy, but he could be strong enough to have stabbed Valentina. The boss said it looked like the killer knew how to stab people effectively, but it may have been just a lucky blow.'

'Well, we certainly can't rule him out. I'll see if his car was picked up on ANPR and CCTV anywhere near the murder scene.'

'Good plan. Now let's get back to the station. I'm dying for a cuppa.'

Chapter One Hundred Six

THE CHARITY'S office was based in a disused shop, the window of which served to advertise its purpose. In front of a backdrop of battle scenes, a mannequin in army uniform, one arm in a sling, held out a hand as if in supplication. A banner bearing the words 'Mexton Says Thanks' stretched the width of the window, with a smaller slogan beneath it saying 'Help those who helped us'. A poster gave details of how to contact the charity and donate to the cause.

A bell jingled as Addy pushed open the door, and again when Mel closed it. They were greeted by a smartly dressed, middle-aged man with a military moustache, sitting behind a desk at the back of the room.

'Hello. Please excuse me for not getting up.'

He gestured to the crutches propped against the wall behind him.

'What can I do for you?'

'Good morning, sir,' replied Mel. 'We're police officers. Are you Mr Angus Johnson?'

The man bridled slightly. 'Major Johnson, if you don't mind. Formerly of the Royal Green Jackets.'

'I apologise, Major,' replied Mel. 'Could you spare us a few minutes? We'd like to ask you a couple of questions.'

'Apology accepted.' The man smiled thinly. 'What's it about?'

'Does the name Valentina Malenka mean anything to you?'

Johnson thought for a few moments.

'No. I don't think so. Wait a minute. Wasn't her name in the local paper? Found dead, if I remember correctly.'

'I'm afraid so,' said Addy. 'She was murdered on the night of the seventeenth of last month.'

'Good Lord. But what's that got to do with me?'

'Your name came up in connection with the investigation. We wondered if you knew her.'

'I certainly didn't. And what's this connection, anyway?'

Johnson became increasingly irritated and glared at the two detectives.

'Ms Malenka was a blackmailer, sir,' replied Mel, consulting her notebook.

'Her cottage was burned down but we retrieved her blackmail material from her cloud account. We discovered your name, along with images of documents that appear to show some suspicious payments from your charity to another account. There was a video, too. Was she blackmailing you?'

'Certainly not. I've never had any contact with the woman.' Johnson's face flushed. 'And there's nothing she could blackmail me about. For God's sake, I took a round in the spine in Afghanistan in 2015 defending our way of life and you have the nerve to come into my office and accuse me of doing something reprehensible. I think you've taken up enough of my time. I'm busy trying to get people like me the help and support they deserve.'

'All right sir,' said Mel, her hands held up in a placatory gesture. 'Just one more thing. Can you tell us where you were on the seventeenth of last month, between ten p.m. and two a.m.?'

'At home. When I'm not here or shopping I'm in my converted flat. And, yes, I was alone. I keep myself to myself and don't encourage visitors. Is that all?'

'Yes, sir. I have to warn you that a financial investigator will be looking at the documents, in due course, and we may need to talk to you again Thank you for your time.'

Johnson glared at the detectives and swung himself nimbly onto his crutches to see them out, locking the door behind them.

'He didn't like that, did he?' said Mel as they walked the few yards back to the station.

'Can't really blame him,' said Addy. 'My dad served in the Falklands and saw plenty of his mates injured and unable to cope when the Army let them go. You can't eat a medal or an honourable discharge.'

'Fair point. But I reckon Valentina did have something on him. I don't reckon him as the killer, though. He may be angry, but he couldn't wield a knife while on crutches. Even if he tried, she would have been able to dodge out of the way.'

'True enough. We'll write this up for tomorrow's briefing. You can get the coffee.'

Mel grinned and swept her card over the keypad that protected the back entrance to the station.

Chapter One Hundred Seven

'So HOW DID you get on with the last of the interviews?' Emma asked, as Mel, Trevor, Addy and Martin joined her in the incident room.

'Nothing concrete, with Councillor Plessey,' replied Martin, 'but he was definitely worried. Valentina may have been blackmailing him, but even if she wasn't, the stuff we mentioned to him provoked a definite reaction. He was clearly scared, so he's certainly been up to something. Playing away or pushing planning applications through for money, possibly. Maybe both. He denied any wrongdoing, of course. But I suppose he could be strong enough to kill if pushed to it, and he gave us no alibi, so I think he's worth a closer look.'

'Right. How about Mr Johnson, Addy?'

'Major Johnson, according to him. Most insistently,' said Mel.

'I think we can rule him out, guv,' Addy continued. 'He was wounded in Afghanistan and can't get around without crutches. He may have been trained to kill but he wouldn't be able to any more.'

'Hang about,' said Trevor, sounding annoyed. 'Didn't you challenge him about the video?'

'No. All it said in the notes was video, shooting, possibly Scotland.'

'Sorry. My mistake. I should have put in more. I was so bloody tired.'

Emma frowned at him.

'A bit of a communication breakdown. I'm sorry,' Trevor carried on. 'The video shows him out on a grouse moor or somewhere, shooting. He's standing up, walking around, climbing into a Land Rover and firing a shotgun. There's no sign of any walking aids. I think our Major Johnson is a fraud.'

'You know the next job, then,' said Emma. 'Contact the MOD and find out all you can about him and his service record. Then we need to take a look at the accounts of his charity. When we've got some more evidence, we'll pull him in for a formal interview. Thanks, you four. It looks like we're getting somewhere at last.'

'Trevor was right, guv,' said Mel, carrying two coffees into Emma's office.

'Ah. Thanks, lass. Just what I needed. Right about the galloping major, you mean?'

'Yes. There's no mention of a Major Angus Johnson having served in the Army in recent years, and certainly not in Afghanistan. He was never wounded in action. What's more, he said he was in the Royal Green Jackets and was shot in 2015, but the regiment was disbanded in 2007, after action in Basra. He's a total fraud. I suppose I should have suspected him. There was something in the way he moved on those crutches that didn't look quite right.'

'So he's perfectly capable of stabbing someone.'

'Absolutely.'

'I heard that,' said Trevor, joining the two women.

'I've had a more detailed look at the bank statements Valentina had in her cloud account. They go back nearly ten years. Most of the money coming in to the charity seems to get diverted to an account in Jersey. Less than a fifth of it appears to be used to help disabled veterans. There were statements from the Jersey bank that showed the diverted amounts. The balance, as of a couple of months ago, was £570,000.'

'Wow,' replied Mel. 'That's a lot of help somebody's not getting. You know we suspected a police officer of being involved, because of the calls to and from Valentina's phone?'

'Go on, Mel,' said Emma.

'Well they could have just as easily come from outside Johnson's premises as from outside the police station. Tracking isn't that precise.'

'Great stuff. I think we've enough to pull him in, on suspicion of fraud and murder. Get over there with a couple of uniforms, you two, and arrest him. And don't forget your stab vests.'

Chapter One Hundred Eight

When Mel, Trevor and two PCs approached the Mexton Says Thanks office, it was closed and there were no lights showing. Repeated banging on the door produced no response, although the shop was still supposed to be open.

'Looks like he's done a runner,' said Mel. 'Can one of you go round the back in case he's here and tries to escape? We'll give it two minutes and then force an entry.'

Two minutes later, PC Halligan used the Big Door Key to smash the door open.

'Police. Show yourself,' he shouted.

Mel and Trevor followed him in and scanned the room. It was obvious that someone had left in a hurry. Either that or the place had been burgled. Filing cabinet drawers were left open, bulging plastic bags leaking fragments of paper stood next to a shredder and the smashed pieces of a computer hard drive were strewn across the shabby carpet. A pair of crutches, propped up in a corner, made it clear that Johnson could walk unaided.

Trevor phoned Emma.

'He's bolted and tried to cover his tracks, guv. The chat we had with him must have frightened him off.'

'OK. I'll get Martin to trace his car through ANPR.'

'One other thing. There's an empty box of cartridges for a twelve-bore shotgun but no sign of a weapon or a gun cabinet.'

'Shit. We need armed support. First step is to check his home address and see if Johnson or the weapon's there. I'll organise it. Come back to the station once you've secured the premises. We may need forensics in there.'

'OK, boss.'

Angus Johnson peered through the window of his flat at the flashing blue lights, two storeys below. He saw the armed officers pouring out of the back of the discreet, dark van and realised that he was facing a life sentence. His claustrophobia would make that unbearable. Sod that for a game of soldiers, he thought, and debated with himself about shooting his way out. Impossible. He had a double-barrelled shotgun and a dozen cartridges. They had pistols and carbines with plenty of ammunition. Anyway, he had no wish to harm the police. The only person he hated was that bloody bitch who had blackmailed him. When he torched her cottage he had been sure that he'd destroyed all the evidence. He even went back to check. Now, he cursed himself for forgetting that she might have stored copies in the cloud. If she hadn't, the police would never have had a reason to suspect him of her murder.

He supposed the financial scam would have been discovered eventually, but he had hoped to go on until he reached a million. It was a nice little earner, but something must have attracted the attention of Valentina Fucking Malenka. So, there was only one thing for it. He could not do prison time. He took a large swig of brandy and, with trembling hands, loaded a single cartridge into the left-hand chamber of his shotgun. He pulled back the hammer, placed the butt on the floor, slid the cold steel of the barrels into his mouth and reached down for the trigger.

Armed officers rushed into the building and up the stairs to Johnson's flat when they heard the shot. Two guarded the lift, and any residents opening their doors were told to go back inside.

'Armed police,' shouted the lead officer outside Johnson's door.

'Come out with your hands on your head and leave your weapon behind.'

Silence except, perhaps, for a faint dripping sound. After repeated shouts, two officers breached the door and sent in a dog. Still no answer. The officers forced their way in, protected by shields, and pulled up short when they saw the scene in front of them. The flat was immaculate, painted in soothing pastel colours, apart from the back wall and ceiling of the lounge, decorated in the style of Jackson Pollock with blood, brain tissue and bone fragments.

'Someone'll have to get down to B&Q for a tin of paint or two,' quipped one of the officers.'

'You're not wrong,' the other AFO replied, approaching the body, after checking the rest of the flat was clear. He radioed the Tactical Firearms Commander.

'Looks like he's shot himself, guv. There's no-one else here. We've recovered a replica revolver but no other weapons, apart from the shotgun he used. I'll wait for the SOCOs and make it safe when they've photographed everything.'

Chapter One Hundred Nine

Day 54

'So, it looks as though we've got Valentina's killer,' said Emma at the morning briefing.

'Well, most of him,' said Mel, prompting a few chuckles from the team.

'It's a pity he didn't go to trial,' continued Emma, frowning. 'We had plenty of evidence against him. SOCOs found a knife of the kind used to kill her in a cupboard. It had been washed, but the lab should be able to get Valentina's DNA from it. They also found a coat, which they're attempting to match to the fibres from Valentina's hand.

'While we wait for the results, we can get back to Karen's attacker and the poisoner. Ricky Marriott is looking increasingly likely. His phone paralleled hers on the night in question but was switched off around eleven o'clock. It came on again at eight in the morning, in the area of his flat. We have no idea where it went between those times, and it's unusual for a journalist to switch off a phone. So, Jack, can you send someone round to Marriott's flat and invite him in for interview? Have him arrested if necessary. You'd better send some bodies to the paper's offices if he's already left for work.

'The DCI is holding a briefing later today. In the meantime, can you all start to get your paperwork in order for the inquest into Valentina's death? It was opened and adjourned pending enquiries. Several of you will have to make statements when it resumes, and there'll also have to be something from us at Johnson's inquest. I'll handle that. Thanks, folks.'

'How was Karen, Trev?' asked Emma, when he returned from the hospital.

'She looked bloody awful, boss. She's in a lot of pain but conscious, although the morphine made her drowsy. She recognised me, which is something, but she couldn't remember anything about the night she was injured. She recalled the interview she and Mel had with Ricky Marriott in the café but didn't think she had seen him since. She had a vague memory of getting ready to go out somewhere, but she couldn't say who with. I took in the photos of the paramedic's uniform that she sent Mel. She said they looked familiar but she couldn't place them.'

'Bugger. Is there any chance she will remember more later on?'

'The doctors said she might recall some things, but the worst bits could be lost for ever. It's a way the mind has of protecting itself. They think she may never be able to testify against her attacker.'

'Shame. I suppose she couldn't say anything about when she would be fit to return? I'm not being callous here, but I know she enjoyed the job.'

'I realise that, boss. I had a word with a doctor, who said she would take weeks to recover physically. She couldn't say how long it would be before she was psychologically fit to come back.'

'OK. Thanks, Trev. I'll make sure she's offered counselling when she's well enough. Are you going in again?'

'Yes. In a few days.'

'I'll be seeing her tomorrow. We'll make sure she gets whatever physio and occupational therapy she needs. It's the least we can do.'

Just as Trevor was leaving, Emma's phone rang.

'DI Thorpe? Yes. Oh shit. Hold on, Trevor.'

The DC turned back.

'Yes, guv?'

'There's no sign of Marriott and he's been off sick for the last couple of days. I'll organise a search warrant. We need to get into his premises as soon as possible. Call the troops together in the incident room.'

'I want Marriott's flat checked over for any signs that Karen's been there,' said Emma, as the team settled down with coffee. 'I've asked for SOCOs to attend, but I'd like Mel and Martin to take a look as well. There may be something there that could indicate where he's gone. The warrant should be available in an hour. Keep this quiet. I don't want any publicity, as it'll scare him off. We'll hold a briefing this afternoon when you get back.

Mel and Martin slipped on blue nitrile gloves as they entered Ricky Marriott's flat. SOCOs had already processed the scene for evidence of Karen having been there, removing items of crockery and also several paramedic's uniforms. Fingerprint powder left abstract patterns on surfaces and the carpet was still slightly damp in places from sprayed Luminol. Mel looked thoughtfully at a poster from Banksy's Dismaland exhibition in Weston-super-Mare.

'Wasn't one of those doubtful cases in Weston-super-Mare?' she asked Martin.

'Yeah. The care home manager.'

'And Marriott did his pharmacy year in the West Country, didn't he, and his MA in Bristol?'

'That's right. So you think he might have gone west?'

'It's a thought. I'll phone Trevor. He might know if there's a connection.'

Two minutes later Trevor phoned Mel back.

'Yesss,' she said. 'Marriott was born in Weston-super-Mare. So he could have a bolt hole down there. Fancy a trip to the seaside? I'll buy you an ice cream or a stick of rock.'

'Maybe,' Martin replied. 'But let's finish searching this place before you start packing your swimsuit.'

'Does Marriott have access to the garden, do you know?' asked Mel, looking pensively out of the window.

Martin shrugged.

'Probably. Ground floor flats often come with a garden. Let's take a look.'

He picked up a ring of keys from a bowl in the kitchen and found one that opened the back door. Much of the garden was neglected and unruly, but a well-dug flowerbed ran alongside a sturdy, padlocked shed. Tall Foxgloves, with their distinctive pink flowers, were easily recognised, but the detectives couldn't identify the others.

'We need a botanist here,' said Mel. 'I wouldn't fancy putting any of these in a salad.'

Martin chuckled.

'You're right. I bet some of his poisons are home grown.

Let's take a look in the shed. There's a padlock key on this ring.'

The door swung open easily and the detectives peered in, coughing slightly at a chemical smell.

'Bloody hell,' said Mel. 'It looks like something out of *Breaking Bad.*'

Along one side of the shed a bench held a range of laboratory equipment, most of which they didn't recognise. Bottles of chemicals stood on top of a floor-standing cupboard, and flagons of water were ranged along the back wall of the makeshift laboratory. A large bucket contained a malodorous liquid, and a face mask and goggles were dangling from a hook beside the door. Two LED lanterns hanging from the roof provided light, and a small gas camping stove sat under the bench, although there was no sign of cooking utensils.

When Martin unlocked the cupboard they both gasped. Jars and bottles with familiar names of poisons, and other things they'd never heard of, filled the top shelf, while plastic bags of plant material lay on the floor. Packets and bottles of medicines sat in a rack fixed to the inside of the door.

'Look,' said Martin. 'Zopiclone. That was in those lads' cider and that care home manager who died suspiciously.'

'We'll need a specialist to deal with this lot,' said Mel. 'We can't let SOCOs at them without a chemist to advise them. We'd better go. My eyes are beginning to sting.'

While Martin re-padlocked the door, Mel phoned Emma and described the scene. She nodded a few times and turned to Martin when the call ended.

'The guv's sending a couple of uniforms to guard the scene until the SOCOs arrive. She's arranging for a Chemical, Biological, Radiological and Nuclear tactical advisor to check the place before they go in and a chemist from the university to help. Meanwhile, we've got to wait, and I'm bursting for a pee.'

'So go behind the shed,' laughed Martin.

'Not bloody likely. I don't know what's growing there.'

'Well hold on and think of deserts.'

Mel blew a raspberry and was about to sit on a plastic dustbin when she realised it could contain evidence. An upturned wheelbarrow sufficed instead and the detectives waited for backup to arrive.

'There's something else,' said Martin. 'There's a key on this ring for a garage. There's a row of them at the back of these buildings. Maybe that's where he keeps his van. I'll take a look when this site's been secured.'

Chapter One Hundred Ten

Day 55

'Ladies and gentlemen,' began Emma, as the team settled down in the incident room. 'Firstly, as you know, Ricky Marriott is our prime suspect for the attempted murder of Karen and the serial poisonings. He's been away from his flat, and his workplace, for several days and his phone is switched off. Mel and Martin searched his premises yesterday and found a frightening store of poisonous material, chemicals and laboratory equipment. Martin also found a lockup containing a dark van. SOCOs looked for traces of Gordon Howell and Karen having been inside the vehicle and found some fibres, which look promising, as well as Karen's pepper spray.

'So, I need everyone working on tracing Marriott as a matter of priority. Talk to his colleagues again. Ask them if he's ever mentioned a country cottage or other bolt hole. Does he have any friends he might be staying with? Check station CCTV in case he's gone somewhere by train. I want him arrested before DSup Regan comes down and makes us all look like idiots. So, get to it.'

'It looks like you've got a reprieve, Emma,' said DCI Farlowe, when she answered her phone. 'DSup Regan won't be coming. He caught Covid at a colleague's leaving do and is off sick. I'm sure we wish him a speedy recovery.'

Was that a hint of sarcasm in her boss's voice, she wondered?

'Sorry to hear that, guv,' she replied, with a similarly ambiguous tone.

'Anyway, do you have anything to report on the poisoner?'

'We believe it's the journalist, Ricky Marriott,' Emma replied. 'We think he has the knowledge to use the poisons and he could have found out what his victims had done through his job and his contacts. The attempt to poison him was a set up, to deflect attention. We also think he put the mercury in Jenny Pike's car. He's after her job. We've searched his premises and found an extensive collection of poisons. Marriott is in the wind and we're looking for him.'

'Good. Sounds like progress at last. Keep me informed, won't you?

'Thank you. Will do.'

Emma cut the call with a feeling of relief. She had dreaded the arrival of the detective from Hampshire. 'We now have a chance to finish the job without hindrance,' she thought. 'And we'd bloody well better get a result.'

Chapter One Hundred Eleven

GRABBING JENNY WAS EASY, although it meant breaking cover and the risk of being spotted. An invitation to Freaking Merlot to discuss a new lead on the poisoner, and GHB slipped in her drink. Just another pissed young woman being helped out of the wine bar by a concerned companion. He steered her into a quiet side street, laid his sleeping victim across the back seats of her own car, pinioned her wrists with plastic cable ties and fixed them to the seatbelt socket so that she couldn't sit up. He took her phone from her bag, removed the battery and then covered her with a blanket. With the driver's seat lowered as far as it would go, and a blonde wig on his head, he reckoned anyone looking at camera footage would assume it was Jenny driving, not her vengeful colleague.

Within fifteen minutes he was out of Mexton and on the A-roads that would take him to the M5 and the deserted premises where his campaign would end. Somewhere on the journey he would stop and use some paint to alter a few of the digits on the number plate. The police might catch up with him eventually. If they did, like the guy in that Australian song, they'd never take him alive.

Jenny Pike clawed her way back to consciousness and was immediately sick. Her head hurt, her mouth felt awful and her limbs were weak. She dimly realised she was in a car, moving fast, and that her hands were tied. She couldn't sit up and started to panic.

'What the fuck's happening?' she slurred. 'Where am I?'

'Stay still or you'll feel worse,' a familiar voice said. 'We're going on a journey and then you're going to set the record straight.'

'Ricky, you bastard. Where are you taking me?'

Jenny's voice became clearer as anger and fear fought with the residual effects of the drug.

'Somewhere private where we can have a nice chat. Now shut up. You're distracting me.'

Ricky put the radio on and the syrupy tones of the Classic FM presenter, announcing Richard Harrison's *Loretta Martin Suite*, filled the car, almost drowning out Jenny's sobs.

When the car stopped, Ricky freed Jenny from the seatbelt socket and produced his replica pistol.

'Get out. Don't try to run and don't scream. I'll happily shoot you if you do.'

'Is that real?'

'Do you want to find out?'

The menace in Ricky's voice chilled her and she complied, leaning on him as her legs could barely function. He pulled open a door covered with painted plywood, led her into a building and sat her in a chair, fixing her ankles to the legs with plastic ties and wrapping nylon rope around her stomach and the back of the chair.

'I'm going to have to leave you for a while,' he said. 'I wouldn't want anyone finding your car. So just to make sure you don't try anything I'm going to send you back to sleep for a while. But I need to make sure you don't make any noise when you wake up.'

He tore a strip of silver gaffer tape from a roll and wrapped it around her face, covering her mouth but keeping her nostrils clear.

"Try not to be sick,' he grinned. 'It wouldn't end well.'

Her eyes widened as she saw Ricky draw some liquid from a small bottle into a syringe.

'Don't worry. It won't kill you. It's just some ketamine. I'm afraid it's not sterile, but I don't suppose that will matter, not in the long run.'

Jenny tried to struggle as he pulled up her sleeve and tied a length of dirty string around her upper arm. He slid the needle into the vein that sprang up and slowly pressed the plunger. A few seconds later, Jenny began to feel drowsy and disoriented. Then her limbs turned to jelly and her head slumped on her chest.

In a secluded lodge not far from Tirana, surrounded by high walls and patrolled by armed guards, three men sat drinking and smoking.

'Kreshnik has paid the price of failure,' said the man sitting behind a desk, obviously the leader.

'We have lost our beachhead in England and hundreds of thousands of euros a month because of his incompetence. Nikolla has made an example of him. It took us a year to set things up in that poxy little country and now we have to start again.'

His manner was calm but there was fury in his pale grey eyes.

'How about the cities? London, Liverpool, Manchester?' asked a bulky man with a network of scars on his face, accentuated, rather than concealed, by a tattoo of a skull.

'They have their own, local, organisations, and other Europeans are also active there. I have said before, we do not want to go to war with other players. At least not yet. When we are stronger over there, perhaps. So, we will find somewhere else to start again. Somewhere like Mexton.'

He spat out the word as if it was a slug that had somehow found its way into his mouth.

'But I have not finished with that shitty little town and its shitty police force. We will pay them back for destroying our operation. Not now, but when the heat has died down and they will not be expecting it. So, finish your drinks. You both have things to do and I must give some thought to Ireland. There could be a market for weapons there soon.'

Chapter One Hundred Twelve

Day 56

'Weston-super-Mare, guv. That's where we think he might be,' said Mel at the briefing.

'He was born there, we found stuff in his flat linked to the town and he may have killed someone who worked in a local care home. Any chance of a trip down there?'

'I'm not sure I can spare you to go paddling at the seaside, Mel, and you can't go alone,' Emma replied. 'We're too busy here. If you find anything else, I'll reconsider. You can give the Avon and Somerset force a ring if you like, in case he's come to their attention.'

Mel looked disappointed but didn't argue. She realised Emma wasn't being deliberately obstructive. A quick call to the local force revealed that Ricky Marriott hadn't crossed their paths and they had no reason to suspect him of anything. The sergeant she spoke to reluctantly agreed to ask patrols to keep an eye out for him, but pointed out that they had plenty on their plate already. Mel thanked him, promised to send him Ricky's photograph, and cursed him under her breath when the call ended.

'Guv. Jenny Pike's missing.' A worried looking Mel knocked on Emma's door.

'She was supposed to come in and give us a further statement about Marriott and she didn't turn up. I phoned the paper and she hasn't been in work all day. Her phone's switched off, too.'

'Shit. You think Marriott's taken her, don't you?'

'Looks like it. I'm sure he tried to poison her and is after her job. Either he's taken her as a hostage or he's got something nasty planned for her. And my money's on the second one. What do you reckon?'

'You're probably right,' Emma sighed. 'OK. Send someone round to her flat in case she's there. Ask Addy to track her car with ANPR. We've impounded Marriott's van for forensics, and his car is still outside his flat. He could have taken hers.'

'On it, boss.'

Mel dashed back to the office and collared Addy. She explained her suspicions to Jack, who sent Trevor round to Jenny's flat. Much as she disliked Jenny's appalling coverage of the police's activities, the thought of the journalist being poisoned by her colleague made her furious.

Emma shut her office door after Mel had left and slumped into her chair. Marriott, if it was him, must be unique among poisoners, she thought. In nearly all the cases she had read about, the poisoner only killed one or two people, usually for money or lust, and was easily caught. Obviously, people like Harold Shipman, the Victorian women who poisoned their babies to collect insurance and the odd maniac like Beverley Allitt and Graham Young didn't fit that picture, but none of these ran around like some toxic vigilante, killing people in ingenious ways and kidnapping journalists. Also, they usually stuck to one poison, although Young used two, not the wide variety of substances used in Mexton. What a peculiar place the town had turned out to be.

'No luck at the flat,' reported Trevor, when the detectives assembled an hour later. 'I borrowed a key from a neighbour and let myself in. There was no sign of a struggle, or any indication she had left in a hurry. The post was on the mat and the bed hadn't been slept in, so she may have been taken last night.'

'Thanks, Trev,' said Emma. 'We'll get on to her phone provider and see if we can track where she went. Any luck with the car, Addy?'

'Some, guv. It was picked up travelling west last night and I followed it into Somerset. Shortly before it would have reached the cameras on the M5, it disappeared. Perhaps Marriot changed the plates or covered them with mud.'

'The M5 goes to Weston-super-Mare. I'm sure that's where he's taken her,' interrupted Mel.

'OK, Mel. You get to go to the seaside after all,' said Emma. 'Go with Jack. Hopefully he won't let you take any risks. I'll let Avon and Somerset know you're coming and ask them to intensify their search for Marriott and also look out for Jenny's car. I wouldn't hold out much hope, though. It's one silver hatchback among hundreds down there, I'll be bound. Right. Off you go.'

Chapter One Hundred Thirteen

When Ricky returned, Jenny was beginning to wake up. She turned her head when she heard the door opening and caught a glimpse of daylight. 'Shit,' she thought. 'I've been here all night.' Ricky hadn't told her where they were, but she could hear the sounds of gulls calling. 'The seaside,' she thought. 'Or a rubbish tip. Gulls get everywhere these days.' She heard the occasional car pass and snatches of conversation outside the building, but nothing distinctive enough to identify where she was imprisoned. Wherever it was, it smelled as though it had been unused for a long time. The air was stale with a slight overtone of damp.

There was little light in the building, apart from a battery-powered lantern that Ricky had switched on when they entered. Its harsh LED glare glinted off a stack of shiny metal chairs leaning against a wall, and she could just make out some metal shelving, holding hard hats and other protective clothing. A row of disused toilet stalls was barely visible at the back of the room.

An aluminium case, of the type photographers use to

carry expensive cameras, sat on the floor a couple of metres from her chair. Ricky saw her looking at the case and smirked.

'Ah yes. My box of tricks. A fine collection of toxic substances I've picked up here and there. Some of them are pure, lifted from the university stores, years ago. Others I've extracted from plants. A few are in their natural state. Organic, you might say, though they're far from health-giving. You'll get a chance to try some later, I expect. For all your clever-clever investigations, you had no idea I was the Mexton poisoner, did you?'

'Now, you're going to do something for me. You're going to dictate a confession, explaining how you stole my work on the poisoner exposé without giving me the credit. You will also apologise for failing to credit all the other work I did, which you claimed as your own. You'll make it clear that I'm a far better journalist than you are. And just to make it easy for you I've written it all down here.'

Ricky unfolded a sheet of paper and held it out.

'You can read it out loud, to rehearse, if you like.' He switched on his phone. 'When you're ready, I'll record your performance and put it all over social media.'

Jenny looked at the sheet of paper. The words danced in front of her eyes but she could make out the gist. Utter rubbish, she thought. She winced as Ricky pulled the tape from her face and glared at him malevolently.

She tried to swallow, her mouth dry.

'C...can't speak,' she croaked. 'Need water.'

'Fuck,' swore Ricky. 'I left it in the car. I'm slipping. I'll get it. Don't go anywhere,' he said, maliciously, as he replaced the tape.

'We've got a hit on Marriott's phone,' called Addy. 'It's in Weston-super-Mare. Near an old pier and a small park, from the look of it. Shit. It's gone off again.'

'Well done,' said Emma. 'Get the details to Jack and Mel and tell them to hurry. They should be near the town by now. Jenny's been gone for hours and she could be in serious danger. I'll get on to Avon and Somerset again.'

Still slightly delirious, Jenny couldn't keep track of time, but realised Ricky had been gone for some while. He must have left the car a long way away, she thought. She struggled with her bonds, but they wouldn't give. She tried sawing the plastic ties that bound her wrists against the edge of the chair seat, but it, too, was plastic and made no impression on them. She started to panic, rocking backwards and forwards in the chair. She realised that she could make it fall over, but there seemed little point as it wouldn't help her escape. The floor seemed hard, as well, and she didn't want to risk a head injury. So, she sat there, quietly crying, until she heard Ricky return.

Ricky slammed the door shut behind him, opened a bottle of water impatiently and held it to her mouth, water cascading down her front.

'Ricky,' she said, her voice becoming clearer as she spoke. 'Why don't you go fuck yourself? You're an irritating little shit and would never have pushed me out of my job. The mercury was you, wasn't it? But it didn't work and now you're going to jail. Still, I suppose you could work on the prison newspaper. I believe they still have them. As to that piece of paper, you might as well wipe your arse with it. I'm never going to read it out.'

Ricky slapped her hard.

'Fuck you,' Jenny cursed. She felt blood in her mouth, its taste metallic. A gleeful expression crept across Ricky's face and he laughed.

'I've got a better idea.'

He opened the metal case, selected a glass jar full of ground-up plant material and tipped some into the water bottle, shaking it up to mix it with the liquid. Standing behind Jenny, he clamped his fingers over her nose and tipped her head back. She jerked and struggled as he forced the water bottle between her lips but she couldn't avoid swallowing the bitter-tasting mixture.

Chapter One Hundred Fourteen

Ricky stood back, looking satisfied. 'You now have a choice. You've just swallowed a fatal dose of hemlock. You probably know that it was the stuff used to execute Socrates. I harvested it on an island not far from here. There's no actual antidote, but if you can get to a hospital in time they can keep you alive until your body gets rid of the poison.'

'Fuck off,' spat Jenny.

Ricky continued.

'You can dictate the confession and I'll call an ambulance when I leave and make sure they know what's inside you. Or I can sit here and watch you die. It's not quick, and you'll be terrified as you lose sensation in your limbs and gradually find it more and more difficult to breathe. By that point, it's probably too late to save you. So, what's it to be?'

'Start recording.'

Ricky smiled and held his phone in front of her face, pressing the record button as she prepared to speak. Jenny cleared her throat, an expression of pure loathing on her face.

'I have worked with Ricky Marriott on the *Mexton Messenger* for a number of months now,' she began. 'During that time, I came to realise that he is a self-obsessed, egotistical, incompetent twat with fuck-all talent. I now know he is a serial murderer, using the cowardly method of poison, and I hope he never gets out of jail. What's more...'

Ricky pulled the phone away and switched it off.

'You stupid bitch. I gave you a chance to save your pointless life. Don't you realise time's running out for you? I'll ask you again when you feel the poison working. Maybe you'll be more co-operative when you can't feel your legs.'

Mel and Jack drove slowly around the area where Ricky's phone had been detected.

'How the hell are we going to find him along here?' groaned Mel. 'There's a bloody great hotel over there, a restaurant, apartments, this park and a couple of odd buildings that look semi-derelict. Where do we start?'

'Well, think about it,' said Jack. 'He's got an unwilling hostage. He won't be in a hotel or anywhere public. He will be indoors, so we can rule out the park, unless he's dumped his phone there, which is unlikely. So, we're looking at somewhere he can hide out without being disturbed. Let's start with that little building over there.'

They drove down a slope and pulled up outside a small shack that looked like a closed-up information centre, Jack thought. Something to do with the derelict pier whose skeletal arms embraced the Bristol Channel.

'There's nothing here,' called Mel, walking round the structure. 'It's locked up and there's no sign of the door being forced. Debris on the ground outside suggests it hasn't been opened for a while.'

'OK,' replied Jack. 'Let's take a look at the hotel. See if they've got any outbuildings he could have got into.'

As Jack drove back up the slope and along the road, Mel scanned the buildings on her side before they reached the hotel.

'Stop!' she shouted. 'Those toilets!'

'Oh, you're not desperate, are you?'

'No, you idiot. They're obviously closed up. But the padlock's missing from one of the doors. I bet they're in there.'

'Well spotted. I'll contact the locals for backup. He's not armed, as far as we know, but it could be useful to have a couple more bodies. We'll park down the slope a bit and approach on foot. We'll listen at the door and wait for the locals to turn up.

Ricky paced angrily around the room like a neurotic hamster, frequently looking at his watch and glaring at Jenny. The noise of vehicles outside made him start and he pressed his ear to the door. Was that a muttered conversation he could hear? He opened the door a crack and caught a glimpse of the two detectives approaching. 'Shit,' he thought. 'Police. They must have traced the phone when I switched it on before. Why the fuck didn't I use a burner?' He jammed a piece of wood under the door to keep it shut and turned to Jenny.

'Not a fucking sound from you, OK? Or I'll really hurt you.'

Jenny looked at him with contempt and took a deep breath, with obvious difficulty. She gave out a quavering scream that resounded through the building, cut short when Ricky slapped her across the face. A few seconds later there was a banging on the door.

'Police. Is there anyone in there?' Jack shouted.

Jenny managed a groan and the banging intensified.

Ricky ran to the metal case, took out a small bottle and swallowed the contents as the door crashed open. He pulled out his replica pistol and aimed it at the two police officers.

'Stay the fuck away or I'll shoot you,' he screamed.

'Come on, Ricky, don't be daft,' said Jack, loudly, while Mel whispered into her radio.

'There's an armed response unit on its way, Ricky,' Mel said. 'They'll be here in a couple of minutes. Put the gun down. We don't want anyone to get hurt.'

'Bollocks they will. They could be anywhere in Somerset, and the chances of them being this close are almost zero. And, anyway, this is Avon and Somerset police not Mexton. You don't have any jurisdiction. I'm not even sure your police radio works here. You're bluffing.'

Mel shrugged.

'You can take that chance if you like, but nobody needs to be shot. Please be sensible.'

Ricky simply sneered.

'So, what's this about, anyway?' Mel asked. 'Why have you kidnapped Jenny?'

'Because she stole my work and made out it was hers. She's full of hemlock, by the way, and slowly dying. If you try to help her, I'll fire.

'You do realise you're going to prison for a long time,' said Jack.

'That's where you're wrong. I swallowed a large dose of aconite when I saw you approaching. I'll never see the inside of a cell. My mouth is tingling already, and by the time I'm too weak to hold the gun, it will be too late. So, stay where you are and watch the pair of us die.'

He waved the weapon at the two detectives to emphasise his point. As he spoke, Jenny Pike started rocking her chair as if convulsing. Mel caught her eye and nodded. Ricky's attention was split between the police and his victim. As Jenny's chair finally toppled, Mel kicked the lantern into a corner, where it glowed feebly. Jack made a dive for Ricky's legs, knocking him backwards. The weapon clattered across the concrete as Ricky crashed to the floor, a stack of chairs tumbling on top of him. Mel pushed the chairs aside, grabbed Ricky's arm, rolled him over and handcuffed him, just as he vomited on the floor.

'How many lives did you lose then, Jack?' she grinned

'None. But I'll need new trousers,' he complained, looking ruefully at the torn leg exposing a tartan sock. 'Now what about these two?'

Chapter One Hundred Fifteen

A LOCAL PATROL car pulled up just as Mel phoned 999 for an ambulance. When she explained that there were two poisoning victims, the call operator told her that an ambulance wouldn't be there for nearly twenty minutes. There had been a major RTC on the M5 near Weston and they were fully stretched. She told Mel to phone the hospital A&E department for advice and said she would try to find an available ambulance car.

'Aconite and hemlock, you say?' said the hospital doctor. 'If the hemlock patient is still breathing when she arrives, we'll get her into ITU and she stands a chance. I'm not so sure about Mr Aconite. There's no antidote, but there are things we could give him to increase his chances.'

'What sort of things?' asked Mel, looking at Ricky's box of poisons.

'Well atropine can help to keep his heart beating.'

'There's some atropine sulfate here, in ampoules. Six hundred somethings. He must have stolen them. And syringes. Can I do anything with them? He's vomiting and I've taken his pulse. It's slow.'

'Desperate measures, I suppose. You're not medically qualified, so I can't actually instruct you what to do. I'd lose my licence if I did. But if someone injected the contents of a couple of those ampoules into a vein it might help the patient. Check his pulse again. If it's below fifty or so, the injections might be a good idea. I'll call for the air ambulance. He'll need dialysis, and our ITU will be full when the hemlock patient arrives. Also, there's a possibility he'll need heart bypass. He'll have to go to Bristol Royal Infirmary.'

'Thank you, Doctor.'

Mel followed the doctor's suggestions while Jack untied Jenny, easing her gently onto the floor. She had hit her head when the chair fell, but was reasonably coherent. When he turned back, Mel was bending over Ricky, a syringe in her hand.'

'What the hell are you doing, Mel?' Jack shouted.

'Saving this bastard's life. Or at least trying to. I'm damned if he'll escape justice.'

Jack stood back and looked disapproving.

'Should you really be doing that? You're not a doctor.'

'Needs must, Jack. He won't thank me, but it's preservation of life, isn't it?'

'I suppose so. Do you need any help?'

'Yeah. Can you clamp his arm so a vein shows up and keep him still?'

The two detectives wrestled with a resisting Ricky until Mel managed to get the needle into a vein and pumped the contents of two ampoules into his arm. Just as they finished, an ambulance car pulled up outside and paramedics rushed into the building. One went to Jenny Pike, oxygen mask in her hand, while the other rushed towards Ricky. Mel explained what she had done, and the paramedic looked surprised.

'Trying to take our jobs, are you?' he said, but a smile showed he wasn't serious.

Five minutes later they heard the air ambulance putting down close by. Ricky was stretchered into the aircraft while the ambulance car took Jenny to Weston General Hospital. Local officers secured the scene and an Inspector questioned Mel and Jack. It was nearly midnight before the two detectives arrived back in Mexton, tired, slightly bruised, but quietly triumphant.

Chapter One Hundred Sixteen

Three months later

THE SOUNDS OF SAWING, digging and hammering drifted across the neighbourhood as builders worked on the aviary for Tom's parrots. Then it all went quiet.

'Err...is that what I think it is?' said Bill to the apprentice, his ruddy complexion paling.

'It's just a Halloween joke, innit?' the lad replied. 'It ain't real. Is it?'

'We'd better call someone. The owners are coppers. We can't pretend we haven't found it.'

Bill reached for his phone and dialled Mel's number.

'Umm...there's something in the garden you should see. You need to come home.'

Mel stared gloomily at the half-buried skull as the forensic anthropologist brushed soil away from the cranium, revealing a suspicious indentation. Half a metre away, the ends of two ribs poked skywards, as if beckoning the sun.

'How long before the guys can start work again?' she asked.

'It could take days to excavate, I'm afraid,' replied Dr Fox. 'We may need to go over the whole garden to make sure we get every bit of the skeleton that's present.'

Mel couldn't resist.

'You mean a fingertip search?'

Dr Fox scowled and resumed her brushing.

'Some people just can't take a joke,' mused Mel, as she phoned Tom with the news. 'Bruce and Sheila will have to wait for their new summer home,' she thought, 'but at least we'll get the garden dug over.'

Epilogue

Ricky Marriott recovered from aconite poisoning and was convicted on eight counts of murder and two counts of attempted murder. He was given a life sentence with a whole life tariff. Mel Cotton and Jack Vaughan received commendations for their part in arresting him, preventing his suicide and saving Jenny Pike.

Three videos from Martina's cloud account, passed by Trevor to the Child Protection Unit, resulted in long prison sentences for the men who featured in them. No-one else was prosecuted as a result of Valentina's blackmail scheme.

The Albanians arrested for possession of Class A drugs with intent to supply, and possession of firearms, received prison sentences ranging from five to twelve years. Five other members of the gang were jailed for running brothels, but it could not be proved that they had trafficked the women themselves. Those arrested for cyber frauds were given bail and skipped the country before their trials. Other suspected members of the gang simply disappeared.

Councillor Plessey was investigated over irregularities in the granting of planning consents. He escaped prosecution but resigned his seat. He was replaced by a Green candidate in the by-election that followed.

Karen Groves retired from Mexton police on health grounds and moved to Southampton, to be nearer her mother's care home. When her health permitted, she joined the Hampshire force as a civilian investigator. Her former relationship with Valentina Malenka never came to light.

Mel was diagnosed with a mild form of PTSD and started a course of counselling.

Jenny Pike recovered in hospital and remained at the *Mexton Messenger,* but was appointed Deputy Editor. She received a substantial advance for her book *Escaping the Serial Poisoner* and the publisher paid for it to be a WH Smith book of the month. Her attitude towards the police was less aggressive for a while, but she still criticised them on occasions.

Valentina's will was discovered when the police received an email, programmed to be sent after three months without her signing in. All her wealth was left to charities supporting trafficked women and drug rehabilitation centres.

Glossary of Police Terms

AFO: Authorised Firearms Officer
ANPR: Automatic Number Plate Recognition (camera)
ARU: Armed Response Unit
ARV: Armed Response Vehicle
CEOP: Child Exploitation and Online Protection Centre
CHIS: Covert Human Intelligence Source
CPS: Crown Prosecution Service
directed surveillance: planned, covert observation of somebody (*see* RIPA)
DSO: Distinguished Service Order, a medal awarded to officers
DVLA: Driver and Vehicle Licensing Agency
DWP: Department for Work and Pensions
ESDA: Electrostatic Detection Apparatus
hang fire: when a cartridge fails to fire immediately when the trigger is pulled but goes off later
HMRC: Her Majesty's Revenue and Customs
MET (the): Metropolitan Police Service
NABIS: National Ballistics Intelligence Service
NCA: National Crime Agency

PNC: Police National Computer
RIPA: Regulation of Investigatory Powers Act
RTC: road traffic collision
SOCO: Scene Of Crime Officer (aka CSI)
SO15: Counter-Terrorism Command

Acknowledgments

As ever, I must thank my wonderfully supportive wife, Jen, for her assiduous editing and invaluable comments, which converted my early efforts on the book into something worth submitting. Also, for understanding that, when I say I'm off to poison a paedophile, I'm not doing something nasty in the woodshed.

I have benefited from expert advice from several sources. Graham Bartlett (https://policeadvisor.co.uk/) provided vital information on police procedures, and Kate Bendelow, SOCO and author, helped with crime scene details. Dr Zac Marriner provided extremely helpful advice on the treatment of aconite poisoning. Of course, any errors are entirely my own responsibility.

I'm grateful, also, to Pete and Marianne McAleer for explaining the nature of the Catholic Mass and putting me right about several misconceptions.

Thanks also to the Birnbeck Regeneration Trust, Weston-super-Mare, (www.birnbeckregenerationtrust.org.uk) for access to the disused toilets, now used for storage, where the denouement takes place. Their efforts to restore this classic Victorian pier are admirable.

Finally, thanks to Rebecca and Adrian at Hobeck for continuing to publish my work, to Sue Davison for her immaculate editing and to Jayne Mapp for another great cover.

Some readers may be tempted to acquire a parrot, having

read of Mel and Tom's pets. Please do not use a breeder or a pet shop, but contact one of the parrot rehoming organisations instead. A parrot is challenging and a companion for life, and many people don't realise the commitment needed.

The Mel Cotton Crime Series

Fatal Trade

'A very satisfying, solid, well-written and gripping thriller.' LOUISE VOSS

'A fast-paced edge-of-your-seat thriller from a major new talent. Gripping stuff!' DAVID MARK

Glasgow, 1999

Reaching the point of no return, Martina is ready to make her move. After years of being the victim, it's now time to turn the tables.

Mexton, 2019

The small grey-haired woman grimaced as she entered the police station, dragging a tartan shopping trolley containing her husband's head.

'What are you useless buggers going to do about this?'

DC Melanie Cotton's fledgling career is about to take an interesting turn. Freshly promoted to CID, Mel is excited by this disturbing and mysterious case – her first murder investigation as a detective.

She's determined to make her mark.

But as she discovers, there's far more to this case than a gruesome killing, and Mel's skills and courage are about to tested to the limit.

Fatal Hate

'This is high quality crime writing. Recommend-ed.' M. W. CRAVEN

'I dare you to try to put it down.' GRAHAM BARTLETT

DC Mel Cotton is back with a brand new case, the murder of Duncan Bennett. But who would want an unassuming ware-house worker dead.

The case soon becomes far more complex and dangerous, with terrorists, a paedophile network and a hitman in town. And against a background of rising hatred and violence, one woman pursues her deadly revenge.

Mel and her colleagues face their greatest challenge yet. Mel's own courage will be tested to the limits. No-one is safe.

Hobeck Books – the home of great stories

We hope you've enjoyed reading this novel by Brian Price. To keep up to date on Brian's fiction writing please subscribe to his website: **www.brianpriceauthor.co.uk**.

Hobeck Books offers a number of short stories and novellas, including *Fatal Beginnings* by Brian Price, free for subscribers in the compilation *Crime Bites*.

- *Echo Rock* by Robert Daws
- *Old Dogs, Old Tricks* by AB Morgan
- *The Silence of the Rabbit* by Wendy Turbin
- *Never Mind the Baubles: An Anthology of Twisted Winter Tales* by the Hobeck Team (including many of the Hobeck authors and Hobeck's two publishers)
- *The Clarice Cliff Vase* by Linda Huber
- *Here She Lies* by Kerena Swan
- *The Macnab Principle* by R.D. Nixon
- *Fatal Beginnings* by Brian Price
- *A Defining Moment* by Lin Le Versha
- *Saviour* by Jennie Ensor
- *You Can't Trust Anyone These Days* by Maureen Myant

Also please visit the Hobeck Books website for details of our other superb authors and their books, and if you would like to get in touch, we would love to hear from you.

Hobeck Books also presents a weekly podcast, the Hobcast, where founders Adrian Hobart and Rebecca Collins discuss all things book related, key issues from each week, including the ups and downs of running a creative business. Each episode includes an interview with one of the people who make Hobeck possible: the editors, the authors, the cover designers. These are the people who help Hobeck bring great stories to life. Without them, Hobeck wouldn't exist. The Hobcast can be listened to from all the usual platforms but it can also be found on the Hobeck website: **www.hobeck.net/hobcast**.

Other Hobeck Books to Explore

Dirty Little Secret

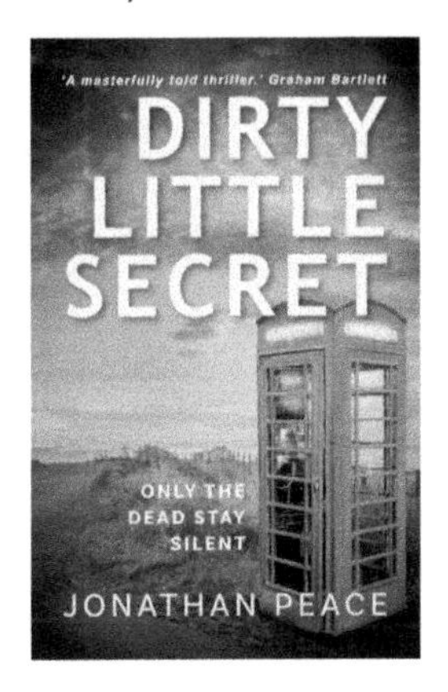

March 1987

Ossett, West Yorkshire
A town of flower shows, Maypole parades and Sunday football games. Behind all the closed doors and drawn curtains live hidden truths and shameful lies.

A body is found
WDC Louise Miller's first case as detective in her hometown is hampered by the sexism and misogyny of small-town policing. Her four years on the force in Manchester have prepared her for this. Along with ally WPC Elizabeth Hines, the pair work the case together.

What truths lie hidden?
As their inquiries deepen, the towns secrets reveal even

darker truths that could lead to the identity of the killer. But when a second girl goes missing, Louise realises that some secrets should stay hidden.

Including hers.

I'm Not There by Rob Gittins

'Everything is cleverly brought together in a thrilling climax.' Sarah Leck

'It has the feel of one of those books that gets a plug and takes off to be a top ten bestseller.' Pete Fleming

'Dark, gritty, well-crafted characters and some gut-punching shocks, first rate crime writing'. Alex Jones

Two sisters abandoned

It was a treat, she said. An adventure. A train journey to the mainland. Six-year-old Lara Arden and her older sister Georgia happily fill in their colouring books as their mum pops to the buffet in search of crisps. She never returns. Two little girls abandoned. Alone.

Present day

Twenty years later, and Lara is now a detective inspector on her native Isle of Wight, still searching for answers to her mother's disappearance.

A call comes in. A small child, a boy, has been left abandoned on a train. Like Lara, he has no relatives to look after him. It feels as if history is being repeated – but surely this is a coincidence?

A series of murders

Before Lara can focus on the boy's plight, she's faced with a series of murders. They feature different victims in very different circumstances, but they all have one thing in common: they all leave children – alone – behind.

So who is targeting Lara? What do these abandoned souls have in common? And how does this connect to the mystery of Lara's missing mother?

Lightning Source UK Ltd.
Milton Keynes UK
UKHW021004050123
414865UK00013B/1801